Helen Harris lives in London, where she has worked as a translator and a tourist information officer, and then as a freelance magazine researcher. She has travelled very widely, including India and the Middle East, and has spent a year living in Paris. *Playing Fields in Winter,* her first novel, was short-listed for the first Betty Trask Award. Her short stories have appeared in a great many magazines and anthologies, including *Punch* and the Penguin *Firebird I* collection.

PLAYING FIELDS IN WINTER

Helen Harris

Futura

TO MY PARENTS

A Futura Book

Copyright © Helen Harris 1986

First published in Great Britain in 1986 by
Century Hutchinson Ltd

This Futura edition published in 1987

ISBN 0 7088 3370 5

Printed and bound in Great Britain by
The Guernsey Press Co. Ltd, Guernsey, Channel Islands.

Futura Publications
A Division of
Macdonald & Co (Publishers) Ltd
Greater London House
Hampstead Road
London NW1 7QX

A BPCC plc Company

'IS THERE any history?' Two doctors stand in the corridor of a dilapidated hospital and an immense Indian sun spills through the windows on to their white coats. A row of large rooms opens on to the inside of the corridor and out of some of them come sobs and sighs. But the doctors are discussing – a trifle dismissively – the occupant of a completely silent room. In it, between listless routine cases, there is an English girl, cast up in their overworked hospital with an initially undiagnosable disease. Their patient is not presenting any of the usual hippy traveller's symptoms; she has not got hepatitis or dysentery or malaria. Yet she is clearly ill. She lies repugnantly white and bony on their much-laundered sheets and tries to roll her eyeballs inwards away from their probing examination. They know it all so well, the doctors: the European female patient's panic at being taken ill here, the hysteria and recoil, the unspoken conviction that their hands, because they are brown, cannot adequately work the miracle of treatment and cure. But this one had said something funny during the examination; she had asked for visitors. As if she could possibly expect acquaintances to visit her here, when they were surely all sitting cosily at home in England, wondering what had become of their adventurous young friend who had gone gallivanting off alone to that fearsome place, India. And they had waggled their heads in amusement and gone on examining her. At which point she had shown that she was simply utterly sick of the sub-continent and, not surprisingly, this had insulted them.

*

At the beginning, there was temptation, temptation to reject the grey with which she had grown up and exchange it for something very bright and shimmering, like a bauble. Oxford in winter was only half alive. There were no leaves on the

5

trees and, in the libraries, immobile figures sat hunched over their books as if they might at closing time shockingly be found to be dead. The college quadrangles, remember, had been painstakingly preserved in the shape of past centuries and from long preservation had imperceptibly lost life, so that every hour on the bell tower was an upheaval and evening chapel a commotion which might shake down the spires. When she rode her bicycle at night through the city, nothing else moved in the streets but cats and she could look into the houses where there were lights on and see motionless tableaux of family scenes.

Sometimes, it seemed, from sheer self-control, the English must erupt. But they never did; break open their dignity, rip off their reserve. They enacted Oxford with elaborate care. The students wore their characters like costumes – they were scholars or aesthetes or drunks. Ultimately they became purely their black gowns or their anachronistic, bicycle-clip-bound trousers. They defined themselves in the security of time and place, as if being in Oxford in their youth supplanted the need to be anything else.

The city lent itself to posturing. It would have seemed an insult to the marvellous scenery of spires against a backdrop of northern European grey not to act out its traditions. But to some of the students arriving in Oxford that autumn, the traditions lacked a vital quality.

*

England was wrapped in an all-enveloping cloud. When his plane landed at Heathrow on that grey October morning, he found a muffled country hunched in self-pity over a handkerchief. It was not gracious or grand, as he had sometimes liked to imagine it as a child in India. The people were all shrouded in a cocoon of selfish privacy, their words and movements muted. He was there for a fortnight before he felt, through the layers of propriety and pretence, that he had really got through to someone.

*

At the beginning, there was the hope of finding that vitality she sought. There was the thrilling feeling that all her life

6

until then had been lived according to a pattern, but that here finally was a chance to evade the pattern and embark on something which no one could have predicted: no romantic maiden aunt inventing a prince for her favourite niece, no part-time clairvoyant at a charity fête. Oxford was so overwhelmingly safe, cushioned in the protective hollow of the Thames Valley. It was gratifyingly ironic that there, in such cloistered safety, she should have managed to find danger nevertheless.

Danger was so tremendous on a morning with ground frost, speeding in from the Victorian suburbs on a bicycle. The road stretched between tall red houses and orange trees. The fallen leaves flared up around her bicycle wheels and the wind scoured her face with a delicious pain. But all there was at the end of that exhilarating ride was a lecture – Middle English or Linguistics – and coffee in a book-lined mediaeval turret and lunch in a monastic hall. She slipped off her bicycle clips, unwound her long striped woollen scarf – sodden with the breath which five minutes before had been exercise and excitement – and sat down in the lecture theatre to listen to an old man talking (with what had presumably replaced passion in him) about vowel formation. In Oxford there were many clock hands which moved in grudging jerks, as if their mechanism resented the need to advance. The clock in the lecture theatre was one of those; it showed a glorious autumn morning as a series of tiny, unwilling concessions to the 1970s. Sitting at the back of the theatre after the soaring bicycle ride, lacking fresh air and space as well as that less definable vitality, she used to have a terrible feeling that she was not entirely alive here either. Somewhere else the world was moving forward, but here in the beautiful archaic city she might get left behind.

There was excitement at the beginning, there was mischief. There was a little girl running in from the garden, clutching a wet frog and crying, 'Mummy, Mummy, look what I've found!' already savouring in advance the delight of her mother's horrified shriek. For she knew from the moment she caught sight of the frog in the grass that he would cause consternation and she could barely wait to carry him into the coffee morning and hear the ladies' upset squeals. Even before she realised that she was in fact *going* to carry the frog into the house, the thought of the squeals alone was satisfying.

There was actually a garden beyond the small confines of her college desk – although it was by no means a miracle like the gardens which came later on – which seemed a triumph over surroundings capable of eradicating the will to create gardens. In Oxford, creating gardens was an obvious thing to do, like decorating your speech with sprigs of Latin or wearing a long skirt to parties. There was the rain and the soft soil of the Thames Valley. The university called out for gardens to surround its libraries with soothing green, to protect its peace. The big trees beyond her window were supposed to harbour prowlers and perverts. They were black firs and cypress. Unable to find ideas for her essays, she would stare out into the winter afternoons and search between the trees for human shapes. But the cold weather and the college's remoteness from the centre of the city kept them away and, although tales did circulate about girls being horribly attacked by rapists who forced their way in through the barred windows on the ground floor, most of the time such danger seemed imaginary.

A long, tidy lawn spread across to the trees, on which girls lay and studied in summer and held decorative tea-parties. A stone sundial at the junction of four gravel paths reported every suspect night-time footstep. On the other side of the trees were the university playing fields where, on winter afternoons, players in bright shirts lumbered up and down, churning up the mud, and from that side of the college, the girls could hear the harsh cries of the men they were supposed to marry.

Behind her, when she sat at her desk looking for ideas in the garden, lay the cold bulk of the college like the shell of some extinct mammoth. Approached from the front gates, it presented a high red wall behind which a hint of turrets and dormer windows gave an impression of possible grace. Coming up from the garden, you saw its angular brick shape devoid of mystery: a great red façade looming above the lawns, which no amount of creeper could romanticise. Its corridors were phenomenal, renowned within the city. A story existed of a new student who had wandered lost in them for days, unable to find her way back to her room and too embarrassed to ask anyone for directions. That and a more light-hearted tale of a visiting male student trying to find his way back from the bathroom to his girl-friend's room in the middle of the night and horrifyingly, improbably, finding himself instead in bed with the junior dean, conveyed the only kind of danger the students imagined. The corridors smelt of disinfectant and left-over years of unappetising dinners.

It seemed an unlikely beginning. But in fact, it turned out to be provocative to give so excessively the impression of a fortress to be penetrated and overthrown.

*

At his beginning, there was curiosity: what were these stiff inhibited young people, yet who clearly thought the world of themselves, like? Could anyone really be as inhuman as they made themselves out to be? The impression of his first weeks gave way to amusement at their naïvety. For all their pretensions, he saw they actually had no idea at all of how the world worked. They put on their acts and mannerisms to hide their gullibility. Good God, he had understood more of life at twelve than these gawky schoolboys did now.

There was a challenge, for never before had anyone implied to him that he might be their inferior. (Except once; he had been about seven at the time, but small for his age. On his way home from school one day, he had got caught up in a gaggle of street children who were pestering a party of tourists outside the grounds of the Residency in Lucknow. As he tried to push his way through the crowd, he heard an English voice exclaim, 'Oh, isn't he sweet?' and, for an instant, he had been filled with a violent rage. Couldn't they see that he had nothing to do with the dirty, squealing urchins? Couldn't they see his satchel and his smart school clothes? Couldn't they *see*?)

Now, he was filled with an urge to pierce that English primness and giving way to his worst feelings, he saw that the girl was one way in. The disdain which he knew he would earn from his compatriot students was a challenge

9

too; he had grown up to think that only run-of-the-mill mediocrities were conventional. And there was too, although scarcely admitted, the fascination of the legend about English girls – that if you wanted to, you could. He felt that he would regret the missed opportunity all his life if he spent these three unique years shut away studying. He owed it to himself to experiment in England; while he was here, he wanted to do everything.

Other chaps who had come home after Oxford had told him about other adventures. Pratap Singh had been to endless parties and got hilariously drunk and smashed things. Joti Verma had tried out all kinds of drugs. But where, he could not understand . . . and when and *how*? He saw no openings in those early days for any sort of adventure and in any case could imagine nothing more wicked in that schoolboys' city than pillow-fights in the quadrangle or a mischievous dousing in the river Thames.

He set his sights on a real adventure, something which would involve risk and compromise to his principles and danger. He turned up his nose at experiments with whisky and piffling little coloured pills; he wanted to try out another life; he knew his years in Oxford would only come to him once and, afterwards, he already knew how defined his life would be.

*

'What will you be when you're grown up?'

'A minister in the government.'

'A minister? Why do you want to be a minister? Not a big-shot general or a pilot or a spaceman?'

'Because I want a big desk – so big – and a nice car with curtains to ride around in and everyone pointing and going "Ah, ah" as I go by because I'm so important.'

'Ha, ha, Kaul Sahib, you have the boy well-trained, it seems.'

'First, let's see if he's clever enough to study and pass his exams. Run along, Ravi.'

*

'What will you be when you're grown up?'

'I don't know.'

'Come on, of course you must know. A teacher? An air hostess? A nurse?'

'I'll be a . . . I'll be Mary Poppins, so I can fly up into the sky with my magic bag.'

'Oh Sarah, stop being silly. You know perfectly well you can't be someone else.'

'I won't grow up. I won't grow up!'

*

The telegram announcing that Sarah Livingstone had been admitted to Oxford arrived at breakfast time. A family argument was in progress over who was responsible for the soft-boiled eggs being as hard as old rubber; and it had grown so acrimonious before the postman rang the front-door bell that bad temper remained in the air even after Sarah had opened the envelope and it slightly affected the celebration. The words on the telegram form did not immediately make sense – little strips pasted together, almost as if in code. But the very arrival of the telegram told the family what it was about and the words only served to define certain secondary details.

'Well, there we are,' her father said, as if it were a family achievement. 'You run along to Oxford, my dear. I'm sure you'll have a lovely time.' And the news had moved him so little that he concentrated on buttering his toast to total smoothness.

'Great! When do we get rid of you?' her younger brother asked.

Only Sarah's mother, flushed by the cooker, had trembled with excitement at the thought of the freedom ahead of her daughter, which her generation had not thought it necessary for her to experience.

They passed the telegram around, joking about the use of Sarah's middle name, about the time at which the telegram had been sent. ('Gosh, so late, you must have been an after-thought!') and even the eggs were accepted under cover of their contentment.

When she looked back on it, Sarah saw that she had received the news rather like instructions; she had duly finished her schooldays and now she was to go to university.

There seemed no comfortable alternatives. At her school, there was one sixth-form pregnancy and three gruesome sufferers from anorexia nervosa. One of these was in the same small class as Sarah, preparing for the Oxbridge exams. At the weeks went by and the prospect grew more and more daunting, so the thin girl dwindled, coming to the class frailer and frailer each day until, only two weeks before the exams, she vanished and they were told that she was being treated in hospital. That girl stayed in Sarah's mind like a thwarted ghost and when she received the telegram, she felt a pang of guilt for this future should really have been given to the thin girl who wanted it so much. Sarah could not make up her mind if *she* did, but something about her family's bland acceptance of the news as the natural course of events irritated her unexpectedly. Looking around at the jolly satisfaction which had replaced the acrimony over the eggs, she felt acutely left out. All this represented was a pattern of which she suspected that she herself was the least part. She said, 'Give me back my telegram,' and taking it, folded it up very small and put it back into the envelope.

Yet she had looked forward to her escape for years, reminded her parents of it in every argument, planned for it and dwelt with relish on its dramatic form. But now her parents seemed to have stage-managed her escape as well; it became just another part of their set-up. At dinner parties, it would fit easily into the conversation: 'You know Sarah's up at Oxford now? Doesn't it make one feel old?' The boundaries of their expectations extended far beyond the house and her childhood. Her escape plans had been detected and foiled long ago.

The house from which Sarah was planning to escape stood towards one end of a white London crescent. On the morning she received her telegram, two other children in the crescent heard that they had been admitted to Oxbridge too. At Number 24 Jonathan Wharton – son of Ian Wharton, the Conservative MP – learnt that he had won a scholarship to Downing College, Cambridge; and at Number 2 Roger Caversham, the son of Miles and Irene Caversham, heard that he had been accepted by his father's old college. Sarah was Sarah Livingstone, the daughter of Gareth Livingstone the photographer.

The crescent being a select London street, the news was not swapped cheerily in front of the spear-headed black railings or passed along by neighbourly exchange. It was learnt, by some silent filtration, over the next few days and no one felt it appropriate to comment or congratulate. The Whartons' Colombian au pair girl, letting herself into the crescent garden early one morning with the family's King Charles spaniel, met the Cavershams' Philippino help struggling almost tearfully with the key and in the course of a halting exchange about their employers, the two girls made the only direct public reference to the recent coincidence. They found the lack of comment peculiar. Then they talked about the smoke from the gardener's bonfire which, rising through the yellow trees, reminded each of them of something different in their own countries.

*

What was it like for him in that other white house beside the gardens when the telegram arrived? It was brought in the very early, pink morning by a 'boy' on a bicycle, who was really thirty-two years old but cowed and thin. There was exhilaration and the proud, nearly dream-like realisation of tremendous powers. He could behave quite differently now; he was about to become part of another world. The words on the telegraph form were so botched and crooked to represent such a huge transformation. Yesterday his life had been one thing: from today, it would be something utterly superior. At the same time he felt calm satisfaction, for the world had only recognised his due – what was to be expected if you were born Ravi Kaul and had servants to cry because you were going abroad. And his father? Had he swollen even greater at this family triumph, jutting his bulbous finger at the sky to show that heaven and he understood one another? And his mother? Had she crept, pressing her sari hood to her mouth, into some back bedroom and sobbed because her eldest son was to travel so far? The pink sun came up and he rang his friends to tell them the news. When they came round to celebrate, a gulf had opened between him and those

13

who were not going abroad, because already their lives had begun to diverge.

The house beside the gardens in Lucknow had been home since Ravi was ten. But it was not profoundly home, the way a house in a city would be if you had been born there and your ancestors had lived in the same place. There was somewhere else, beyond reach, that was really home – Delhi, where the streets were wider and his parents were in a better mood – and Lucknow had always been second best.

Ravi and his brother Ramesh, and later his two little sisters, had grown up feeling that they did not quite fit into their surroundings. Not only were they a Hindu family in a very Moslem city, they were a sophisticated metropolitan family in a provincial capital. Ravi had done well at school; that had been his revenge: better and better at school, to serve everybody right. In summer, when it was really too hot to study, he had continued studying to confound them. He had sat in his bedroom – actually Ramesh's bedroom too – and scowled down at his books for hours, too hot and sweaty to take anything in but satisfied by the sounds of his mother fussing from the doorway – she would not have dared actually to come in and disturb him – and by the imagined vision of his name at the top of the termly class lists once again. Tributaries of sweat and water like the rivers whose names he memorised ran down his scrawny neck from the wet towel he wound around his head. His legs stuck painfully to his wooden chair. When his mother finally tiptoed in with a cold drink, he ferociously ignored her. His diligence naturally paid off in time. First he got into the college in Delhi and then, gloriously, Oxford. And all along no one knew, least of all his proud parents, that his motives were so unscholarly. It was not academic success he was after but his rightful horizon, which would reduce Lucknow to a picturesque childhood memory.

When he was very small, Ravi had had a recurring nightmare. This had been brought on, he thought, by an incident on a bus journey. Where they were going or why, he could no longer remember, but he knew that the journey had been the cause of a great upset in his family; they should have been travelling in a private car and not by public bus,

14

crowded together with all sorts of people in the worst of the hot weather. His mother was tense and upset and her unhappiness had communicated itself to him. Somewhere along the way, the bus had stopped at a roadside snack stall and his mother, screwing up her face in disgust, had taken him into the public lavatory. It was a fearsome place. There was no light in the low hut, but a fierce smell which seemed to make the darkness blacker. Small barred windows high up in the wall let in two square rays of light which showed, once your eyes were accustomed to the darkness, that around the lavatory hole the sloping floor was awash with faeces. So that he should not spoil his shiny shoes by paddling in the excrement, his mother had stood at arm's length from the frightful hole and held up little Ravi over it to do his business as best he could, squawking and terrified.

In his nightmare, Ravi fell and flew sickeningly down into the smelly dark shaft, falling further and further away from the light and his mother, into a bottomless black pit which he knew would eventually come out on the other side of the world.

How many times he dreamed that dream, he had no idea, for it was reinforced so often in his waking hours. There was a dark world of dreadful filth which lay in wait for him outside his safe, clean home. There *were* holes in every public lavatory which led through to the other side of the world. And it was only by turning up his nose at it and sticking fast to what his parents taught him that he could steer clear of the abyss.

*

The college reminded her of school on the dull October day she arrived in Oxford. There was a familiar institutional smell in its long corridors – which aroused memories of lack of affection – and a disembodied jabbering, not produced by any particular voices but apparently generated perpetually by the community of females.

She was given a room overlooking the garden. It was on the top floor of the least popular wing of the college and as well as the corridors, visitors had to negotiate a steep and rather forbidding staircase. It was room Number 102, but

15

the girls on either side had already put up little cards saying 'Jacqueline Poliakoff' and 'Clarissa Rich'. Clarissa Rich knocked while Sarah was beginning to unpack and already giving way to a fantasy of not opening her suitcases at all but seizing what she cared most about and running away. She had found a hot-water bottle in a crocheted woollen cover lying forgotten in the wardrobe. It seemed to predict such chilly, spinsterish winters in the secluded room that she had thrown it into the waste-paper basket and now she was unwilling to put her belongings into the traces left by her predecessor. Clarissa Rich put her head round the door when Sarah answered and, seen without her body, it was a slightly unnerving sight; she had a large, nearly lunar face, surrounded by an aura of pale frizzy hair. She said, 'Hail and well met, stranger. We're neighbours.' Her body, which followed, was very broad and draped in a floor-length purple smock. Standing in the centre of the empty room she said, 'Yes, just like mine, except that my bed's over by the desk, more to the end. I think it's nicer that way; you can use the desk light to read in bed.'

'Have you got yours all fixed up then?' Sarah asked. 'Are you unpacked?'

'Oh goodness, yes,' Clarissa answered. 'I came up three days early so that I could get all that out of the way before the work started.' She looked at Sarah curiously. 'What are you reading?'

'English,' said Sarah. 'And you?'

'History,' replied Clarissa, 'although I must admit I am tempted by philosophy.' She went over to the window to see if the view differed at all from hers and then turned and asked a little awkwardly, 'Would you like to come and have tea?'

Because it had seemed short-sighted to offend her neighbour on the first day and so as to get out of the chilling room, Sarah followed Clarissa. She seemed very pleased to have enlisted Sarah. She showed her where the kitchen and the bathroom were. On the way back they passed a small, rather pretty dark-haired girl, who was being helped with her luggage by two laughing young men. Clarissa contented herself with a 'Hail and well met, stranger!' and a wave;

16

then she ushered Sarah proprietorially into her room and commented, 'Oh dear, one of those. I hope we don't have too many of *them* on our corridor.'

Oppressiveness spread from Clarissa's pimpled forehead and sternly parted, rather oily hair. Sarah thought that maybe her mother had been right when she said it was important to get in with the right people at the very beginning. She did not want to be drawn into Clarissa's musty orbit; it would be awful if she was seen with her at the start and considered by the interesting people to be like her.

Clarissa offered Sarah home-made flapjacks from a big tin and took two, which she chewed with relish. 'It's a wonderful feeling, starting here, isn't it?' she said. 'There's so much exploration and discovery ahead of us.'

*

Although his college in Delhi had modelled itself on one of these, Ravi Kaul was not prepared for quite how closely the university resembled its caricatured versions overseas. It was like moving into a textbook, taking up residence on a well-worn page with all the illustrations austerely correct: chapel, quadrangles, High Table, gowns. It was astonishing how dotingly the traditions were maintained, how cosily the young Englishmen stuck to them. And Ravi, who had assumed that he knew as much about them as any John Smith, and would therefore take to them with ease and panache, found to his dismay that he disliked them intensely.

'It's eight o-clock – sir.'

'Oh gosh, is it?'

'It is – sir. I presume we're up to opening our curtains this morning?'

He had an ancient cubby-hole of a bedroom during that first year and an ancient college servant, a scout, to go with it. His name was Mr Gregory Rainbow and he waited on Ravi Kaul with resentment.

'You're from India, then, if I've got it right?' he asked one morning, after bringing in Ravi's frequent air mail letters with their Hindi cyphers.

'That's right, Mr Rainbow. Have you ever been there, by any chance?'

'Indeed I have – sir. I was there in the Army, as a matter of fact, before the war.'

'Did you like it?'

'I wouldn't say "like" was quite the word for it. It was an interesting experience.'

'Would you go back there?'

'I would not.' The stocky old man deliberated in the doorway – a rustic figure, Ravi thought, whom he liked to imagine leaning on a country gate and chewing a straw, as in a poem by Mathew Arnold or Thomas Hardy. Then, turning, he delivered a ripely matured retort, 'I hardly need to, do I, with so many of you over here?'

*

Straight away Sarah found herself a boy-friend, a taciturn, blond boy-friend called David Whitehead to whom she conscientiously lost her virginity half-way into her second term. Although 'lost' was hardly the right word because Sarah jettisoned the virginity, whatever it was, quite deliberately. She calculated the precise circumstances in which this would take place (before David's electric fire on a long Saturday evening) and together with her new friend Emily Williams analysed and assessed its consequences and advantages. In return, David Whitehead presented Sarah with his complete inability to give or receive emotion. He had been brought up in boarding school dormitories and all-male common rooms; he was the son of the convention that it is weak and debilitating to show one's feelings and even when a little emotion would have been permissible, he could not produce it. His feelings had been permanently doctored. His attachment to Sarah was mainly negative; he did not repel her with sarcasm, he did not leave her room at night. Sarah was unclear about the exact nature of her feelings for him. She found his silences appealing, because they seemed to her to show he was withholding something from the unworthy world. He had a schoolboy hero's hair. But there was never any upheaval between them. Each acquired the other gravely as a new aspect of university life, and each knew privately that they were only trying the other out . . . like a new

18

subject, like another society, like most things in that first year.

Her first year was certainly quite safe. Beginning so inauspiciously on that wet October day, it remained circumscribed and traditional, a game with antiquated rules. In later years, in fact, she often forgot about it completely when she recalled the university. She overlooked the part it must surely have played, with its dissatisfactions and limitations, in bringing about what came afterwards.

Sarah watched the faces of the first evening develop into a narrow range of English fictional characters: the earnest, ugly blue-stocking; the socially successful but malicious beauty; the vamp. As the daughter of Gareth Livingstone, the photographer, she found herself cast as sensitive – artistically bad-tempered. In spite of herself, she had hung on her wall the two photographs which her father had given her to take to college. Her visitors said, 'Gosh, what amazing pictures – they're by Gareth Livingstone, aren't they? Goodness, is he your father?', and she thereby managed to distinguish herself from Clarissa Rich on her right and Jacqueline Poliakoff on her left.

She did what everyone else did – joined societies, drank coffee and argued until two in the morning about Platonic friendships and the existence of God. She experimented with different, rather amusing personalities as the year went by; she was the sour and knowing cynic, the popular party-goer whose mantelpiece was lined with invitations, or from time to time the library recluse.

Each night there were the decreasingly palatable dinners for which they had to endure a Latin grace in Hall, Clarissa Rich's frizzy hair left coiling in the bath at the end of the corridor and the noise of Jacqueline Poliakoff copulating excruciatingly through the thin partition wall. There were evenings as blank and desolate as the winter lawns, as cold and isolated as her college room, when everything seemed so ordered and so staid that Sarah longed for a disruption.

Not only did their past dominate their present, it cast its massive shadow on to their future too and seemed capable of dictating what Sarah Livingstone would become and who her friends would be for ever. Like the owner of the crocheted hot-water bottle cover before her, she would sit with her knees drawn up by the two-bar fire and console herself by numbly eating chocolate biscuits.

*

Ravi, shivering, appalled, caught every germ malingering in the damp Thames Valley. He had only to open his mouth, it seemed, for a new permutation of cold, bronchitis or influenza to glide in; the college nurse expressed the opinion that his origins were to blame. His nose became almost Englishly pink. And then finally he must have run through the whole range, for he acquired immunity and the illnesses stopped. It made him quite cocky for a while.

He had never been a weakling child. His brother Ramesh had been the sickly one, stealing more than his fair share of their mother's attention. For Ravi, an illness was a rare calamity and he hated England for having attacked him in such an underhand way. It was an insidious germ warfare, which undermined his very character and confidence. For here there was no one to bring him sweet milk drinks with cinnamon and rub his temples with tingling balm. He lay in his mediaeval bedroom and coughed and listened to the bells chiming; he thought he had never been so lonely and forlorn in his life.

*

It was a closed world. Was it three or four weeks after the first night dinner that her new friend Emily Williams knocked on Sarah's door, gulping tears, at half-past one in the morning? It was a Sunday night. Her boy-friend from Surrey had come up to stay for the weekend, as promised, but after seeing her new environment and the kind of topics which were going to occupy her for the next three years, he had announced that evening as they packed up his things for the coach that he and Emily were through. She had lain in her room for two hours crying and then come running across the dark quadrangle, hating the very gravel screeching under her feet, to wake Sarah. Now she sat huddled in Sarah's armchair, shaking with her crying and the cold as she repeated, 'I can't bear it, Sarah. I'd rather have him than all

20

this. Honestly, I shall have to leave. I just can't stand it here without him.'

Sarah filled her kettle and then, theatrically, poured out two glasses of sherry as well. She had bought the bottle a week or so earlier and had put as much thought into arranging it with the new little glasses on her coffee table as if they were ornaments. By means of objects like the sherry glasses and her ivy, she was after all turning room Number 102 into her own backdrop, distinct from that of Clarissa Rich or Jacqueline Poliakoff. She put Emily's glass on the table near her and sat down on the other chair opposite her, wrapping her dressing-gown closer. She noticed on her bedside alarm clock that it was nearly 2 am and felt a pleasant sense of drama.

During those early days, Emily Williams had been her one source of drama. In the first week of meetings and book lists, Emily agonised loudly over which subject she should read and whether or not she was at the right university. In the second week, after they had been set their first essay, Emily had fallen dramatically ill and then accused the college nurse of dangerous incompetence. She had had her transistor radio stolen and later escaped near rape by an engineering student at a Freshers' party. Sarah saw that friendship with Emily would ensure some excitement, while Emily found in Sarah the impressionable audience she needed for her dramas.

She wept in front of Sarah but, after a while, started to apologise for keeping her awake.

Sarah said, 'That's all right. I couldn't sleep anyway.' Insomnia was one of the discoveries of that period – provoked at first by the unfamiliar sounds of Jacqueline Poliakoff's pleasure and then sustained by the thought of the three hundred women lying sleeping around her.

'Why not?' asked Emily, who hoped for distraction.

So Sarah invented a reason. After all, she did not want to be invariably the one who listened and consoled, but never had anything to weep about. She said, 'I've met this man.' And Emily listened. The man – who had in fact barely made any impression on Sarah at all – was a History student called David Whitehead. (Or had it actually been Whitechurch? Remembering him years afterwards, she had a sudden doubt.

21

No, no, it must have been Whitehead, with that fair hair.)
She had met him at an audition for a student play; he was
going to help with the lighting and Sarah was auditioning for
some minor part. So she told Emily that she had sensed
something between them at once. It did sound plausible. She
was making it all up, but Emily encouraged her. The thrill
of misfortune and the possibility of Sarah also becoming
involved in it comforted them. They drank another glass of
sherry and soon Emily started to giggle through her tears.
By the time she felt confident to leave and Sarah went back
to bed, she really could not sleep for wondering if there
might not perhaps be something between her and the History
student after all.

*

Repelled, tantalised, Ravi was faced with plate upon plate of
gristly English meat. He did not eat meat and his throat
involuntarily constricted at its evil savour. But something
perfectly silly forbade him to go to the Bursar and request
Colonel Webb to order him a vegetarian diet. He would not
single himself out among these pink, meat-eating English
boys; he would not act the traditional delicate part of the
good Hindu boy abroad. So he ground the foul fibrous stuff
untasting between his teeth and left most of his meals
uneaten. But he had not had to appeal for special treatment
over something with which these hearty boys could cope.
And the thought of the pious horror of his mother and his
aunt at the sight of him eating steak and kidney pie perversely
spurred him on.

*

In the afternoons, there were tea-parties. Every afternoon,
in every room in Oxford, there were tea-parties. Amidst a
mess of coffee mugs and gaping packets of biscuits, Sarah
Livingstone and her friends discussed the question of Arts
versus Sciences and whether or not to build a Channel tunnel.
They toasted crumpets on unwound paper clips attached to
the grilles of their two-bar fires. Late in the afternoon, they
switched from tea to sherry and left for dinner, striking poses
and howling at jokes which lasted for a term at a time.

Friendships began or ended at these tea-parties, love affairs were surreptitiously advanced and once – carried away by the warmth and intimacy of the gathering – Clarissa Rich recounted how she had been 'tampered with' as a child by her father. In David Whitehead's room in the city centre, above a shop which sold running shoes and rucksacks and camping stoves, Sarah ate ginger nuts and drank tea from a particular kind of pottery mug which she would ever afterwards associate with tedium.

David's friends formed a small, close sub-group. Membership was by vocabulary and however congenial a person might be, admission would only ever be granted if he used the right words in the right way. There was Anthony – whom those in the know called Ant – who would one day be a distinguished barrister and grow immensely fat; Nigel, who drank such quantities that his closest friends were scared for him; Simon, Tim and Christopher Lee-Drake. Tolerated, but never really belonging, there was also occasionally Ali, whom they had for unconventionality and flavour because he came from Pakistan.

At their tea-parties, they did not actually talk very much, being able to convey all they wanted to one another with just one or two of their private words. They lay on the floor and savoured their exclusiveness. Sarah sat with her back against the bookcase and got a reputation for being argumentative. David's friends said to one another what a pain she was as, warmed by mugs of tea and crumpets, they went out into the mist.

*

Ravi had never imagined he would joyously sit down with a circle of assorted Indians to a meal of vegetables and rice prepared in a mucky kitchenette. He had never imagined he would ostentatiously relish chappals and kurtas just because they were Indian or bring up geographical irrelevances in his economics tutorials in order to see his impeccably English tutor, Professor Elstree, force himself to reply with feigned courtesy. He had intended to explore. But he ended up going with a party of other Indian students to a shabby cinema in a cheap district of the city, where they saw rubbishy Hindi films shown for the benefit of immigrant workers. The students went because they were homesick and the little cinema smelt wonderfully authentically of Indian crowds and paan. They sat together at the back and jeered – just as they had done as boys in their various home towns thousands of miles away – and the rest of the audience, for whom the films were intended, turned round and cried at them to shut up.

Ravi became one of the group of expatriates who met for meals in stuffy little Indian restaurants and made fun of the badly-spelled menus, who played sitar records and argued Indian issues together. He still believed that he would integrate into the city, but for that to happen, the city had to show some sign that it was interested in letting him in.

*

Of course, that first year had a summer too; it would be wrong to portray a country of constant winter. It began suddenly, over about three days, and after those three days – even though the cold weather periodically returned – it was still unquestionably summer. The winter receded into the dimmest corners of the libraries, where only those who liked nothing else sought it out. The term they called Trinity was given over almost entirely to enjoyment. The college garden, on which Sarah had looked out in gloomy animosity since October, now became a scented expanse of rolling couples. Only occasionally a grey female don would scurry between them, almost guilty to be a reminder of study. There were parties all the time: outdoor parties on the lawns, strawberries and cream parties, vicars-and-tarts parties, boating parties. The river, which had wound brown and uninterestingly until then, became the centre of the summer as the students floated along it in punts and held more parties on its banks. There was a visible, hilarious outburst of loving. At night, with the windows open, you could almost always hear gasping in the dark.

In a straw hat and a long Edwardian skirt, Sarah enjoyed everything. She rode on her bicycle from one party to another, holding up her skirt to the handle-bars.

David Whitehead came into his own, for a boy-friend was

an important prop for the summer. He was someone to lie with beside the river, endlessly to propel a punt. Sometimes, out of idle curiosity, Sarah must have closed her eyes and imagined that he was someone else; she could not have said who, but someone less clear-cut than David who eluded her. And since by then they were both growing a little tired of each other, David probably did so too. But they looked a convincing couple and appearances were all-important in the summer. After a winter wrapped in shapeless woollen clothes, people put on flamboyant summery outfits and David and Sarah, blond and blue-eyed, looked utterly appropriate in cricket whites and Edwardian dresses. Bizarrely, incomprehensibly, someone called Verity Claybody tried to kill herself in one of the sunniest weeks.

Of the many parties that term, one should be mentioned in particular because it was the scene of the first gap in that closed society, although no one involved ever remembered it later. David's friend Simon was giving the party – or maybe Simon's friend Tim. At any rate, it was a staircase party, with more than one host; everyone living on Simon's staircase had invited their friends and, as a result, there were a great many people there and no one clearly knew whose guests they were. The table bearing the drink was at the innermost end of three adjoining rooms and was soon drained. But David and Sarah had brought a bottle, which they kept and drank themselves. The three rooms were horribly crowded; music nearly blotted out the conversation and heat and cigarette smoke formed a further barrier. So they stayed near the door, held their bottle of wine and drank it. Before the party, they had had an argument and now the shared bottle was their main reason for standing together. They talked little; each hoped to drink their fair share of the acrid wine and they both looked absently about the room. David looked for Simon or Tim, because the two of them could then exclude the party from their conversation. He did not especially like parties, unless there was really plenty to drink, but he came to them because it would have seemed defeatist not to. Secretly he harboured an image of an ideal party, at which there would be no music and so no obligation to dance – in fact, no explicit jollity at all, but only a small group of carefully chosen people discoursing brilliantly, ironically in some select location. (He would have to wait over fifteen years to realise this fantasy, almost without recognising it, at a drinks party in a government building known by its number only.)

Sarah looked for a distraction, in the vague hope of upsetting David by somehow involving him in the party. Over the closely packed crowd, she could see heads bobbing in the next room where people were dancing. Emily Williams, well on the way to being incapably drunk, was spreadeagled against the wall embracing a man Sarah did not recognise. There was a foreigner by the fireplace, standing alone and looking left out and slightly disapproving of the party around him. Sarah noticed him briefly; for one thing, he was a different colour from everyone else and his brown face stood out between the pink ones, flushed with exertion and drink. He was looking around the room with his chin up, either haughtily surveying the crass jollity or concealing the fact that no one had come up to talk to him behind an aloof expression. As he was rather short, he was only revealed by a gap in the crowd and after a moment the gap changed shape, leaving Sarah a view of his face alone. It was a good-looking face, with strong black eyebrows and what seemed in the party lighting to be quite black, shining angry eyes. A thought surfaced in Sarah's fuddled brain, which could best be expressed as, 'So not everyone in the world is English.' This sounded ridiculous, but allowing for her drunkenness it must have meant that particular group of university friends rather than the entire world. And she looked on for some other way to upset David.

They left the party early. An alternative would have been to stay extremely late and obliterate their disagreement with fatigue and alcohol. Instead, to round off their argument, they each went back to their own college. David found his friend Simon Satchell in his room and challenged him: 'I thought you were supposed to be giving the party?'

'I am,' Simon said. He was virtually lying in an armchair. 'I'm waiting to see how long it takes before someone notices I'm not there.'

They opened some beer and sat companionably in silence

for a time. After a while Simon said – just to point out to David that his evening did not appear to have been completely successful either – 'What have you done with Sarah?'

David laughed, to give himself time to arrange the right answer, then he said, 'Sent her home to bed. I needed some peace and quiet!'

Simon chuckled understandingly. For lack of any impulse to move, they sat there together until half-past three.

*

Sarah thought of dropping in on Emily Williams to ask her about the unknown man, but she had not come back to her room. In the room next door to her own, Jacqueline Poliakoff was being simultaneously tickled and throttled. Impetuously, Sarah's winter dissatisfaction returned. She considered crying, but felt too lazy, so she made herself a cup of coffee and went to bed.

The next day, or the day after, there was a picnic to which Sarah and David had already agreed to go. When they met they made no reference to their argument; they usually dealt with their difficulties that way. They joined their friends at one of the boat-houses and loaded the picnic into two punts. But as everyone got in, it occurred to David to climb into a different punt from Sarah so as to show her that all was not forgotten. She pretended not to notice but when the two punts came together at their destination, having separated on the way, he saw that she had her head on his friend Nigel's shoulder. They set out their picnic in a field, overlooked by ponderous cows; it was not a bright evening and almost as if they felt the whole exercise was too serious, too staid, before they ate someone produced two frisbees and they all shrieked and played. They were aware that they presented a happy, bucolic scene to other punts passing down the river and that was a major part of their enjoyment. They had a red and white checked tablecloth and long loaves of French bread. But midges rose up from the river in a spinning cloud and when they had eaten, they realised that the field was damp. Coming back, did David get into the same punt as

27

Sarah and when it was not his turn to punt, sit next to her and put his arm around her in the dark?

*

'Honestly, I love the way you just assume I'm coming with you to the Ball. Don't bother to actually ask me, will you?'

'For Christ's sake, what do you expect me to do? Go down on bended knee and beg you? If you don't want to come, if you'd rather go off to your wretched Starvation Supper, all you have to do is say. It's no skin off my nose. Twenty pounds saved!'

'Oh, you weren't actually going to pay for my ticket, then? We'd be going Dutch?'

'Yes, of course we would. Catch me shelling out twenty pounds on you!'

'Huh, charming! Well in that case, let's just forget about it then, OK? I don't particularly fancy paying twenty pounds for the privilege of spending an evening with you. Balls are supposed to be memorable.'

'Oh, have you been reading your Mills and Boon again? Are you after some True Romance?'

'Oh, piss off, David. Who'd want to dance all night with a berk like you?'

On the last night of term they walked beside the river, in an evening which the English had the cheek to call close and sultry, but when that term ended they already knew their makeshift intimacy was over.

*

Returning to Oxford to begin his second year, Ravi Kaul made a resolution. He had become too entrenched in his group of Indian friends, he decided. He would never live up to his early intentions of sampling what there was to be sampled in England – which, naïve as they were, had some good sense in them – if he spent all his time with Sunil, Dev and Rajiv. They had been a fine cocoon to help him while he found his feet, but now it was high time to shake them off and be a little adventurous.

He knew one chap who was in with a tremendous lot of English students – Ali Suleiman from Pakistan. So on his second day back he called on Ali, who was surprised and flattered by the visit. The other Indian and Pakistani students usually treated him with barely concealed contempt, as an ingratiating Anglophile chameleon. As he was leaving, Ravi said, 'By the way, Ali, you know a hell of a lot of people here, don't you?'

'Do I?' asked Ali, waiting to hear what would come next.

'Yes, of course you do,' Ravi said. 'You know all sorts of people. Dev Mehdi and I were talking about it just the other day. You don't just hang around with your fellow sinners. Who are those guys at Magdalen you're always with? Tatchell? Latchell?'

'Simon Satchell,' Ali said correctly, 'and Anthony Crowmarsh. Do you mean them?'

'Yes,' said Ravi, 'probably. You're really "matey" with them, aren't you?'

Ali hesitated, for now he realised that something would be asked of him. He started to balance his head dubiously, but ended up proudly nodding 'Yes'. 'Of course,' he added quickly, 'they're not the only ones.'

'I'd like to come along and have tea with them one day, you know,' Ravi said disarmingly.

Ali giggled and asked, 'Why?' This was one favour he really did not want to grant; despite what he had implied to Ravi Kaul, he knew that his position in that group was actually false. With the heightened sensitivity of people who are often subjected to slights, Ali was quite aware how patronisingly they treated him. He saw that he was a useful symbol for boys pretending to be broadminded. But at the same time, he was genuinely fond of them. Perhaps he made the situation out to be worse than it was, as he imagined Ravi Kaul seeing it. And it was gratifying to have someone as arrogant as Ravi asking him a favour.

'Why not?' Ravi answered. 'It would be interesting to get to meet them.'

Ali pretended to be weighing up subtle issues. Then, just to show Ravi that he preferred meticulous English arrangements to slapdash verbal agreements, he said he would let him know when by means of a note in the inter-college mail.

'Pompous arse,' said Ravi in the passage.

29

The tea, a few days later, was not a great success. Ali was on edge and showed off embarrassingly. Ravi, already regretting what he saw as the grovelling which had been required to secure the invitation, was unnecessarily debonair. And the English boys were ridiculous.

That afternoon the subject under discussion was rustication, a lovely word. Someone had been rusticated for taking a pot-shot at one of the deer in the college deer park with an air-gun – did this constitute sufficient grounds for being sent down? Ali and Ravi arrived extremely late because Ali had insisted it was the thing to do. The room was ankle-deep in discarded coffee mugs and there were no biscuits left. A curly-headed chap, the Tatchell-Latchell whom Ravi had remembered, was sitting in the main armchair telling the story of an even worse offence he knew of, which had not warranted rustication. Sitting back-to-front on the two other chairs were what Ravi thought of as rugger types, listening with their arms folded along the chair backs. On the floor, there were five or six more fellows sprawled or lying with their legs jutting up into the air. There was only one girl in the room, a fairly pretty blonde girl, who was ostentatiously reading a book.

'Anyway, he actually attacked a person,' Tatchell-Latchell was saying as they came in, 'not just a sodding deer. He actually assaulted a bloody don, for heaven's sake, in the middle of the front quad!'

Ravi sat down on the floor near the bookcase where the fair-haired girl was sitting. This was not a deliberate move; there was an empty space there. The girl looked up from her book and smiled at him quite welcomingly – because he was a stranger, he imagined; she would not have stopped reading if he had been one of the familiars.

'Hi,' he said and immediately began agitating for some tea, since he hated to be thought ingratiating. It was coffee and the open jar was thrust at him from the middle of the floor. As the most recent arrival, Ali had gone down the corridor to refill the kettle.

'But he was pissed out of his mind,' someone said contentiously. 'Surely that's mitigating circumstances?'

A few of them laughed, uncertain whether or not he had spoken seriously.

'Wasn't Larkin pissed?' asked another, Larkin being the man who had shot the deer.

'Larkin's always pissed,' Tatchell-Latchell cried, to general approving laughter.

'Maybe that's it,' said one of the rugger types solemnly. 'The deer was just the last straw.'

The conversation continued like this for quite a while. Then Ravi felt obliged to butt in facetiously: 'Maybe it is your well-known national concern for animals which is responsible. Perhaps there is a strong anti-hunting lobby on the governing board and they actually feel more enraged at an attack on a deer than on one of their own number.'

This was met with an embarrassed silence, as if none of them could tell whether or not he were joking.

A little recklessly, Ravi pushed on, aware that he might be exposing himself to their ridicule. 'I mean cruelty to one another is an everyday occurrence, is it not? Whereas cruelty to a deer is quite another matter.'

Help came unexpectedly from the girl, who suddenly announced, 'I think he's right. There's a sense of outrage over a defenceless deer, which there certainly isn't over fat old Dr Percival. I mean, killing Dr Percival could actually be considered a humane act.'

'Oh, Sarah,' one or two people said, as though she were known for her outrageous statements.

'Go back to your book,' said a blond boy derisively.

'I wouldn't go that far,' Ravi said to the girl mildly, 'but you take my point.'

That was Ravi's main contribution to the tea and afterwards he did not feel encouraged to make any more. The conversation picked up again in the same jocular way. In their corner, Ravi and the girl began to talk, stiffly, seriously.

*

That experience drove him back to Sunil, Dev and Rajiv. Term got under way and he was busy choosing courses and fixing up classes. In the Long Vacation his friend Ved Sharma, a graduate student, had gone back to India and got married. He now lived out of college with his wife and they gave a superb party for all the Indian students. Ravi's resolution lapsed. He was quite surprised when a scribbled note from Simon Satchell invited him back to tea. He was inclined not to go. But he did not receive many notes like that – and on the day in question it was bitterly cold and he felt like a cup of coffee.

Again, the room was crowded. Ali Suleiman pretended to be pleased to see Ravi there, but was privately jealous. Some were born with a silver spoon, it seemed. Good-looking Ravi Kaul had only to lift a finger to get where he wanted, whereas he – short and plumpish and unimposing – might struggle all his life for nothing.

But although they had invited Ravi, none of them seemed particularly inclined to welcome him. As before, they lay about on the floor and only talked sporadically, their conversation verging on the incomprehensible. No one tried to include Ravi in it, perhaps because they did not want to fall into the usual English error of being too polite and patronising, but perhaps because they just had no idea how to approach him. He sat on the edge of things, growing more and more impatient and eventually concluded that Ali Suleiman must really be a fool to seek out this set. He looked around at the ruddy faces and he did not care if his disdain was visible.

That time, the fair-haired girl was not there. Not that he had looked forward to seeing her, but it was an even less interesting group without her. It occurred to him to ask Ali Suleiman about her afterwards.

'What's become of that girl who was there before?'

'Sarah?' Ali said familiarly. 'David Whitehead's girl?'

Ravi had not even identified David Whitehead among the taciturn guests. He tried to imagine which one of them the fair-haired girl might possibly belong to. 'Yes,' he said, 'that's right, Sarah.'

Ali giggled mischievously. 'They're through,' he said. 'Finished!' He wondered momentarily whether to let Ravi in on their gossip and then went on, 'Of course, old David hasn't let on; he'd never talk about that sort of thing. But it's pretty obvious if his lady vanishes off the face of the earth that all can't be well between them.' He added, to convey to Ravi how much more he knew of the story than Ravi did, 'He's better off without her, if you ask me. She's a trying girl.'

'Trying?' asked Ravi.

'Yes,' Ali said. 'She could be very difficult. Not my sort at all. Always raising heavy issues when you felt like relaxing, never content just to sit and let things be.'

Only because it was Ali Suleiman who was doing her down, Ravi defended the girl. 'I don't know, she seemed quite pleasant to me.'

'Well, you hardly met her,' Ali said crisply.

'Yes, but one gains an impression.'

'A wrong one,' said Ali. And, with a knowing lift of his eyebrows, which he often assumed as a worldly expression, 'She is,' he added, 'too scrawny.'

Ravi did not intend to return to that gathering, although now he easily could have unasked. He caught sight of Simon Satchell once or twice in the library and deliberately made little effort to say hello to him. Since Simon behaved like that to everyone, they stopped acknowledging each other and soon all contact between them ceased.

Ravi did not give Sarah another thought. He had sniggered slightly when Ali Suleiman told him that her surname was Livingstone because of the obvious adventurous connotation, which somehow confirmed his own impression of what kind of a girl she must be. He had come across them quite often here – tense, possibly pretty but above all intellectual girls, who seemed to sense there was something missing here, could not identify it and consequently thrashed about a lot trying to make sense of their predicament. They lived out of town in those grim women's colleges whose corridors smelt quite excruciatingly dreary and they ranged in type from positively forbidding to desperately oversexed. After a little consideration, Ravi put Sarah Livingstone towards the kinder end of the spectrum and then forgot about her.

What happened next was a coincidence but, in a small city, perfectly feasible. Ravi was walking along the street to an economics lecture with Dev Mehdi and Sunil Sircar. They turned to cross over and he saw Sarah waiting at the traffic lights on her bicycle. She was looking at him with an expression that included recognition and apprehension, but she did not call out 'Hello' – possibly because she was not sure if he would remember her. She might also have been embarrassed to be met on her bicycle wearing – he could not help noticing – bicycle clips around her jeans. She looked rather dashing, actually. The temptation to show off to Dev and Sunil was too much.

Ravi called out, 'Hi Sarah!' and saw a look of relief cross her face. She answered, 'Hello!'

He gave her a cheery wave and walked on with his friends.

'Who was that?' they both asked in Hindi. In their group, they knew all of one another's friends.

Ravi said, 'Sarah Livingstone. A girl I know slightly.'

'Aha,' said Dev Mehdi, 'but whom we don't.'

'A clandestine association,' commented Sunil Sircar, joining in the teasing. 'What exactly are you up to, Mister Kaul?'

Revi laughed, enjoying the game. 'Now, wouldn't you like to know?'

'Well, your nefarious pursuits are no concern of mine,' said Sunil.

'Just don't think they've escaped our notice,' said Dev, and they all laughed.

'Sarah Livingstone,' Sunil repeated with relish. 'And which college is she at?'

It was only then that Ravi realised that he didn't know.

Ali Suleiman knew, but Ravi was quite sick of that prig's company. In any case, why should he want to find out? It was not as if he were going to march round to Sarah's room and have afternoon tea with her; he had had enough of that scene. By and large, the girls he had met in Oxford did not appeal to him and after the disappointments of his first year, he had no intention of letting himself in for any more. The girls were mostly too explicit; like a display of bright sweets spread too long in the glaring sun, they did not rouse his appetite. After a few exploratory encounters at the beginning, he had wryly recalled a vague promise made to his father before leaving India that, whatever youthful excesses he might succumb to while he was away, he must never forget that his ultimate duty in that respect would always be awaiting him at home. At the time Ravi had laughed to himself, partly because of the roundabout way in which his father – a pompous man – had broached the subject and partly because he had no intention of being so unimaginative. He had talked to chaps who had been away and he knew what treats were in store for him, if he so chose. It was all part of the adventure of three years abroad, although he could hardly expect his reactionary father to understand that. But as it happened, he was not often tempted to break his promise. First-hand experience changed his views; treats there might be – and he knew one or two guys who availed themselves of these quite shamelessly – but they were not for Ravi.

There was another obstacle as well. Most of the girls he had met here could not shake off a severely limited attitude towards him; an Indian male was somehow not quite a normal male in their eyes and they behaved on the whole much more primly towards him than to their own kind. The one thing that he found secretly thrilling – their visible generosity with their favours – was not usually offered to him.

Ved Sharma had had a fling with an English girl before he went home to get married. None of his group had thought much of her or, for that matter, of Ved either, who was generally thought to be making a classic fool of himself.

A girl whom Ravi had nearly gone to bed with in the first term, out of sheer excitement, had utterly repelled him as they lay entwined on the floor of her room by saying, 'Oh Ravi, this is amazing! I've been with two white guys, a black guy and now an Indian. All that's left now will be a laid-back Chinese!' Two other girls, who had been very friendly to him early on and had sent him invitations to coffee, had later turned out to be keen on converting him. The rest simply were not interested; they consorted with their own kind and, sexually speaking, they looked through Ravi, as if he were made of a completely unfeasible material. Of course, he found them mainly unattractive in any case. They tended to wear unflattering clothes; they went in for freakishly bushy, far-fetched hairstyles; above all they made an awful lot of noise, screeching and cackling and thrusting themselves forward in discussions in a loud, abrasive way.

Ravi remembered all this and then curiosity got the better of him. Sarah Livingstone *had* seemed more interested than the others. After all, he kidded himself, she was a way of widening his circle of acquaintances too. So he dropped in on Ali Suleiman.

*

Sarah's room was right at the top of one of the grimmer buildings of the women's colleges. He had not sent her a note beforehand, in case it looked as though he were unsure of himself and since he was a little, he told himself as he knocked that she would be out. But she was not; he liked the way she shouted, 'Come in?' It sounded as if she was glad to be interrupted at whatever it was she was doing. She was sitting at her desk by the window, with the chair half turned round to see who was at the door. When she saw it was Ravi, she got up quickly.

He said something pitifully silly, which had occurred to him when Ali told him Sarah's surname, but which he had promised himself on the way over that he would not use. 'Ah, Miss Livingstone, I presume?'

She went 'Tsk!' She must have heard the quip a hundred times before, but she smiled, at herself and at him. 'Come in, sit down.'

Ravi did both. 'You remember, we met?'

'Yes, of course. At Simon's. We talked about hunting.'

Ravi smiled, then heard himself say something appalling: 'Now I expect you think I've come to do some hunting myself.'

Sarah looked taken aback, but quickly said flippantly, 'So long as you haven't come armed!'

They faced each other. For a moment, it seemed as if they were going to dislike each other after all.

'Only with my monetarism file,' Ravi replied in kind. 'I was on my way back from a seminar,' he explained untruthfully, 'and I thought I remembered this was your college. Not the most welcoming of entrances, if I may say so.'

Sarah agreed readily, clearly relieved that Ravi had moved

on to such a simple subject. 'It's ghastly, isn't it? You know it used to be a lunatic asylum?'

'No!'

'Yes, it did. At least, that's the story – well, not this wing, but Quincy opposite. Did you see it on the way in?'

'The older one?'

'Yes, that's right. It's supposed to be haunted; apparently a mad woman in a long white dress sometimes walks and weeps there at night.'

'You're having me on.'

'No, no, that's what people say. Mind you . . .'

They both laughed. For a moment, there was nothing to talk about again. Then Sarah said slightly artificially, 'I don't remember – which college did you say you were at? Have you got any ghosts?'

'Only live ones, as far as I know,' Ravi said.

'Oh, we have them here too,' said Sarah, gesturing distastefully at the wall. 'In fact, I've got one next door.'

'Ah, I passed a rather funny-looking female on the way up,' Ravi said. 'A moony sort of girl. She looked a little like an exhibit gone missing from a waxworks museum.'

'Oh, lovely!' Sarah said. 'In a long purple dress? That was her.'

She poured coffee and put Ravi's mug on the low table in front of him.

'I'm afraid I haven't got any biscuits. I'm frightened of keeping them in my room.'

Ravi laughed. 'How funny; you seem quite cool about ghosts, but biscuits really rattle you!'

Sarah was reaching out onto the window-sill for a carton of milk. She straightened up to explain seriously, 'Ghosts don't contain calories. They're not fattening and I'm petrified of getting fat.'

'Well, you don't need to worry about that,' Ravi said. 'You're very thin.'

Sarah looked delighted. 'Thank you,' she answered, although in fact Ravi had not especially intended the remark as a compliment at all.

'Being fat is really an obsession here, isn't it?' he asked. 'You're all so guilty about your size. I mean, even a slip of a thing like you. Everyone is weighed down by a great burden of guilt they're trying to shake off. What is it? A bad conscience as an individual or a historical legacy?'

Sarah considered the issue. 'But why is it almost exclusively women?' she said. 'If it's a matter of guilt, why should we carry all the burden?'

There was something very nice about the way she said that, Ravi thought, leaning forward and challenging him with her pleading eyes.

'I don't know,' he replied. 'Maybe because the women here are more sensitive than the men, more susceptible to moral qualms.'

Sarah gave a flattered, disbelieving laugh. 'Do you find them insensitive, then?' she asked him. 'The men here?'

Ravi barely hesitated. He had thought about the topic so much. He knew this girl would relish an attack on her own kind. 'Totally,' he declared, 'and proud of it!'

'You're in your second year, aren't you?' she asked and that annoyed him; checking up on his right to make such an accusation, aligning herself with those he attacked.

'Yes,' he answered drily. 'My comments are the considered judgement of a year's observation.'

Sarah smiled, embarrassed by his touchiness. 'Go on,' she said, 'I'm interested.'

And Ravi swallowed her unintended insult and continued. So what if she first felt it necessary to check on his credentials, he could shake her from her smugness. Vengefully, he launched into one of his withering verbal caricatures of Oxford. He showed her an antiquated city, peopled by museum exhibits who went through the motions of being alive inside the safety of their glass cases. As he talked, instead of dismay, he saw Sarah Livingstone's face light up with the joy of recognition.

They led each other on to wilder denunciations. It was as if, for the past year, they had been waiting on the sidelines, filled with self-righteous indignation at the pageant in front of them. And they loved denouncing it – witty, unkind jibes seemed to come naturally from both of them.

'We should talk again,' Ravi said easily when he decided

38

to leave. Briefly, they had really enjoyed themselves and now they exchanged slightly self-conscious smiles.

'OK,' agreed Sarah.

Ravi felt rather pleased with the way things had gone; virtually no awkwardness, no artificiality – they had just had a good time together. But because he did not want to seem eager or enthusiastic, he left without arranging anything further.

The door of Sarah's room opened behind him as he walked away down the corridor and her blushing, flustered face appeared.

'Sorry!'

Ravi waited.

'I'm terribly sorry, but I just realised that I don't actually know your name!'

It came like a blow beneath the belt and left Ravi momentarily too winded to reply. Why hadn't she said anything earlier on? The revelation undermined his impression of the whole afternoon; why had she sat there right through their conversation without asking him? If he had been one of her English chums, she would have said straight away, 'What did you say your name was?' And why had he not thought to introduce himself, instead of confidently assuming that she would remember his name? Of course, anything other than English certainty was unpronounceable. The little bitch! She had been so full of unctuous eagerness, of Girl Guide brightness that she had quite forgotten he was an individual with anything so distinctive as a name. She was just being nice to a poor foreigner; she was no different from all the rest.

'Ravi Kaul,' he said stiffly and then continued a little abruptly down the corridor.

It was only as he walked back into town, through the transparent drizzle, that it struck him that Sarah had had no need to reveal what she had done. She could perfectly well have stayed quietly ignorant in her room. The fact that she had come out after him to retrieve his name meant that she expected to see him again.

*

The arrival of the good-looking Indian from Simon's tea-party at her door had astounded Sarah. They had had a rather stilted social conversation together and she had registered almost nothing of his personality at all. She remembered only that he had been slightly aggressive, which she had liked, since this was directed at David's friends. He had also seemed somehow rigid, she recalled, as though he were keeping his real reactions in check. She had not noticed any sign of interest in her which might have led her to expect him to turn up at her door.

She said, 'Come in, sit down,' a little at a loss.

Very formally, he said, 'You remember, we met?'

'Yes, of course,' Sarah said quickly. 'At Simon's. We talked about hunting.'

She wanted to put him at his ease by showing what a clear impression he had made on her. Apparently flattered, he giggled and quickly showed her that he was quite at ease and she need not have made the effort.

'Now I expect you think I've come to do some hunting myself?'

'Oh God,' Sarah thought. 'I'm not going to be pursued by one of those, am I?' By which she meant a poseur, a social performer who would pester her with visits and letters, but nothing racial at all.

'So long as you haven't come armed,' she responded flippantly.

She had hoped he might be excitingly unconventional – being Indian, she felt he ought to be – but this was an opening of the most predictable kind.

Hostility flickered momentarily between them and a little resentfully – she had been trying to write an essay – Sarah started to prepare coffee. They made small talk about the college buildings, about the other students. Since she now thought he was bound to be a traditional sort, Sarah apologised for not having anything to offer him for tea.

To her surprise, he started to make fun of her. Her initial behaviour, she realised, had been patronising, but she was still slightly annoyed to be seen so unquestioningly as a typical English young lady, who entertained gentlemen to afternoon tea and whose social behaviour was totally governed by convention. When he began to make fun of the university, she felt oddly defensive even though she knew that in principle she was equally fiercely against what he was mocking. That was because he included her in it.

They had a keen discussion and to make it quite clear to him that she did not care a great deal for the university either, Sarah even overdid her criticisms. He was certainly very funny and his caricatures of Oxford were vicious and astute. In the relief of finding common ground, they seemed to encourage each other in overstatements.

'You walk around in glass cases, it seems to me. You're all petrified of bumping into one another on your little island.'

And Sarah replied, 'Would you want to bump into some of the characters strutting around here?'

'We should talk again,' he said, when eventually Sarah stood up to switch on the light. She had not really intended this to be a hint, but he seemed sensitively to interpret it as such.

They had talked for over an hour. It was nearly dark in the room and unwittingly an atmosphere of intimacy had been created.

'OK,' Sarah said guardedly, for while she had ended up enjoying herself, she could not help wondering if the Indian might not become a strain on further visits.

She had tried to manipulate the conversation in such a way that he would mention his name, which she could not remember. She was embarrassed to ask him, and now she felt she had left it too late. At the beginning, it might have been discouraging. Later, it would have been out of place.

He thanked her for the coffee and as he stood at the door, about to leave, he flashed her a bright, mischievous smile.

It was only when he was already out in the corridor that she was struck by a way of sabotaging that irritating parting impression of intimacy. On an impulse, she opened the door and called out. He turned.

'I'm terribly sorry, but I just realised that I don't actually know your name.'

It was almost as though she had kicked him and Sarah immediately regretted her unkind impulse. He mumbled something which she just distinguished as 'Ravi Kaul' and went on his way.

She said, 'Oh, OK, thanks', but he walked on without any response. She realised that his offence might dissuade him from ever coming to visit her again and felt a quite unexpected pang of regret.

*

Ravi mulled over his mixed feelings about Sarah Livingstone for nearly a week. She had let him down; she had been silly. A flush of embarrassment still spread over him at the memory of Sarah's face bleating from the doorway: 'I'm terribly sorry, but I just realised that I don't actually know your name.' Until then, they had got on so well. She was quick and spirited and there had even been a moment – as she told him feelingly about her reactions to her first night in the college – when he had felt that they had something in common. He regretted the possibility of not seeing her again. Before her disastrous postscript, he had really thought that he liked her.

'How's Miss Livingstone?' Dev teased him. 'When are we going to be introduced?'

In the end, Ravi came to the conclusion that he and Sarah had got on best at a level of joky repartee. He decided that an approach on these lines might be a way of getting his own back on her, so he sent her a note:

Dear Sarah,

The Film Society is showing an extremely interesting Russian film this Friday: *The Battleship Potemkin* by Eisenstein. Would you like to come and see it? We could perhaps have a meal together afterwards.

Yours, Anonymous

And Sarah, who of her own accord would never have dreamt of going to see some obscure Russian film, considered his invitation and then wrote back:

Dear Anonymous,

I'd love to see *The Battleship Potemkin*. How, when, where?

Yours abjectly, Sarah Livingstone

After the film, Ravi took Sarah to one of the little Indian restaurants. It was a slightly aggressive thing to do; he would enjoy rubbing her nose in his pungent origins. But as he pushed open the door of the Shah Jehan and inhaled its warm fuggy air, he wondered if bringing her there was not a silly mistake.

The waiters, crude boys, did not conceal their amusement at the sight of their regular client Ravi dining with Sarah and – as ill luck would have it – Ved Sharma and his wife came in soon after them. Ved looked intrigued but made a great display of waving discreetly and not coming over to talk to them. His new wife stared at Sarah quite openly.

'Mm, I love curry,' Sarah said as they read the menu.

Ravi suppressed a pedantic wish to explain to her that the word 'curry' was a British over-simplification which had nothing to do with Indian cooking at all. But her eager appetite for what he was offering her encouraged him. He felt quite benevolent now. He was aware of Ved and Amrita discussing what he was up to on the other side of the restaurant but he rather relished the reputation he was about to acquire.

'Do you eat Indian food quite a lot, then?' he asked Sarah.

'My father loves it,' she answered, having unwittingly shown by her choice of dishes that she knew nothing about it at all. 'He's spent quite a bit of time in India.'

'Has he?' said Ravi, feeling hostility instantly well up inside him. 'In the army or with some government outfit?'

Sarah's laughter took him aback. How could she possibly know the image which he had in mind as he asked that question? But it turned out that she was laughing at the idea of her father, whom she described as 'wishy-washy', being in the army.

'No, no,' she explained. 'He's a photographer; Gareth Livingstone – you might have heard of him.'

Ravi had not, but already he imagined the photographs: India summed up in a number of big, high quality, award-winning pictures – temples, children, inevitably children, and if Mr Livingstone had been brave enough to leave the big cities or to travel by train, some austere artistic shots of the Indian landscape. So those were the images which Sarah

43

Livingstone had of India. Well, he thought wryly, probably better than Oxfam advertisements.

'Do you like his photographs?' he asked patronisingly. 'Are they any good?'

Sarah recoiled a little, as though he had really asked her something rather shocking, but considered his question for a moment before she replied. 'Well actually, they're all rather similar, you know. I mean, people can tell if a picture's taken by my father whether it's in India or in Hyde Park. It's as though he sees the same things everywhere.'

'How can that be?' Ravi joked. 'Mughal monuments, yogis, elephants?'

Sarah smiled. 'Don't you think,' she said, 'that some people take their country with them everywhere?'

Their food arrived as she started to tell him about her parents and her younger brother John, their house in the white London crescent. It turned out that she was pretty curious about Ravi's home and family too. Even if she had viewed him as a lone outsider in a vacuum to begin with, now she was clearly intrigued by the faraway place he came from.

All the dishes at the Shah Jehan were basically the same and Ravi felt a little ashamed of the way Sarah enthused about them. When they had eaten, he thought of inviting her back to his room for coffee, but rejected the conventionality of the gesture and walked back to her college with her. As they approached it down the silent suburban street, Ravi thought he sensed Sarah growing tense with suspicion. Surely she didn't imagine he intended to try anything on, did she? She made an unnecessary reference to something she had to do rather early the next morning and annoyed, Ravi said facetiously, 'Don't worry, I'm not going to try and insinuate myself into your bedchamber.'

Sarah looked round at him in the dark, taken aback by the irritation in his voice. 'Oh, but do come up for *coffee*,' she said.

Ravi was quite disgusted by this remark. Primly he replied, 'No thank you.'

When they reached the great front gate, he wished Sarah good night a trifle stiffly, standing very straight in front of

44

her. Just after she had answered 'Good night – and thank you', the clock boomingly struck midnight right overhead and they both laughed spontaneously. Sarah scuttled in through the gate as an elderly porter came out to close it and Ravi, looking back automatically as he walked away, caught sight of her fair hair glinting in the bright gateway.

✳

'Well, try anything once, I suppose,' Sarah had said to Emily Williams when Ravi's invitation to the film arrived.

From Sarah's description of his visit, Emily said that the Indian sounded intense, but concluded that Sarah would probably like that.

'Is he good-looking?' she asked and when Sarah nodded vigorously, she exclaimed joyfully, 'Well then, go – for heaven's sake, go! They don't exactly grow on trees around here, do they?'

Sarah discussed most things with Emily Williams, liking the brash comments which Emily offered. The successive disappointments of Emily's first year had made her cultivate a cynical stance.

'Ah well,' said Sarah now, 'try anything once.'

She went straight up to her room after the meal with Ravi at the Shah Jehan, but then decided to go and talk to Emily after all. She had intended to tell her what a fascinating evening it had been, how refreshing it was to have a new angle on everything. But Emily forestalled her; she had caught sight of Ravi Kaul by arrangement when he arrived to collect Sarah and she had found him ravishing. Now, having sat by herself all evening, feeling lonely and fed-up with the limitations of her life, she found the very idea of Ravi Kaul ravishing and she greeted Sarah crying, 'He's gorgeous, he's absolutely delectable!'

Quite unintentionally, Sarah abandoned what she had been going to say about how stimulating it had been talking to Ravi Kaul and found herself instead enthusing about his eyes and his hair, his unusual Indian shirts and the wonderful way he threw back his head when he laughed.

The idea that she could conceivably fall in love with an Indian only then occurred to Sarah – so far, she had thought

45

of Ravi Kaul as a diversion. It landed on her mental landscape like a bomb. It blew out the confines of her future, destroyed the stacked years of duller expectations. But of course, Ravi was the antithesis of David Whitehead. She found the idea so exciting that she could not sleep that night for thinking about it. Lying in her lumpy bed in the dark, where David Whitehead had always complained that the broken springs hurt his rugby injury, she tried to imagine the contrast.

*

Ravi had planned to invite Sarah Livingstone to a concert of classical guitar music the following Friday, but she pre-empted him. On the Tuesday morning, he received a note from her in the inter-college mail, asking him to a tea-party which she was giving that Thursday. He was highly delighted by this gesture and also surprised by the promptness with which Sarah had let him know that she was interested in him. The note flattered him and it only occurred to him very briefly to wonder if he might be about to get into deep waters. But he was also vindictively glad of an early opportunity to remind her of his dignity. Although he would have quite liked to go to the tea-party, he was pleased that it coincided with a seminar on the recession and he was able to write back briefly saying that he could not come.

*

His two-line reply offended Sarah deeply. She had made a brave gesture, she felt, in asking him to tea and now, in her terms, he was playing hard to get. It did not cross her mind that Ravi's behaviour might be quite straightforward and governed by nothing more than honesty. She decided that he was trying to lead her on.

She spent much of that week contemplating her image of a love affair between herself and Ravi Kaul. It was an alluring vision in which she, as well as her surroundings, was somehow transformed into something more elegant and interesting. Ravi she only saw as a dark foreigner and a glamorous seducer. He had no particular personal features yet; he was just the path that he could lead her down. She

46

was, in fact, perhaps not thinking about Ravi at all but only about her own adventure.

He arrived unexpectedly on Sunday morning, when in theory visitors were not allowed into the college. Later he claimed that he had told the portress that he had come all the way from Delhi. His first words did not placate her.

'Tut, tut, not at church?'

It was Remembrance Sunday. In the city, near the War Memorial, a cannon had just begun booming and its solemn thuds made their conversation seem sillier than it was.

'I never go to church,' Sarah said defensively.

'I never for a moment thought that you did,' Ravi answered lightly. 'We are two heathen together.'

He appeared not to notice Sarah's bad temper and his cheeriness made her feel she was being crabby. She smiled. 'You aren't at all religious then either?'

To her puzzlement he seemed embarrassed by the question, although their exchange had been after all quite light-hearted. When he replied, 'No, no, not at all,' it sounded like an evasion.

They heard the cannon stop and the Silence began.

'Did the tea-party go well?' Ravi asked. 'I was sorry I couldn't make it.'

'Oh, it was nothing much,' Sarah said. 'Just a few people. But it was a pity you couldn't come; Ali Suleiman was here.'

Ravi suddenly glared at her. 'Well, in that case, frankly I'm almost glad I wasn't here. I've had more than enough of Ali Suleiman recently.'

Sarah said, 'I thought you were good friends.'

'Whatever gave you that impression?' Ravi snapped. 'Just because we're both the same hue doesn't mean we must like each other, you know.'

'Oh God, why do you have to attribute such stupid motives to me?' Sarah exclaimed. 'You must think I'm a total moron.'

Ravi jumped. 'Nothing of the sort,' he answered. 'In fact, quite the contrary. But why should you think I was such good friends with Ali Suleiman? Do we seem at all similar to you?'

'No,' Sarah said. 'Yes. You came along to Simon's

together. You're both – serious about things. You both – you both like issues. And he's always talking about you.'

'Is he? *Is* he? What does he say?'

'Well, at tea on Thursday, when I said I'd asked you but you couldn't come, he told me I should take you with a pinch of salt, that you gave a very suave impression but really it was all a big act.' She giggled.

Ravi swore under his breath; then he threw back his head, struck his knee and started laughing. 'And you really thought he could say that and still be a good friend of mine?'

'Well, men are always trying to do each other down, aren't they? Anyway, isn't it obvious? He's jealous of you.'

Ravi looked astonished. 'Jealous? You think so?'

'Yes,' Sarah said, 'I do.' It annoyed her that, despite her intention to humble Ravi Kaul, he was coming out of this conversation better than she was. 'I'm surprised you haven't noticed. If you want my honest opinion, I think he's a bit pathetic; he takes himself so seriously and he doesn't realise that everyone's making fun of him.'

Such mixed feelings met on Ravi's face that for a moment his expression curdled.

'If you must know,' Sarah went on, 'I really only invited him because I felt a bit sorry for him and I thought that if you were there, it would be a good sort of bridge.'

'He's a pompous arse,' Ravi said. 'Really, he's ridiculous! Who does he think he's fooling? "Take me with a pinch of salt"! I'm amazed you should think we were friends.'

'Well, I thought you were both exiles in a foreign land. And he brought you along to Simon's that time, didn't he? I thought maybe you had taken him under your wing or something.'

They united in attacking a third party, as their attack on the university had united them before. The easy game of doing down poor Ali Suleiman, who had played a fool's part in bringing them together, put an end to their hostility. Ravi dealt with his single twinge of guilt by thinking that Ali was a pretty low sort of character in any case.

When it was nearly lunchtime, he suggested that they walk to a country pub for lunch. On the way there they were still self-conscious, aware of the quarrel they had just patched up. They were too obligingly amused by each other, too jovial, while at the back of both their minds there was still a score to settle. But the pub was busy, it was a favourite Sunday lunch-time outing and it took them a while to order drinks and food and to find a place to sit down. By the time all that was done and they were wedged beside each other on an antique wooden seat, they seemed to be like minds once more in a laughable universe.

Ravi said with amusement, 'Ploughman's Lunch!' and lightly prodded his plate of symmetrically arranged cheese.

Sarah had a sudden insight then into what it was to be a foreigner in her own country. The sight of Ravi Kaul looking down laughing at that blandly mundane object made a lasting impression on her. Even as she giggled appreciatively, she began to see how time spent with Ravi Kaul would be time in a different country; England would not be familiar and hidebound any more, seen through Ravi's eyes.

Out of keeping with her thoughts, her mouth said, 'What would that be in India? A ploughman's lunch?' And when Ravi snorted sardonically and started to explain to her how meagre and frugal it would be, she tasted another aspect of the future – how enjoyably she would do penance for the historical legacy of guilt which Ravi had identified in her.

She ate his pickled onions, which he left, and was aware that, for some unknown reason, he found this little piece of flirtatious greed immensely pleasing.

'Have some more,' he said. 'I'll order you a whole plateful.'

'Oh God, no! You'll have to walk upwind of me all the way back.'

'And, above all, not try to kiss you.'

'Oh, were you planning to?'

'Do you like sharp tastes then? I have a pickle sent to me from home which you must try if you do. It's my mother's speciality; one little bite and you can never forget it. I think she sent it to make sure I didn't forget my home.'

'Does she send you lots of stuff?'

'No, no, only when someone comes. You can't send things

like that through the post, you know. Your customs men don't like these dirty, unhygienic foreign treats . . .'

'They're not *my* customs men. They wouldn't like my treats any better if I tried to bring them back from abroad.'

'That's what you think. Anyway, they *are* your customs men. They are protecting the sterility of your sceptred isle. And Indian pickles in unlabelled jars are a threat which might pollute it. We have to hide them in our washing.'

'Well, I dissociate myself from them.'

'That's fine by me, Sarah.'

'Does she think you might forget your home, then? Or were you just joking?'

'Well, four thousand miles is a long way, you know. I wouldn't be the first to forget his way back.'

'Do *you* think you might?'

'Never. I mean . . . sometimes, obviously, I imagine it. I imagine staying here or going on to America and the idea seems quite fun. But after all, India's where I belong, isn't it? Would you ever leave England and go off for good and settle somewhere else?'

'Oh, tomorrow.'

'Tomorrow? That's what you *say*. But you've never tried it, have you? I bet you'd find you couldn't, actually. You'd wake up one morning in Timbuctoo and find you missed something which you just couldn't get there. And you'd have to go home to find it.'

'Like pickle?'

'As a symbol, pickle will do.'

'Well, I think you're wrong. There's nothing English I would wake up craving for in Timbuctoo.'

'Ah, that's so easily said, Sarah. It's nice to imagine you're quite fancy-free. But what about afternoon tea or face flannels?'

'Face flannels?'

'Face flannels – that's what you call them, isn't it – have always struck me as being quintessentially English.'

'I could manage perfectly well without face flannels.'

'Well, if you're so certain, then maybe you should try it out one day and see.'

'I intend to.'

They grinned at each other across the pub table, flanked by contented Englishmen with beer mugs – taking each other on as a challenge, as a dare.

*

Ravi returned to his college and, to his slight annoyance, found Sunil Sircar in his room, lying on the bed with the radio on, waiting for him to come back.

'The man himself! Where have you been?' Sunil asked, scarcely glancing up from a book of Ravi's which he was reading.

Although Ravi usually enjoyed the conviviality of Sunil's and Dev's long visits, for once he would have been glad to have his room to himself. He had been taken almost unawares by his liking for Sarah Livingstone and needed to work out where it left him.

'To London to see the Queen!' he snapped.

Sunil looked up from the book and asked, 'What's bitten you?'

Ravi took off his jacket and glared at Sunil. 'Nothing,' he said furiously. 'Maybe I would just like to lie down on my bed, read a book and listen to the radio.'

Sunil gesticulated generously and rolled closer to the wall. 'There's room for two here.'

'For heaven's sake,' said Ravi, 'you're the end!'

Sunil narrowed his eyes. 'Has something happened?'

He pushed away Ravi's jacket – which landed over his face – and burst into a loud, smug laugh.

'Shut up!' Ravi cried and told him to go away and leave him alone, which offended Sunil, privacy being a taste which Ravi Kaul had only very recently begun to develop.

*

Sarah locked her door and did not answer when Emily Williams knocked on it. She wanted to relive the pub and the walk again in her memory, so as to be certain of what she had felt: aghast excitement and fascination with the foreign profile beside her. Ravi Kaul must be the more interesting version of her life for which she had long hoped. Although she had boasted to him that she would leave

51

England without a backward glance, now she was frightened by the prospect of even looking out to sea.

It was almost, ridiculously, as if both of them knew and were terrified that already they had gone too far.

For the rest of that term, they continued to meet tentatively once or twice a week, quietly amazed to feel their interest growing to obsession.

Afterwards, it seemed to have been a time of caution, approaching each other with infinite care. Ravi sent notes and paid visits; Sarah still deliberated if she would be in or out. But things which they could not predict made all their caution ridiculous – the joy of their own contrast when they began to walk side by side, she so blonde and he so dark and different; the sound of the other's voice infinitesimally mispronouncing their name and the dangerous, irresistible depths of a person inside whom was an unknown country.

*

In the last week of term, Sarah invited Ravi to a mince-pie party given by a girl called Joanna Richardson. As he walked out to her college in the dark, it occurred to Ravi that this would probably be the last time he and Sarah saw each other before the end of term and he could not help feeling a little relief, as well as wistfulness. It was all tremendous, but it was getting out of hand. He was fond of Sarah and Sarah was undoubtedly fond of him, but would it not perhaps be better to leave it at that? Student couples passed him in the dark, holding on to each other and laughing loudly to parade their happiness. Ravi imagined what it would be like to be fully part of the strolling street. No, it would be small-minded to back out now.

The party was held in Joanna Richardson's room after dinner, with records of Christmas carols and candlelight. Joanna was a large, clean-faced, kindly girl who seemed too motherly for an environment of spinsters. Her guests sat on the floor, their faces shining with the season as they laughingly recalled Christmases of their childhood. Joanna passed round trays of her sugary, white misshapen pies. Whether he wanted to or not, Ravi stood out like a ghost at their feast and inevitably drew Sarah out with him. Sitting in her room beforehand, waiting for him to arrive, she had enjoyed the realisation that she was very much looking forward to it. She had also enjoyed arriving at the party with Ravi, her friends' momentary and almost imperceptible confusion and their instant reassessment of both of them. Now she sat close to him and enjoyed the way his presence separated her from her companions. Ravi had not known the shape of a tangerine in his stocking on a peculiar morning, nor the annual bilious excess of sweet mincemeat. When Joanna Richardson asked him with painstaking politeness, 'What festivals do you celebrate?', Sarah enjoyed the collusion with which their feet impulsively nudged. Although she did not know which festivals Ravi celebrated either, they had already made fun of that politeness; they called it 'Feed the Faint and Hungry Heathen' and Sarah would never use it again. Ravi told Joanna one or two strange names and she exclaimed, 'How interesting!' Sarah smiled condescendingly at her and felt proud to have access to Ravi's world. This must be the crossing-over time, she thought, feeling stranded in a heady vacuum; she had left England behind her already, but she had no idea of India. She watched Ravi's laughing face in the candlelight as he listened to the distorted schoolboy versions of Christmas carols; *she* knew what he was laughing at, but the singers raising their glasses of mulled wine and roaring, 'A *bar* of Sunlight Soap came down and they be*gan* to scrub,' had no idea. She let her gaze feed on Ravi's brown face and the twin pinpoints of light in his eyes. She saw in them such a potent, such a huge alternative to the faces of the roistering chorus that she was transfixed. Feeling her stare, Ravi turned and read in it such an extent of unuttered longing that he was shaken. Moved by affection, gratification and pity, he reached over and vigorously squeezed Sarah's hand.

It was wonderfully cosy going back to her room together afterwards, drinking coffee and making fun of the mince-pie party. Sarah was elated because she imagined then that she had escaped at last. Ravi kissed her goodbye slowly and carefully and, walking back to his college, he whistled in the night.

*

53

And then there was Christmas, bloody Christmas, just as things were getting exciting. Sarah went home to a house about to be cheerily decorated with crêpe paper and tinsel, with a lighted tree in the living-room and holly around the frames of her father's favourite photographs. Ravi went to stay with a friend's cousin's family in Sheffield into whose hermetically Indian home, despite many children, Christmas hardly permeated at all.

Sarah thought about Ravi every day. Ravi thought about Sarah less, not because he was any less interested at that stage, but because for him she was part of the university and the university did not extend as far as Sheffield. For Sarah, the university was that period of her life and she took it with her everywhere. Mr and Mrs Livingstone entertained a good deal at Christmas time and as Sarah had once gloomily predicted, they brought her into the conversation with, 'You know Sarah's up at Oxford now? Doesn't it make one feel old?' Sarah smiled and held out trays of canapés to personalities her father had photographed and did her best to convey the impression that away at university she led an exotic secret life. She imagined Ravi surveying her parents' parties with amused scorn and she surveyed them with amused scorn in his place. In Sheffield, Ravi saw a different England. He had few reasons to venture out into what seemed to him a hostile Northern city. His friend's cousin's family wrapped him in the continuous round of their activities. Late one night, a shaven-headed boy spat at him as he walked home and jeered, 'Paki!' Ravi told this story afterwards in Oxford, laughing so as to obtain the maximum discomfort from his English audience. He lay on his bed and read. The vacation lasted six weeks.

*

The sight of each other on the first day of the next term put an end to their caution. A few hours after they arrived back in Oxford, Ravi set out on foot to Sarah's college and Sarah got onto her bicycle to ride round to his. They met at the corner of two central streets and broke into a helpless grin at the ridiculous recognition of their happiness. Sarah looked just as Ravi liked to think of her – pink-cheeked with cold

54

and exercise, her fair hair ruffled by her bicycle ride. She was the picture of a jolly English girl on a hockey pitch who, by some freak of fortune, had landed in his path. And Ravi stood on the kerb as he had stayed all through the vacation in Sarah's imagination – the foreigner who was going to transform her and her surroundings.

'Ravi!'

'Sarah!'

Her bicycle wobbled in to the kerb. A delivery van, driven by a malignant grocer who hated students, braked excessively sharply and hooted at them.

'Look out! You'll get yourself knocked down.'

'Who cares! Did you have a good vac?'

'So-so. And yours?'

'Dreadful. Tedious. Boring. I couldn't wait to get back.'

'That bad?' He asked mischievously. 'Didn't you enjoy your Christmas?'

'Oh, *Ravi*—' Sarah was still on her bicycle, beaming at Ravi as he stood by the handlebars and grinned back at her. He flipped her arm teasingly and as she made to return his nudge, they toppled into the beginning of an embrace.

'Hello, hello!'

'Get off your bike before we have an accident. Imagine the indignity; having a bike accident when you aren't even moving.'

'I'd blame it on you. Let me get off then.'

Ravi's arm around Sarah's shoulders, Sarah's arm around Ravi's waist, they walked to his college which was the nearer. As they came into the front quadrangle, Dev Mehdi saw them linked for the first time and a new era began.

They went up to Ravi's room and he made tea. But he kept interrupting to look round at Sarah and grin. Everything was so funny – the thick dust of his uninhabited room, the lack of milk. They examined each other with delight. The Christmas vacation behind them was their joint achievement and they wanted to crow over it.

'I was coming round to see you,' Sarah admitted.

'Were you?' Ravi exclaimed joyfully. '*Were* you?'

'Yes, really I was. I bet you were on your way out to see me? Admit it.'

'No, actually, I wasn't. I'm sorry to disappoint you, but actually I wasn't . . . Mind you, I probably wouldn't have been long in coming.'

'They've repainted my corridor.'

'A treat in store for me.'

'They've painted it the colour of grass-snake's puke. I don't know who chose it; it's disgusting.'

'Well, maybe you'd better continue to come round here instead.'

'I see. Any excuse for not trekking all the way out to college. What if I can't be bothered to come here either?'

'I shall die of a broken heart,' said Ravi, spooning three steep heaps of sugar into his tea.

They laughed triumphantly and Ravi said, 'Sit closer.' He could not help marvelling at the uninhibited promptness with which Sarah did. Experimentally, he put his arm around her shoulders again and started to muddle her hair. She looked round at him and giggled.

'Tell me what you did in Sheffield.'

'Not a great deal. You know, it's not much of a place.'

'I've never been there. I don't know the North of England.'

'No? It's not very far away; but I think it's another country. The people I met seemed quite different from you snooty lot down here. They're more friendly, I think. At least, some of them. But you know someone spat at me one night and called me "Paki"?'

'No! Ravi, that's terrible.'

'I think it's rather funny. "Paki"! I could hardly stop him and give him a little lecture about Partition. I don't think he would have taken that very kindly. I must remember to tell Ali Suleiman that I've been promoted to be his honorary compatriot.'

'Ugh, I think that's horrible. How can you joke about it?'

'Why are you getting so upset? You must know that kind of thing happens all the time.'

'What was that you said – partition? What is that? Is it like apartheid?'

In the shadow of the winter afternoon, the distance between them was suddenly vast. 'You haven't heard of Partition?'

'I told you, I don't know anything about India. You'll have to teach me.'

'This involved Britain as well, you know.'

'Did it? Oh dear. Well, I'm afraid I'm terribly ignorant. Is there a good book I could read about it?'

Was the most dangerous difference between them this – that Ravi knew about Sarah's origins because they were laid out all around for him to see, but Sarah had no idea of what had given rise to Ravi? If so, Ravi was at an advantage from the beginning.

'I'll lend you one. If you really want to read about it.'

'I do, I do. It's awful how little I know.'

'Awful,' Ravi agreed teasingly, taking a strand of yellow hair and twisting it between his fingers. 'But I'll forgive you.'

'That's as well. Make me some more tea, then.'

'Why was your vacation so dreadful? Didn't you have a good time at home?'

'Oh Ravi, you can't imagine what Christmas at home is like. My parents invite all the most inane people whom they couldn't bear to entertain all the rest of the year and they have these big boring parties where everyone circulates, repeating to one another what the last person has just said to them. Oh God! I only got through it by imagining what we'd make of it if you were there and having this satirical running commentary going in my head.'

'Really? You invited me along in spirit, in other words?'

'Well, yes. Did you think about me at all in the vac?'

'Not at all,' Ravi answered with mock gravity. With another shout of jubilant laughter, they grabbed each other and fell giggling across the carpet where they sat.

*

In those days, Sarah's sum knowledge of India could have been catalogued something like this: Capital – Delhi (New Delhi), although whether or not there was also an Old Delhi she had no idea. It had once been ruled by Britain for a stuffy and easily mocked period called the Raj, during which there had been a Mutiny, sparked off by Hindu sepoys refusing to bite off the ends of cartridges because they believed they had been defiled by beef fat. In India, the cow was sacred. Sacred cows wandered amid the traffic of big cities and often caused dire traffic jams because if they lay down in a main road, no one dared to shift them. The climate was dreadful; the heat was horrendous and there were monsoons. The Prime Minister was Mrs Indira Gandhi, who had bizarrely black and white striped hair like Cruella de Vil in *A Hundred and One Dalmatians*. The population was enormous; millions, starving millions who conjured up the haggard faces on an Oxfam poster. They tried to stop people having so many children there, but it was no good; the idea that having lots of children ensured a comfortable old age was too deeply rooted in the poor people's beliefs. Colouring the whole catalogue with the queasy taint of guilt was the message of the posters: poverty.

Of course, when Sarah first began to grow interested in Ravi Kaul, he seemed to have nothing to do with India. He was a foreigner, but it hardly mattered to her which country he came from. His skin alone made him exotic and probably she did not think about the rest of him at the beginning. When she came to know Ravi a little better, and his friends, the country they came from did not seem a real one either. It was a looking-glass country which sent bright, shimmering reflections across the English winter. The Indians were like humming-birds beside the dowdy pigeons who were their English contemporaries. It took Sarah years to realise that Ravi Kaul was not gloriously alone in the world, but part of a pattern no less pervasive than her own.

*

When he got back from eating with Sarah in the Shah Jehan that night, Ravi went round to Dev's room and accused him of being a meddling old woman.

'You couldn't leave me alone, could you?' he shouted. 'You had to hang about in the front quad to spy on me!'

'I was on my way to see you,' protested Dev. 'We haven't seen each other for a while.'

Ravi was not seriously angry and Dev knew it. He was too pleased by the direction developments were taking to get seriously annoyed by his friends' reactions. In fact, Dev shared his glee; when all was said and done, this was an exhilarating start to the term. But he pretended to be hurt.

'If you're intending to drop us all, now you've got other acquaintances on your mind—'

'What nonsense!' Ravi exclaimed, sitting down on Dev's bed. 'Why not just behave normally about things? What exactly is supposed to have happened, anyway?'

'I've no idea,' Dev shrugged, 'since you seem to want to keep us in the dark.'

'For heaven's sake,' said Ravi, 'do I have to keep you informed of my every move? At four pm I shall go out for tea. I intend to return by six-thirty. I will be at such and such college and on my way back, I will stop at the Co-op shop to buy a packet of ginger-nuts, price twenty-five pence!'

'Some of your moves aren't so innocent,' Dev said mischievously.

'Oh, make me some coffee, you idiot!' Ravi answered.

Sunil joined them. He also was amused by the new turn of events and after his first mug of coffee, he asked Ravi flippantly if he was thinking of taking a leaf out of Ved Sharma's book. Dev stiffened in alarm and Ravi, sprawled complacently across Dev's bed, looked furious.

'What exactly do you mean by that?'

'Well, unless I'm much mistaken, young Sarah looks as though she's here to stay, doesn't she?'

'I don't see what Sarah Livingstone's got to do with Ved Sharma, quite frankly,' Ravi said bitterly. 'If you can't see the difference between an intelligent person like Sarah and that silly Penny, then you need your head examined.'

Sunil tittered significantly to Dev. 'Oh naturally, utterly different,' he agreed.

'Well, can't you see?' Ravi exclaimed. 'She *is*! That Penny had about as much brain as a soft-boiled egg.'

'Smitten,' Dev commented with mock gravity, led on by Sunil who, plopping sugar into his second cup of coffee, commented, 'Ah, it's her brains you're after, is it? More on the lines of scrambled egg?'

Ravi swore furiously at his friends in Hindi. 'What are you two? My aunts? Why are you turning this whole thing into an issue anyway? What's it got to do with you?'

'We have your welfare at heart,' Dev said sententiously.

'Well, I'm fine,' Ravi snapped. 'Better than you'll ever be.'

His friends chuckled and Ravi was so annoyed that he sat up. 'For heaven's sake!' he cried. 'What d'you think I'm about to do? Marry her?'

Long afterwards, he lay awake and tried to recall his evening with Sarah from behind the irritation which Dev and Sunil had superimposed on it. She was so lively and forthright, there was so much fun ahead of him. His friends' concern just showed how conventional they still were at heart. They were decent fellows, of course, but when it came to certain things they just hadn't shaken off their inherited prejudices. He looked forward to the next day and as he began to feel drowsy, thought ahead sleepily to the spring and summer, to the remainder of his two years in England. Sarah Livingstone gave them a whole new dimension. He only thought again very briefly about Sunil and Dev, almost pityingly. He would dare to live so much more than they would in England and, afterwards, his memories of his time abroad would be much richer.

*

It was nothing to do with the new paint ('Grass-snake's puke,' Ravi repeated, giggling, when he saw it. 'It *smells* of grass-snake's puke') but Sarah did begin to visit Ravi more often than he came to her. She preferred his room.

It was never cold there. Although the room was in one of the dampest seventeenth-century buildings, with the electric fire and a supplementary radiator on at full capacity, Ravi simulated another climate. He often kept the curtains drawn too, in the daytime, which excluded the city completely. His friends, who all spent a lot of time there, helped to create their own environment. From the regulation furnishings of a student room – utility desk, bookcase, single bed – they made something else: a refuge from the winter city, whose occupants braced themselves when they went back outside.

The room had its own smell also – sweet, weird and distinctive – which years later in other cities would still make Sarah breathe in with longing. She found it a bit cloying at first and suggested frankly to Ravi that he should open the window more often. But she grew to identify its constituents – a brand of cigarette, certain spices, a medicinal balm – and became fond of it, even trying to reproduce it with joss sticks in her own room. She liked Ravi's room.

It was such a lively room, unlike her own which was frozen between his visits. There was usually music, high mournful music, and, several times a day, the radio news. People would eat there at inexplicable times, bringing in take-aways or pans of lentils. An Indian girl called Nanda who, for some reason, took against Sarah from the first day, cooked complicated meals in a kitchenette and laid them out pains-takingly in Ravi's room. Nanda was the only discordant note in the harmonious way of life, so far as Sarah was concerned. She flirted coyly with all the men in what Sarah considered a ridiculously old-fashioned way and giggled furiously when complimented on her cooking. She seemed to disapprove of Sarah no end. There were long, heated discussions about places and subjects of which Sarah had never heard. The language switched back and forth between English and Hindi. The first Hindi words which Sarah learnt were 'Chai' (tea) and 'Chini' (sugar). She used them to gain laughs.

At first, Ravi's friends seemed uncertain how to react to Sarah, uncomfortable. It was as if they did not know how long she would be there and could not decide whether to include her in the conversation. Later though – when she had become, as Sunil jokingly put it to her, 'a part of the fixtures and fittings' – they seemed to absorb her into their company happily enough and to include her without reser-vation in what went on. She thought she blended in pretty well.

*

The next day, Ravi did walk round to Sarah's college. This was not out of guilt because of the small lie that he had told her; but the previous day had left him with more misgivings than Sarah about their friendship, which he wanted to resolve by seeing her. He was certain that his behaviour could not be defined by his friends' crude image of it; he was not just planning to have a good time with Sarah, not like that, not in the way Ved Sharma had with his silly Penny. In fact, he

61

was disgusted by his friends' failure to recognise that relations between him and Sarah could possibly take place on any other terms. For them, it seemed, such a liaison could only be an amalgam of unprincipled male lust and female immorality. He walked through the suburban streets fired by righteous indignation and arrived in the red front quadrangle of Sarah's college in a state of fervent sincerity. Because his feelings for Sarah were not like that – not at all what Dev and Sunil imagined – they grew as he justified them. He nearly ran up the stairs to her room.

Sarah was waiting for him. She had been waiting since she woke up at nine that morning and lay still in bed so as not to lose a wonderful dream in which she and Ravi were together on a train, travelling through a snowy, mountainous landscape. Ravi was pointing out the landmarks and explaining to her what they were. He kept telling Sarah that the country outside was India, even though she knew perfectly well that it couldn't be. But because it was a dream, she believed him. 'It's not at all like you expected, is it?' he kept saying. 'I told you so.' It felt so wonderful and momentous on that train, cold and spectacular as they swept through the beautiful scenery. In her dream, she hoped they never reached their destination.

The rest of the day was quite overshadowed by the dream and the excitement of Ravi. She met her tutor and arranged to work on 'Charles Dickens and the novel as a social message' that term. But she paid almost no attention to the term beginning about her; so far as she was concerned, this term would be Ravi's.

When at last he arrived, she was playful, to hide her contentment and to pay him back for keeping her waiting all day.

He asked, 'Well, how has your first day been? Have you got everything fixed up?'

Sarah adjusted his collar flirtatiously. 'Everything.'

Ravi waved at a stack of library books, just brought in and still in a haphazard pile on Sarah's coffee table. 'You've got your work all mapped out?'

Sarah giggled. 'Yes. Have a look.'

There was a volume of Dickens and two critical appraisals

at the top of the pile, then A. K. Coomaraswamy's *Introduction to Indian Art*, *An Indian Summer* by James Cameron and *Indian Temples and Palaces* by M. Edwardes.

Sarah burst out laughing at Ravi's astounded face. 'I've got my work all mapped out!' she crowed.

But Ravi looked serious. 'Why have you got all these?' he asked sternly.

'Goodness only knows,' Sarah said sarcastically, 'but I've developed this sudden interest in India. I can't think why.'

'But what about everything else you have to read? There's nearly a week's reading here.'

'Oh Ravi, don't be so priggish. Aren't you pleased that I want to learn about India?'

'Of course, of course I'm pleased. But you mustn't let it interfere with your work. I mean, after all—'

'After all, what? I don't give a damn about *Hard Times*. This is much more interesting.'

'Anyway,' Ravi said abruptly, 'these books are all wrong – not what you ought to read if you really want to learn about India. They're comfy, pretty armchair books. If you want to learn something about India, then you must read some proper stuff. I'll get you some decent books from the library.'

'OK, fine,' Sarah said a little sulkily, 'but there's no need to trample on my good intentions.'

Ravi fondled her hair. 'No, of course not,' he said. 'I'm sorry.'

They sat on the carpet and looked at each other until they were almost overcome by their proximity. The winter afternoon was already growing dark. At such moments, the limitations of only having known each other for a few weeks were nearly too much to bear.

'Shall we go out for a walk?' Sarah suggested, driven by the excitement for which there was as yet no outlet.

'All right,' said Ravi, although he was content and also warm inside. He thought he understood that Sarah was afraid of intimacy growing in the dark.

They put on their coats and went out into the premature twilight. The wet air clung to their faces and their hair. The college garden was sodden.

'In India,' Sarah said, 'what would the weather be like now?'

'It depends which part,' said Ravi. 'It's a big place, you know.'

'Oh, don't be so patronising,' Sarah said. 'I have realised that much! I mean in your part, of course. I'm not interested in the rest.'

'In the North?' Ravi said. 'It's the cool season right now; it would be about in the seventies during the day, but cooler at night. It's winter there, too.'

Sarah gave a little laugh of astonishment. 'Gosh, do you wish you were there?' She wrapped her coat more tightly around her and shivered.

'No,' Ravi said, 'I don't.' But thinking about it, almost involuntarily his teeth chattered.

They both laughed, then Ravi put his arm around Sarah and said sweetly, 'There are reasons why I'd rather be here.'

They walked out on to the playing fields. In the thick grey light, the painted lines of the boundaries and the goal mouths showed up like large primitive chalk drawings. Ravi and Sarah walked around the edge, where it was less muddy, making fun of the desolate stretch of ground which seemed so glorious to the boys who played on it. The goal-posts stood like the remains of an abandoned religious ritual. The netting sagged.

They walked, impervious to the desolation. As clearly as the ruled white lines in front of them, each saw and felt their joint future. With overwhelming certainty, each realised that he held the hand, encircled the waist, felt the breathing of his future lover. And for possibly the first time, each knew that the other must realise it now too, which made them quiet and taut with apprehension. If one of them – confronted with that picture – shied away, the other would be wounded. So they said very little, afraid of harming the picture, and out on the cold playing fields they walked round and round, mesmerised and terrified by the picture of their future happiness.

The cold brought them indoors again: Sarah coral-faced and sweating with emotion, despite the cold, Ravi so chilled he thought he could feel each individual bone turning to ice beneath his skin. They went carefully up to Sarah's room, carrying with them the new realisation. She put on the light and the fire and drew the curtains on the view of the playing fields through the sombre trees, almost as if embarrassed by what they confirmed. Ravi stood in front of the fire and rubbed his hands.

'Are you frozen?' Sarah asked. 'Shall I make some coffee?'

'Do you find this temperature invigorating?' Ravi asked. 'You always look so pink and glowing in it.'

'Pink?' Sarah said. Half-jokingly, she looked at her face in the mirror.

'It's sweet,' Ravi said. 'I like it.'

He caught her as she made a face at herself and affectionately stroked her nose.

For a moment, they looked minutely at the effect of cold on their different faces. Holding the jolly English girl from the hockey pitch, Ravi saw that the pink could be made to climb under her susceptible skin. Through nearly motionless lips, without a sound – so that if anything were later to go wrong, it could always be claimed that the words had never been spoken – Ravi's mouth said, 'I love you.'

And loud and irretrievable, Sarah answered, 'Oh, Ravi, Ravi, so do I.'

And their fright swamped them. Terrified, they clung to each other and giggled in high-pitched shock. Then as normality returned, the girl who had grown up to stint and suppress her emotions broke away to make coffee and wondered, 'Does he? Could he? Is this real?' While the man who had become resigned to seeing his years of foreign freedom pass in sickly, studious loneliness, felt an elation which transcended words but said something like, 'Oh, this is glorious, glorious!'

There was a knock as they drank their coffee and Emily Williams came in. They were so overwhelmed by their emotions that they appeared almost to welcome her.

Ravi had met Emily Williams already and was surprised that such a thinking girl as Sarah should have such a silly best friend. But he imagined that friendships between women here had flimsy foundations. Sarah and Emily were only friends because they happened to be at the same college at the same time and shared a taste for poking fun. He was slightly stiff in front of Emily.

Emily thought Ravi Kaul was wonderful. She had encouraged Sarah in the adventure from the moment she had first seen him across the quad. In fact, on meeting, she had found him a little disappointing; he was a bit stiff; he did not quite live up to her vision of a glamorous Oriental boy-friend. But she was determined that he should do so; when she and Sarah talked about him, she dwelt on his luscious black eyes and his incredible lashes and she never let on to Sarah that he did not. She said he was 'gorgeous' and 'delectable'; well, for Sarah he might very well be. If she herself had decided on an Indian romance, she would personally have preferred someone a little more foreign and flamboyant, and also a little taller. But, despite her reservations (why was he so keen on Sarah anyway, what was he after?), she pushed her friend eagerly into the adventure. Although she would not have dared to get involved with an Indian herself, it flattered her that she was friendly with someone who would. Almost subconsciously, she was shocked, for Ravi and Sarah transcended a barrier still firmly planted in her brain. And anything shocking should be encouraged. She would never have expected it of Sarah Livingstone, actually; she had always thought her rather staid where emotional risks were concerned. But now that Sarah had surprised her, she wanted to reward her with encouragement. Also, Emily had made a fool of herself over men so often already; it would not upset her if Sarah were now to do the same. Naturally, she would comfort her when that happened. And she did not see how else it could end.

She grinned when she saw them both sitting blushing on the carpet.

'Oh, do send me away if I've come at the wrong moment,' she exclaimed theatrically.

Sarah and Ravi laughed.

'What nonsense,' said Ravi.

'Do you want some coffee?' Sarah asked.

Emily plumped herself down in the armchair. 'Are you sure? I mean, I'm quite happy to go away again if I'm interrupting. I was just dropping in.'

66

'Shut up,' Sarah said.

Ravi chuckled. 'You'll embarrass her if you keep on like that.'

Emily giggled conspiratorially. 'Well, guess what? I've just picked up a very interesting little titbit on the grapevine.'

'Ooh, what?' asked Sarah.

'Can I speak quite freely in front of you, Ravi? You won't be shocked by our decadence? Louise Cotton is having it off with Dr Latour!'

'You're joking!' Sarah exclaimed.

That, Ravi thought, was a prime example of his reasons for disliking Emily Williams: in her company, Sarah reverted to a tittering English schoolgirl. His face stayed solemn.

'No, I promise,' Emily continued. 'According to a reliable source, they were seen leaving his rooms at half-past nine this morning. His Pop Art tie is apparently on display in her room. Honestly, that girl!'

'What a slag!' Sarah said. She turned to Ravi: 'You haven't met Louise Cotton, have you? She's slept with nearly everyone who's taught her, but no one below the rank of a college Fellow.'

'And what's this Dr Latour like?' Ravi asked a little stiffly.

Emily and Sarah hugged their knees.

'He's gorgeous,' Emily answered. 'He's the archetypal vague, blond intellectual heart-throb. We've all had our eye on him.'

'You too?' Ravi said jokingly to Sarah.

'Oh yes,' she answered provocatively. 'I think he's lovely.'

All three of them laughed.

'Still, you can't have your cake and eat it, can you?' Emily said to Sarah in a mock reproving voice, giving a mischievous nod in Ravi's direction.

They laughed again in satisfied acknowledgement of Ravi's new position.

When Emily Williams had gone (to spread the glad tidings down the corridor, Ravi commented dryly), they were left with their realisation. The afternoon seemed to have lasted an extraordinarily long time and Ravi's misgivings were already out of date. The new situation had overtaken them and now he and Sarah had to learn how to face up to it. They agreed to meet for lunch the next day.

*

'How come you're so against England when you're so English?' Ravi asked Sarah.

They had eaten lunch in his college dining hall for three weeks running, surrounded by young sportsmen and the portraits of their florid-faced ancestors. Sarah had kept up a cheery commentary on their characters and conversations, on the similarity between the slabs of steak and kidney pie and the faces above them.

'I'm not *so* English,' she answered defensively.

'Yes, of course you are.'

'No, I'm *not*. Do I neigh with laughter? Do I toss my mane and whinny?'

'That's beside the point, Sarah. You *are* English; in some ways, you're the absolute epitome of the English—'

'Huh, thank you very much.'

'But somehow, you seem to have disowned the place. Why?'

'I don't want to be defined by *here*. Being English isn't enough. I mean, here we are on a foggy little island, sinking down fast into the nineteen-seventies, at the end of our era of greatness, and it just seems so . . . so pathetic to pull up the drawbridge and wallow in it. Don't you ever feel that being Indian isn't enough? You must do, or you wouldn't be here.'

'That's not why I came here,' Ravi protested indignantly.

'Then why did you come? Wasn't it to escape from a stereotype and get a chance to be something different – more?'

'No! I came . . . because I'd have been a fool not to – but I didn't come to change my nature or to reject what I was.'

'But you don't intend to go back unchanged, do you? Or just keep your old self safely intact somewhere? I mean,' flirtatiously, '*do* you?'

'Of course not. Naturally I'll experiment, I'll explore. But that doesn't mean I have to reject everything in my life up to now, does it?'

68

'Well, it does a bit.'

'How can you reject something "a bit"? Either you reject it, surely, or you don't?'

'No, that's what I'm doing; I'm rejecting England a bit. Maybe one day when I'm middle-aged, I'll start yearning for Home Counties respectability and face flannels. But I doubt it.'

'Well, I shan't put on some plummy-voiced personality or turn into a substitute Englishman like Ali Suleiman either.'

After lunch, in the slight privacy of his room, Ravi's finger found the back of Sarah's bra under her pullover and greeted it with a playful ping.

*

'Those people who gave the party where I first met you – Simon Satchell and his lot – did you ever really like them?'

They were walking back to Sarah's room after a supper party with friends of hers and Ravi chose the dark to ask his question – not so much to spare Sarah embarrassment as to hide his own discomfort. He felt it was really a dishonourable and prying question to put to her, but something in the memory of that group nagged him persistently.

Sarah considered her answer and characteristically, Ravi thought, it was honest when it came. 'No, not really, I don't think so. I wasn't actually part of that group. I went around with them quite a bit last year, I suppose, and I went out with one of them.'

Ravi had prepared other, more delicate ways of obtaining this reply: 'Don't get annoyed, but there's something silly Ali Suleiman once said to me.' 'You won't be cross with me, will you; is it true you were . . . friends with one of them?' He was startled by the promptness with which Sarah gave him his answer. Obviously she saw no need for coyness or concealment. (But would he ever have told her about the crazy girl Shakuntala when he had been at college in Delhi?) He walked on a few steps in a silence intended to be casual.

'Which one?'

'Are you jealous?' Sarah joked.

'Why should I be jealous? He hasn't got you any more and I hope I have.'

'His name was David, David Whitehead. Did you meet him?'

Ravi pretended that this name was strange and new, although he had in fact remembered it with odd clarity ever since Ali Suleiman had casually referred to Sarah as 'David Whitehead's girl'. The name had aroused antagonism in him then, conveying the image of a lumbering figure with thatched fair hair like a country cottage roof, and he did not like the sound of it any better now when spoken reminiscently by Sarah.

'What did he look like?'

'Blond, quite tall I suppose, with blue eyes, but not really what you'd call good-looking.'

'Um, I don't think I did meet him.'

'He would have been at that tea-party.'

'Yes, but they all looked pretty much alike to me.'

Sarah gave a triumphant little skip and laughed. 'That's what English people are supposed to say about you – that you can't tell one brown face from another.'

'That's not what I meant, Sarah. They weren't so much physically alike, but they all behaved in the same way. They had the same voice and manner. That's why I asked if you really got on with them; they seemed so narrow and self-satisfied.'

Again, Sarah considered her answer. 'In a way, I did. I mean, it was nice to have a toehold in a group that was hard to get into. But I'm not sure if I ever fitted in. I think they thought I was a bit of a pain, actually. I was really only there because of David; it was an immature relationship.'

Something about the way she said that repelled Ravi unreasonably and he gave a wry little nod. He did not like to hear Sarah dismiss a whole romance in those terms. For all his antagonism towards the thatched blond boy, he felt momentary sympathy for him; Sarah had made their feelings for one another sound like a mere aberration, a discarded garment which she had outgrown. He was moved by something like premature jealousy. Would she one day dismiss him in the same way?

They returned to her room. A little more boldly than so far, Ravi reached inside Sarah's blouse as he hugged her good night.

'Of course we like her,' Sunil told Ravi in the last week of that term. 'What rubbish! If you don't mind my saying so, you're becoming completely paranoid, old chap.'

'Well, if you like her,' Ravi answered, 'why can't you make more of an effort to let it show? You know what she said to me the other day? "Do Sunil and Dev resent my being there?" You make her feel uncomfortable with your censorious attitudes.'

'I don't know what you're talking about,' Sunil replied. 'What have I said or done that's censorious?'

'It's the way you react if she's there when you come in. You know perfectly well what I mean; you put on this polite, tut-tutting sort of face . . .'

Sunil burst out laughing. 'Rubbish, nonsense!' he cried in Hindi. 'You're just imagining these things because you feel guilty.'

*

'So things are really hotting up with Ravi?' Emily Williams asked Sarah at the start of the summer term.

She had recently embarked on an adventure herself – with an eccentric postgraduate music student – and it bothered her faintly that Sarah's initial impetus seemed to have slackened.

Sarah nodded happily.

'Great,' Emily said. She stirred her coffee. 'Soon?'

Sarah fidgeted. 'I'm not going to give you a time and a place,' she demurred.

'Sorry, sorry,' Emily apologised. 'But you must admit, it's so romantic.'

The two friends laughed. Sarah was enjoying being a subject of college gossip. She knew, pleasurably, that when she and Ravi walked into the front quadrangle with their arms around each other people noticed them. People who previously had had no idea who Sarah Livingstone was, now knew of her attachment. Ravi remained anonymous; the mere sight of him with his arm around Sarah constituted his interest.

Sarah's friends thought Ravi was terribly sweet. While

all of them could have given a reason why he was not for them – too argumentative, too suave to be trustworthy, too short – they all agreed he was *sweet*. They rather admired Sarah for falling in love with him and were more tolerant of her character failings now that she was known to be daring.

*

'Will you come round to my room tonight or shall I come round to yours?'

'Will Sunil and Dev be there?'

'Most likely.'

'Oh, come to mine, come to mine for a change. Then I can have you all to myself.'

'Aha, and what, pray, do you intend to do with me?'

He did not yet know when he could expect to get into bed with Sarah. She had a timetable, but he was not to know that. Sarah's timetable planned the event provisionally for the start of summer proper, but she expected Ravi to initiate it. Ravi was confident that the event would surely take place soon, but he was not clear when he could expect Sarah to consent to it. He had never slept before with a girl who loved him.

'I'll seduce you, of course.'

'Will you indeed? I must remember to change my shirt before I come over.'

The weeks had brought them enjoyably closer. Their friends, by their lack of understanding, gave them the closeness of isolation. And their private enjoyment of discovery united them until, in the end, it seemed that only days, as thin as nylon, separated them.

*

'What does "satyagraha" mean?'

'Oh gosh, you're not still reading those wretched books, are you? Doing your background research on Ravi Kaul?'

'Come on, come on, shut up. What does "satyagraha" mean?'

'Passive resistance.'

'Passive resistance? That sounds awfully provocative; like

fending someone off with one limp white hand but lying back and letting him have his wicked way all the same. Have I said something wrong? Why are you looking at me like that?'

'Sometimes you come out with the most incredible statements! You can be so silly, you behave as if you had only one thing on your mind.'

'Oh, but I *do* have only one thing on my mind. Don't you? Ow, get off! No, stop it Ravi, I'm reading. I'm reading about passive resistance. Oh my God, what a moment to choose. Listen Ravi, you'll get more than you bargained for – I warn you, I'm not going to offer you any passive resistance!'

*

Sarah could not have explained at the time why she panicked. It seemed to be outside her control. Perhaps it was a final farcical attempt by the pattern to reassert itself, before lying low for years until a more propitious time. But one night she ran away from Ravi. They had lain side by side in front of his fire for hours. It was really late, after one or two in the morning, and getting out of his college had been a frightful business. But she had insisted. Gripped by panic, she had taken her bicycle and ridden back to her college in the dark. She was pursued by a vision of her lunacy; what, for God's sake, was she doing? Why ever had she allowed things with Ravi to get this far? Now everything, everything was out of control and she was obviously on the verge of a disaster. The glaring clarity of her madness astounded her. Yes, she must have been out of her mind to have imagined that she could take up with Ravi Kaul as if he were another blond schoolfellow. He was from another world and she knew nothing about him at all. She could not sleep for the proximity of the danger, and next day she was still awed and shaken by the enormity of it. She tiptoed around the city with frigid care, cringingly aware of how close she had come to abandoning it.

Ravi was staggered. As far as he could work out, there was no earthly reason why Sarah should suddenly have run out on him. It was a horrible, crazy thing to have done.

They had been enjoying a wonderful evening; gloriously, endlessly rolling and kissing and fondling on his floor, while the clock covered giant circles of time and the electric fire scorched one side of them. He had told Dev and Sunil that he had an urgent essay to write and he had locked the door. That night, he had thought, the grand finale could not be far off. He had been so sure, he thought, of what Sarah felt for him. In a period somewhere between midnight and one o'clock, it seemed to him that he had as good as made love to her already. She had never objected to his probing fingers; she had taken them and welcomed them to her body. She had enjoyed his fingers. She had let him reach into her under-clothes. She had risen and wriggled appreciatively. He recalled that maybe she had stiffened ever so slightly when he first reached inside her pants, but that was only natural; a little modesty was necessary after all. Perhaps her conscience had fleetingly stirred, had reminded her of her upbringing, reminded her that what she was about to do would have scandalised her forebears. But she seemed to have overcome it. She had held Ravi close against her and relished him. Their tongues had seldom left each other's mouths; afterwards his face was sticky and stiff with repetition. As far as he could see, in a few days – in a week at the very most – Sarah Livingstone would be his.

But now that prospect had been snatched away and he racked his brains trying to work out what he had done wrong, but could not think of anything. He was at a loss. Had Sarah misled him with her seeming acquiescence? Was she – impossible – not intending to come to bed with him at all? Was that not part of her idea of their adventure? Or had she had second thoughts about him at this late stage? He felt humiliated. On the way out they had passed Dev, wide-eyed, returning from the vending machine with his hands full of chocolate and he had beamingly offered them a bar. Ravi felt a sudden surge of anger at Sarah; what the hell was she playing at? Up till now, he had thought he understood exactly what was happening. He had known where he and Sarah were heading and he was enjoying the journey. Now he was stumped.

His bewilderment kept him awake and, in the morning,

turned to anger. Sarah had no right to do this to him. He thought of her across the city; she had become a picture again, as at the very beginning, for he could not imagine what she must be feeling this morning, what she could be thinking. He saw an agitated blonde girl at a breakfast table, confiding her night's escapade to her tittering girl-friend Emily. The girl at the breakfast table was not nearly as brave and unconventional as she had made herself out to be; beneath her daring exterior, inherited prejudices still held her in their sway.

His anger grew and, by the afternoon, became a decision to confront Sarah. She jolly well owed him an explanation and he would make her tell him what was up. As late as possible, for he had told himself that he would get it over with before dinner, he walked out to her college. On the way he stoked his rage with the blithely weaving cyclists and the rain, but still he felt fearfully apprehensive as he drew nearer. What if she threw a screaming scene? What if she just refused to let him in?

She knew he would come. Of course she knew he would come. She had tried to prepare the scene a dozen times, but there was a point at which her imagination stuck: how would she feel when Ravi walked into her room? In her mind, Ravi climbed the stairs again and again. (In desperation? In anger?) He knocked at her door. (Timidly? Furiously?) And he came in. There she stopped, because she could not imagine what that moment would feel like. With her eyes shut, she tried to see Ravi's face. To her astonishment, she could not. The shape of his hairstyle formed around his dark face; she could catch bits of his features, his nose, his teeth, but the real expression that was Ravi would not come. As an experiment she reproduced in her head the faces of her parents, of Emily Williams, even of David Whitehead, and they all swam up obediently from the dark. She tried to make Ravi's again, but only his would not appear. Peculiarly upset, she wondered if this was a sign of subconscious racial prejudice which she had only now discovered.

She went to the college library, like a coward, so that if Ravi called she would not be in. But forgotten objects, like notebooks, kept bringing her back to her room just in case he did. She got no work done and by the late afternoon was utterly wretched, undecided, had no idea what she felt about Ravi at all. The surroundings she had fled back to now repelled her. At one point she even thought of rushing out to Ravi, flinging herself on him and asking for forgiveness all the same. Then the thought of that made her shudder. She was standing miserably at her window, undecided whether or not to turn on the lights, when at six o'clock Ravi knocked and opened the door.

'Oh God.'

'May I come in?'

'Yes, of course. Oh God.'

'Stop saying "Oh God". What's going on?'

'Oh, Ravi, I . . . sit down, let me make you some coffee.'

'I don't want any coffee, thank you. I have come . . . I would like an explanation, please. I'm afraid I don't quite understand what happened last night.'

'Neither do I.'

'Neither do *you*? Well, who the hell *is* supposed to know, then?'

'I don't know. I don't know why I did what I did. It – it just happened. I don't know what's going on. I'm in a most awful state. If you've come round to be tough with me, then you'd better go – I can't take it.'

'Tough with you? *Tough* with you? Don't you think you were maybe just a little tough with *me* last night?'

'I didn't mean to be. I'm sorry, Ravi. It just all sort of got on top of me suddenly and I had to get out.'

'What did? What got on top of you?'

Simultaneously, they glimpsed the first possibility of humour in the past anguished hours and both giggled unhappily.

'Oh Ravi, it's not what you think. I wasn't just being a prim little English prude, scared stiff at the prospect of sex. I promise you it wasn't that.'

'I didn't think it was.'

'Didn't you? Then why did you think I did it?'

'I've no idea; that's what I've come to find out.'

'I really don't know why. I just suddenly felt that I didn't know where I was any more. I can't explain it. I thought everything was fine up to then, you know I did.'

'I *thought* you did.'

'I did, I did! But last night I suddenly thought: what's happening? I mean, what are we doing? It seemed as if we didn't know each other at all yet and there we were – where are we going? Suddenly, everything seemed peculiar.'

'Suddenly, everything seemed peculiar.' Ravi wasn't mimicking her, but the repetition of her words made Sarah writhe.

'I know, I know it sounds stupid, but I'm trying to explain what I felt. Can't you imagine what it's like for me?'

Because Ravi had the role of the wronged party, he could afford to stay calmer. He sat and listened in injured silence while Sarah thrashed about on the hook of his presence.

'But why couldn't you tell me that you were scared?'

'How? It was *you* that I was scared of. You . . . and what you mean . . .'

'Me? You felt scared of me?'

'It's not that I feel any differently about you or anything. You do believe that, don't you?'

'If you say so.'

'Oh Ravi, you know I don't. It's not fair – why should I have to defend myself like this? What have I done wrong?'

In the middle of that turmoil it struck Ravi as strangely delightful that even in love, Sarah should use the vocabulary of the playing fields: 'It's not fair.' And he was distracted by it enough to answer, mimicking her in kind: 'I'm not sure if you've been playing straight with me.'

'I *have*!' Sarah burst out. 'I have. I just don't see where it will end.'

She had failed to hear the borrowed vocabulary. It was an accusation she responded to with tears of instinctive outrage.

Ravi wanted to comfort her. He felt like reaching out his hand and patting the upset schoolgirl to console her, to reassure her that the end – wherever it came – would not be devastating, would not destroy her.

Sarah met his hand and held on to it with relief. He forgave her; she had not repelled him. The essential was secure, the rest could be dealt with later. So again they sat beside each other on the carpet, silent for fear of damaging their happiness.

It was far too soon after the crash, too close to the rift for them to talk about it. They did not dare touch it in case it split open again. But they stayed there side by side long after it was completely dark, holding on to each other, depending on each other's shape and breathing to carry on.

When Ravi had left, promising that they would meet straight after his politics tutorial the next day, Sarah threw herself on to her bed and wept at the release from tension. Then she wept with vast and desperate regret because Ravi was gone.

She knew then that he had won, for in the end it had turned out that he mattered more to her than her own ground. For him, she was prepared to leave safety and dignity behind after all. He would doubtless require huge and unknown sacrifices from her in the future and she would joyfully consent to them. Through her wild crying, she enjoyed one last flurry of false regret; she was actually looking forward to it.

Sarah missed Ravi for most of the night, but she must have slept a little between half-past three and five o'clock because, suddenly she was aware of a bird cheeping in the college garden and the dark beginning to thin out on the other side of the curtains. She stroked her face with one hand, pretending that it was Ravi's hand, and mouthed the words he had spoken when they kissed for the first time: 'One all.' His voice had sounded low and lilting in the dark and his inflection made the words impishly his own. When he looked at her, his eyebrows arched in mocking query over the eyes on which she had nearly turned her back because they were not blue.

In the morning she went to meet him after his politics tutorial. He did not hug her in greeting because Sunil and Rajiv Mehrotra were with him and later, in his room, they were both still cautious and a little ill at ease. In the evening though, they went into college dinner with Sunil and Dev and Sunil entertained them with his inspired imitations of college Fellows feasting at High Table on venison and quail. Ravi and Sarah nearly choked with laughter.

They did not solve the problem straight away, of course. For almost a fortnight they waited, creeping cautiously back to where they had been before. Ravi especially was careful, for fear of setting off another panic; if Sarah had run away again, he would not have gone after her. She became impatient with his caution. Although she knew perfectly well that it was she who had provoked it, now she felt that Ravi was punishing her with his reticence. He tended to keep his hands in his pockets when they walked together and left without hesitation once he had kissed her good night. She wanted to show him that he did not need to be so cautious any more and she felt she ought to reward him for his patience. So in fact it was Sarah who initiated the act which put an end to caution.

It happened in the last week of May. She would remember the day and date for ever afterwards because, when it was over, she thought her life had changed and opened her diary to see the date on which that had occurred.

She had spent the afternoon in Ravi's room, listening to a lady called Lateh Mangeshkar singing on the stereo and drinking very sweet tea with cinnamon in it. Outside, it was the sort of day which alternated violently between heavy squalls and white unripe sunshine. People coming into the room reported that outside it was April, May, June. A high-pitched hilarity connected to the coming summer was in the air.

For part of the afternoon Ravi was not even there – he had had to go off to some seminar – and Sarah had stayed and waited for him with his friends, finally feeling quite accepted by them and enjoying her position there. Only the girl Nanda occasionally still made her feel uncomfortable: prim and formal with Sarah, either resentful that Sarah had trespassed into her flirtatious monopoly or obscurely disapproving. Sunil, Dev, Rajiv and Dilip all seemed quite reconciled to her and Sunil gave her one of his small foul cigarettes – a bidi – to try while Ravi was out.

When Ravi came back, pleased with his success at the seminar, Sarah slung her arm around him and crowed, 'Look, I've been picking up filthy habits from your friends!'

Everyone laughed and Sarah stuck the bidi sluttishly in her

mouth like a comic charlady. Later, she winced at the memory of what she had said and wondered if anyone had taken the remark badly.

She sat next to Ravi on the floor and pressed the full length of her leg against his. He squeezed her hand hard in return.

Because it was a Saturday night, they all decided to go and eat together at the Shah Jehan. Walking there in a noisy party through the quiet streets, Sarah exulted; she was part of their group now, she was part of them. Once upon a time, a group of Indians larking about in the street would have seemed flamboyant, undisciplined and foreign. Now she was one of them, she thought, and it was the streets which were foreign. She walked hand in hand with Ravi and he exulted too, to see her beaming in the dark.

They seemed to fill the little restaurant and the waiters rushed to and fro, bringing them more and more dishes. A favourite ploy, Sarah noticed, was to slip in extra dishes which no one had ordered, but none of the others seemed to mind. They peered at the new mixtures, consulted and invariably laughingly told the waiters to leave them on the table. Without alcohol, a drunken hilarity spread over them. People shouted and delved experimentally into one another's plates. They called along their adjoining tables and cracked side-splitting jokes. At the climax of the hilarity, someone proposed a toast to Sarah in tea.

She did not say anything to Ravi when he waved good night to the others afterwards and turned to walk back with her to her college. Something in the way he publicly turned his back on them, put his arm around her and hugged her to him told her that that night marked a change. All the way back, her body felt quite hollow in anticipation. But just in case – just in case she was mistaken – she took Ravi's hand as they reached the front gates and pulled him to her saying, 'About time too, Mr Kaul!'

It was cold in her room and she flicked the switch of the electric fire before hugging Ravi. Then they took each other – neither knowing who took first – and enclosed each other in a long embrace. Ravi's right hand reached inside Sarah's duffel coat, but Sarah's hands undid Ravi's collar. Their mouths met in a warm, slippery, prolonged kiss. Ravi's hands reached under Sarah's pullover and Sarah's hands slid around Ravi's neck. Their chests met, then their stomachs and they adhered to each other length to length. Their feet got in the way. Standing embracing in the middle of the room, each delved further inside the other's layers of clothes as they rolled their heads, round and round on the soft pivots of their tongues. They bore against each other and their arms held each other fast. Their hands laid claim to the hollow of another back, to curves they could explore and acquire. Their hands felt for more territory, encountered fastenings.

They stood apart to undress. Silently, tidily, they took off their clothes and laid them on the chairs. Sarah was ready first and hopped quickly into the bed. Ravi, in the centre of the room, turned away slightly to hide his nudity, so that Sarah could watch uninhibitedly as his brown body emerged from his white underwear. Then he came over to the bed and slipped into it at the very edge. Sarah was waiting, rigid with apprehension on the cold sheets. Ravi threw back the sheets suddenly and uncovered their naked bodies. He looked down at Sarah's, and he said gloatingly, 'Miss Livingstone, I presume?'

They clutched each other. They fell laughing onto each other. And then each began to look seriously at the new body they had acquired. Ravi was opaque and smooth. Sarah felt herself momentarily repugnantly white and bony on the much-laundered sheets. But Ravi explored her. He put one finger to her acutely pink nipples and slid his palm down over her pale stomach. And Sarah, gradually thawing out of her nervous stiffness, reached over to discover him too. Their faces were deadly serious and this went on for a long time.

It was no one's decision when Ravi moved inside her. He did not offer, she did not invite him. His hand was already long between her legs and all of her appreciating him. He entered her, and in the moment while he felt and found, during the gap between his fingers and himself, they looked into each other's eyes and grinned.

Then it was nothing like being with David Whitehead, Sarah's only other lover. It was nothing like being a receptacle, a sack jolted up and down in a series of sore, mechanical jerks for a few perfunctory moments. Now she was an orange, whose segments were separated by feeding fingers. Now she was waiting earth in which a man was planting a tree. Inside her, the trunk of the great tree swelled and its branches stretched out; her body, the branches, her hands, fingers, twigs, leaves in her heart. Now she and the tree were the same substance, the same movement as together they grew and spread. There were all the seasons, fast after one another and at once, buds and thunderstorms, and there were roots tickling her and nothing, everything. She and the tree, she and the tree, she and the tree burst into flames.

In the dark, two people, stranded, thrown up by a typhoon, lay one of top of the other and did not say a word. Hot, sticky and wet, they lay breathless and their lives from beforehand came back to them.

'Ravi?'

'Sarah.'

'Oh, Ravi.'

'How do you do?'

Later, they talked. Later, they said they loved each other, that they would not let outside things intervene any more and that, from now on, the two of them would be stronger than everything else. They said that they would surely not last out the summer vacation apart. And Sarah foresaw, jokingly, her parents' reaction when Ravi came to London to visit her. They laughed at themselves, because it seemed typical of the way they were determinedly at odds with everything that when at last they had managed to achieve this triumph, there were only three more weeks of the term left.

*

Ravi went back to his college in the morning. Walking through the faint mist, he felt thrilled and smug and secretive and tired. There was an uncanny absence of friends in his room. He had a shower at the end of the corridor, humming under the hot stream and then, shutting the door of his room on everyone, sat down to work with gusto. In the late afternoon Dev wandered in and, from his evasive manner, it was obvious that he had guessed. He sat down on Ravi's bed and, for a moment, pretended to look at the books scattered over it. Then he tilted his head at Ravi and at first Ravi raised his chin defiantly but then, succumbing to camaraderie, pretended to put on a show of modesty and sheepishly grinned.

Dev stroked his small moustache with the tip of his index finger. It was the slightly self-conscious gesture of someone too plump who has just eaten a most enjoyable sweet.

*

Clarissa Rich looked down from the library window at the dappled lawn. That silly blonde Sarah Somebody, whom she had lived next to in the first year, came sauntering across it arm-in-arm with her Indian boy-friend. Clarissa's attention left her Stoics text – which truth to tell was not tremendously stimulating although she was glad, she was glad she had changed to Philosophy – and she stared out intently at the pair of them. They zigzagged across the lawn, going nowhere, clearly quite absorbed in their own contentment. Sarah looked up at the Indian boy, laughing, and he ruffled her hair. Clarissa watched them greedily until they disappeared, frolicking, around the corner of the college boat-house. She could tell by the way they walked what had recently happened between them. She recognised the moment when two people walking together quite publicly became one. She drew herself up stiffly and went back to her reading. But, suddenly, she felt herself engulfed in a wave of despair; oh God, would anything like that ever, *ever* happen to her?

*

In the exhilaration of their progress, they expected sunshine but for a while it stayed cold. Improbably, auditions began for open-air productions in the college gardens at the end of term. All the gauzy clothes bought for imaginary summer days hung pathetically inside the musty antique wardrobes. But then on about the seventh of June, something happened; the sky turned blue and from a thin haze, the sun shone out on the city. By two o'clock in the afternoon, the lawn under Sarah's bedroom window was dotted with girls on rugs, still wearing cardigans but doggedly making the most of the sunshine. Half the windows in that wing had been opened wide and cheerily assorted music could be heard.

Sarah cycled over to Ravi's college, tilting up her face at the sunlight. Exclaiming, 'Oh isn't this gorgeous?' she raced into Ravi's room and flung open the window. She stuck her head out into the sunshine again and savoured the light. 'Mmm!'

'Isn't what gorgeous?' Ravi asked from his desk, watching Sarah's antics with affectionate amusement.

'Wake up!' Sarah exclaimed. 'It's summer! Look, come and have a look.'

'Summer?' Ravi said, joining her at the window. 'Where?'

Sarah seized him exuberantly. 'Don't be so snobbish, Ravi. It's wonderful!'

Ravi shook his head disbelievingly. 'We'll have to get you to India one day, so that you can see what a proper summer is like,' he said. He was quite unprepared for the way his comment made Sarah, over-excited as she was, fling her arms around him and cover him with kisses.

It stayed fine – in Sarah's terms, gorgeous. For three or four days the sun shone steadily, the temperature rose and the city was transformed. Sarah persuaded Ravi – reluctant to admit that anything as slight as this should be welcomed so extravagantly – out into the garden, the park. Her pleasure infected him and they fell on to the grass (damp, Ravi warned) and gave in to exuberance. Sarah held up her white arm against Ravi's, rejoicing, 'If it stays like this, I'll start to go brown too!'

'I had forgotten,' Ravi said wonderingly, 'how everyone goes crazy here at the first ray of sunshine.'

And they did go crazy. By the end of the first week of the fine weather, girls were appearing in backless T-shirts, cut-away dresses and gaudy, flowing ethnic skirts. They bicycled through the streets with a beatific look on their pale faces. Then they came out into the college gardens in bikinis, displaying their impossibly white skin to an equally pale sun.

Ravi watched them with amusement: the white larvae of the winter disporting themselves in the sunshine. He found them funny, but also a little touching; their happiness was so earnest. Physically too, the girls were transformed.

Perhaps the sunlight showed up shades of difference which he had not noticed before. He saw dull hair flare into splendid yellow and puddle-brown eyes turn out to be green. All of them went an excited pink. He made fun of them; their sillier excesses were extraordinary, but he also felt a pitying fondness for them all, driven crazy by such a small promise of summer. Blithely, they were utterly unaware of how ridiculous they seemed.

Sarah started to experience a new source of discontent around this time; she wished that she was not white. There were various incidents which prompted this; Nanda comparing their bodies when Sarah tried on one of her saris for fun, waggling her head and exclaiming, 'So – oh pale!'; Ravi commenting jokingly again on the pinkness of her nose on a cold day. Being white began to be associated for her with being vulnerable and ridiculous. Her skin could not conceal its flustered reactions to climate, to emotions, to Ravi Kaul. In bright sunshine, she would burn. She was condemned to silly transparent obviousness. The Indians, with their camouflage of opaque skin, were more at ease in the world than she was.

She had an urge to buy herself some new clothes. Last summer, she had mainly worn a broderie anglaise Edwardian outfit alongside David Whitehead's cricket whites. But this now seemed quite inappropriate. So she went to a boutique and bought a dress of Indian fabric – thin, violently coloured cotton with small circles of mirror sewn to the skirt. She put it on as a surprise for Ravi when they went together to a party given by Ved Sharma to celebrate the news that his wife Amrita was expecting a baby. To Sarah it seemed a remote and unlikely theme for a party, but it was a festive occasion. All the Indian students she knew were there and Amrita, the star of the evening, served them delicious snacks and smilingly received their compliments. Sarah enjoyed the feeling of privilege which came from participating as a member at someone else's private ceremony. It made up for the earlier disappointment, when Ravi had reacted almost teasingly to her enthusiastic new dress.

Most of the parties that summer were different. The garden parties, the strawberries and Pimms parties went on, but

Sarah felt she was on the outside of them now and no longer part of the fun. She strained to experience the parties as Ravi must experience them. Often it seemed that Ravi enjoyed them in the end much more than she did, for he could be quite spontaneous whereas she felt obliged to monitor her every move.

One evening, going down the river in a punt with Ravi, Sunil and Dilip Joshi, she saw David Whitehead and Simon Satchell punt past them. On the one hand, she felt glad and defiant that David should see her sitting happily next to Ravi, but on the other she felt a moment of sneaking embarrassment that David should punt so expertly past them, while Sunil splashed experimentally along.

*

'Tell me more about your family. You've got two sisters, haven't you?'

They were lying in bed in Sarah's room one Sunday morning and summer rain was spattering the window. By keeping the curtains drawn, they could pretend they were somewhere else.

'Yes, and a brother Ramesh.'

'How old are they all?'

'Oh, goodness! Ramesh is nearly nineteen, Asha's fifteen and Shakuntala's thirteen, I think.'

'Do you get on quite well with all of them?'

'Yes, actually I do. I mean, it's a bit difficult with Asha and Shakun; they're a lot younger and I was always away from home so much when they were growing up. I think they look on me as much as an uncle as a brother, you know; a distant figure returning from afar and bringing gifts.'

'Do they look up to you?'

'Well, yes, if you put it like that, I suppose they do. They're awfully sweet and fight to look after me when I come home.'

'Huh, no wonder you're so spoilt! Do you have people waiting on you hand and foot?'

'Naturally. We live like maharajahs, you know.'

'No, don't make fun of me. I mean, do you have servants?'

'Three.'

'Three? Is that all? I imagined lots. Are they faithful family retainers? Or sort of short-term, like au pair girls?'

'No, they've been with us for years. Ila cried when I came to England.'

'Ah, how touching; the young master leaving the family home. It's like a Victorian novel.'

'But Sarah, she was really sad. You don't understand how strong those ties are there. It's nothing like you imagine.'

'Well, I certainly can't imagine any of our au pair girls shedding bitter tears if I was going off to India. Tell me about your brother. What's he like?'

'Ramesh is a good sort. He's very serious, though, not like me at all. He takes everything terribly seriously and always weighs up all the pros and cons before he acts. He should have been the eldest; I think he considers me a bit of a tearaway. We're very different, but he's a great chap.'

'What does he do?'

'Oh, he's still at college in Delhi, the same college I went to actually, trying to live down his big brother's terrible reputation.'

'*Did* you have a terrible reputation?'

'Oh, not really, I was just very argumentative. I wouldn't accept all the rules and regulations without a fuss. We were a group, actually, about ten of us, and we started a kind of reform movement in the college. A lot of the students there had a terrible bureaucratic mentality; they were just interested in sitting on their backsides and getting a piece of paper at the end to show that they had done it. They only studied within the strict limits of what was laid down in the curriculum; they weren't interested in branching out, leaving the beaten track, beaten to death, and – gracious! – possibly discovering something! And most of our teachers were just as bad. They kept to the narrow path of their textbooks, never looking up, never looking out, teaching in a vacuum, never incorporating a scrap of contemporary comment into their classes. So the group of us devised a new method of non-violent protest; it was intended to draw those imbeciles' attention to what was going on around them in the country, to the fact that you can't teach all subjects in a vacuum, that sometimes you have to take day-to-day events into account.

We used to smuggle a radio into the classroom and turn it on suddenly full volume for the news, disrupt all that dead rote learning with the clamour of outside reality. That was the idea. We kept it on just long enough for the first headlines – usually that wasn't long enough for the lecturer to pinpoint exactly who was responsible – and then we'd snap it off. Everyone knew who it was, but we took it in turns to hide the radio so they could never put the blame on just one of us. And it shook them. It was such a prestigious place, you see. We were supposed to be grateful to be there and concentrate on our books, not actually agitate for improvements. Once one of the history lecturers – he was the worst offender – did something particularly blatant: there had been a decree in Parliament the very day before his class, which had direct relevance to the subject he was talking about – and he ignored it. He talked for a whole hour – skirting round the issues, nimbly dodging every possible reference to the decree and never once suggesting that the topic had anything to do with our lives. Even some of the duller students saw what he was up to. That night, we cut all the pages dealing with the decree out of the newspapers and went and stuck them over the windows of his college room – he was a widower, you see, he lived in the college and supplemented his salary with disciplinary duties – so that in the morning when he opened the curtains, he couldn't see out because all the headlines about the decree were glued fast to the pane.'

'I wonder if I would have liked you if I'd met you then.'

'Why do you say that?'

'Well, you sound so cocky and arrogant. I mean, I don't think I'd like you if you were like that here.'

'Like what? I'm exactly the same here as I was over there . . . I think.'

'You can't be! You'd never have anything to do with the people who do things like that here.'

'Ah, that's only the context, Sarah. I'm exactly the same here, but my surroundings are different. Pasting over someone's window here might be an obnoxious thing to do, but it would be done by drunken rugger types after a party, wouldn't it, and they'd stick up pictures from girlie mags. That's the difference, surely, not me?'

'I see what you mean. I think I like you anyway.'

'I'm glad to hear it. Because, actually, I think this place could do with a little of the clamour of outside reality too.'

*

'Show me where you live on the map. It's in the North, isn't it?'

The blue sliver of an air-letter, used as a bookmark, frequently reminded Sarah of the country she knew nothing about. Even the air-letter paper was different from the smooth blue she was used to; it was rougher and grainy, with incomprehensible Hindi ciphers, and where Ravi opened it impatiently the paper always tore.

'Yes, roughly.'

'Show me on the map.'

'You get the map. I feel too lazy.'

'Here. There – India Plains, plate thirty. Is it on this page?'

'Yes, there. That's where I live.'

'Lucknow. Is it nice?'

'On the whole, no. The part we live in is lovely though. It used to be called the City of Gardens. Now it's more like the City of Shacks. But our neighbourhood is still pretty nice.'

'Tell me about it. Tell me about your house.'

'What do you want to know? It's nothing special.'

'No, but describe it to me. I want to be able to imagine you there during the Long Vac.'

'Goodness!'

'Well, go on, it's only fair. You know what my home's like.'

'Well, it's in a district a little way away from the centre, quite near the river. The houses are mostly quiet, white bungalow-type places in gardens. Ours is one of those.'

'Is it quite big?'

'No, not really. In fact, you'd probably find it rather small by your standards.'

'But it has a garden?'

'Goodness, you're really interrogating me.'

'Well, I want to know. I can't imagine what it's like there. I mean, you might as well come from the moon for all I know about it.'

'Oh, the moon's more romantic.'

*

'I heard from my father this morning.'

'Did you? What did he have to say?'

'Nothing much. He hopes that I'm working hard and making the most of my time here.'

'Well, you are, aren't you?'

'Yes, I suppose I am. Though not exactly what he had in mind.'

'How would he feel if he knew about us?'

'Oh, he'd be horrified. He'd probably think I was on the road to ruin.'

'Does he write to you often?'

'On the first of the month.'

'Really?'

'Yes. It's hardly a letter actually, more of a bulletin. I mean, it's not written because he felt like sitting down and writing to me or because he has anything in particular to communicate; he writes because it's the first of the month and when I left, he *said* he would write to me on the first of the month.'

'Good heavens! Do you get on well with him?'

'What do you think?'

'Well, I don't know. I think he sounds rather daunting.'

'He's not daunting; he's too predictable to be daunting. He's just very stuck in his ways and clings on to all the old traditions. He's petrified of letting go in case he finds himself adrift in a world he can't cope with.'

'What does he do?'

'He's a civil servant, he works for the State government. What exactly he does, I've never been too clear. When I was little, I thought he just drove around in a big car with net curtains, shooing people off the road. Maybe I was right.'

'How about your mother? What's she like?'

'She's wonderful, a real darling.'

'Does she write to you a lot?'

'Sometimes.'

'More or less than your father?'

'Oh, much less.'

'Why, if she's so much nicer? Why doesn't she write to you on the first of the month instead of your father and just let him send you an occasional sermon?'

'My father doesn't know she writes to me. She's very shy and secretive about her letters and she gets one of my sisters to post them without Daddy knowing. They're her little indulgence.'

'But, good heavens, you're her son. Why shouldn't she send you letters?'

'Oh, my father would insist on reading them if he knew.'

'*What!*'

'Don't sound so amazed. In India most fathers are tyrants, especially fathers like mine who feel threatened by the big wide world. They like having a little universe in which they can be top dog.'

'But why does she put up with it?'

'She has no option.'

'But—'

'But what? Of course it's shameful, but after all, there are worse things. He's not an unkind man, he's not harsh to her, he's just a petty dictator.'

'But, Ravi, it's such an intrusion; it's as though she had no right to her own affairs.'

'Of course. But you know, he's not unique. Lots of husbands in India are like that, in his generation anyway. He doesn't see anything wrong in what he's doing and I'm not sure that she does either.'

'Does he read the rest of the family's mail as well?'

'Oh yes, I'm sure of it. I get two quite different kinds of letters from my sisters – those written for Daddy's inspection and those they've smuggled out. You can tell the difference straight away.'

'Gosh, I think that's awful!'

'The close-knit Indian family.'

'It sounds suffocating.'

'I suppose it must to you. It can be, of course. But you

don't know the positive side of it; people aren't so lonely there.'

'I'd rather be lonely.'

'Would you? Would you really?'

'Yes, I would! I mean, I just can't imagine my father spying on my mother's correspondence. Frankly, he couldn't care less; it wouldn't even bother him, I don't think, if she was writing passionate love letters to someone. He wouldn't even notice.'

'There you are! Is that any better?'

'Yes, it's infinitely better.'

'I'm not absolutely sure.'

'How can you *say* that?'

'Sarah, you don't know anything about India; you've never been there. You know, you can't judge everything over there by the standards you would here. In a way, you can't judge *anything* by the standards you would here.'

*

The final weeks of term were wonderful. As well as garden parties, there were dinners of vegetable curries and lentils, gatherings to share newly arrived Indian sweets or rare records or letters of common interest. Sarah was taken to the shabby little cinema in the outskirts and found herself the only non-Indian in the audience. It was a revelation, showing her that her geography had been self-imposed all along.

The background stayed the same. One particularly warm evening, David Whitehead saw Sarah and Ravi walking hand in hand on the opposite side of the river. He found the sight oddly satisfying and gloated over their silly, oblivious smiles. If Sarah Livingstone was now going around with that Indian chap, then as far as he was concerned she could be after only one thing – and if that was what she was really like, then she could never have been up to much after all.

There was still punting and cricket in the park. Sarah and Ravi lay on the grass and made fun of the cricketers. At first, it struck Sarah as funny that Ravi should know the rules of cricket so much better than she did, but he got quite angry with her when she laughed about it. It stayed fine and Sarah wore her Indian dress and open sandals. Ravi wore his light muslin kurtas and later Sarah wore one of them too. The weather was exceptionally warm, almost close. They went to an open-air performance of Chaucer's *The Franklin's Tale*. In the middle of the play a thunderstorm broke and they giggled at the way the audience stoically brought out umbrellas and plastic macs and no one ran away. After the thunderstorm the weather cleared again and, in the morning, the smell of lukewarm drying grass was nearly intoxicating. It was warm enough for picnics, warm enough for bare arms at night. Bizarrely, incomprehensibly, someone called Verity Claybody tried to kill herself in one of the sunniest weeks.

But in that similar summer, Sarah was travelling. Apparently stationary amongst the same quadrangles and the same cavorting, she felt her distance from them grow. She could even less wholeheartedly be part of all that, now that she was part of Ravi. A childhood memory of carrying a frog into one of her mother's polite fund-raising coffee mornings and all the ladies recoiling in squeamish alarm surfaced strangely when she arrived at a certain kind of party together with Ravi. She sensed the same instant of shock, the same social perplexity over what would be the right reaction. And then the swift efforts to crowd around the frog and cry, 'How sweet, how educational!' also echoed that earlier memory. Sarah felt she was on the brink of a departure. But it was in fact Ravi's departure for, on July the first, he would be going back to India for the Long Vacation.

*

Ravi felt that the summer was closing in on him. It was gorgeous (to quote Sarah), it was beautiful, but it was closing in on him and he was secretly looking forward to flying home. His affair with Sarah Livingstone had been like a second private summer, running alongside the risible public one and giving it a mischievous capering shadow. It had turned the long succession of floral hats and strawberries into a celebration in which he could smilingly participate. He had never imagined that he would live like this. When he woke up in the morning and found Sarah beside him, smiling in her sleep, he could still hardly believe it. When she came running into his room, where her intimate possessions lay openly for everyone to see, each time he felt a jump of joy. He would catch sight of her in the street, across gardens, as though they were total strangers, smiling and chattering, and the connection between them repeatedly amazed him. She was tremendous. The ease, the happiness with which she had taken up his way of life here touched him deeply. It was a compliment to him, he knew, to see her mixing rice and vegetables on her plate with her fingers or kicking off her sandals to sit down barefoot on the floor, even if it looked a little silly. He had had to accommodate to her ways really remarkably little. What was the point, when she was so eager to shake them off? The two of them enjoyed their private summer and Dev and Sunil, who had begun by looking askance, now watched his happiness with envy and admiration.

But vaguely disquieting – no, almost too unimportant to be disquieting – was any suggestion of permanence, any accidental assumption by Sarah that this idyll would continue elsewhere. Ravi knew that it was inseparably part of the university, as much as the student plays and the garden parties. Like them, it would be inconceivable outside the city. They both knew this, of course, must know this, but on some of the more rapturous nights it would have been so easy to forget it. By himself afterwards, Ravi sometimes worried that Sarah had long forgotten it and that it was really his duty to remind her. But he had been drawn to her originally for her independence, her bright resilience and he reassured himself now that those qualities would see her through when it all came to an end. Besides, how could anything so good-humoured possibly end in acrimony? When their different destinations inevitably recalled them, Sarah would cope. This was not the first time for her, after all. So he said nothing to remind her; it seemed unkind. By going back to India for the summer, he thought, he was doing enough to remind her that he belonged somewhere else.

*

She went to see him off at the airport, a forlorn ritual which only reinforced the impression of Ravi's debonair departure and her sad remaining. When he had gone, she shut herself in a lavatory and cried. Outside the door, a grey mop pushed by a doleful-eyed Indian woman slopped to and fro and when Sarah came out of the cubicle, red-eyed, the woman stared at her with an unremittingly gloomy gaze. Sarah cried not only for the loss of Ravi, which was awful enough, but also for the return to monotony, for the humiliating relapse into everyday blandness which enclosed her as she rode back into London on the Underground.

*

'So tell us more about him, darling. He sounds quite fascinating.'

'Oh, Mummy, he's not some exotic creature! You don't have to talk about him as if he were an unusual specimen of pond life.'

'But Sarah, I'm not doing anything of the sort. We just need to know a little more about him, don't we, so that we can make conversation when he comes here. You said he's reading Politics and Economics?'

'You don't need to "make conversation", Mummy. Can't you just be perfectly natural with him? He doesn't need to be handled with kid gloves.'

'I'm not going to handle him with kid gloves. Gracious, you're so prickly and over-sensitive these days, Sarah. Whereabouts in India did you say he comes from?'

'Lucknow. But originally—'

'Lucknow!' Sarah's father interrupted joyfully. 'God, I remember Lucknow. I could tell you some funny stories about Lucknow . . .'

*

4 July, London

Darling Ravi,

How can I *possibly* last until September 30th? It is only three days since you left and already I miss you so much that I can't concentrate on anything. (I hope it wears off!) I should be reading on 'The Modern Novel', but instead I'm afraid I'm just drifting around the house wishing it were already August, because then at least I'd have my holiday with Emily to look forward to. As it is, everything feels really *moribund* here; a lot of people are away and I'm pretty much cloistered in the house with my dear Mama, who is driving me slowly berserk. She keeps cross-questioning me about you, *viz.* 'Does he drink? Does he smoke? Is he a vegetarian? Oh well, it'll give me a chance to try out some of my new wholefood recipes. Is he very pernickety about his food? They usually are, aren't they? Is he frightfully well off?' She imagines you are some kind of maharajah, I think, since she supposes that's the only kind of Indian who comes to Oxford. (She's got no idea about scholarships.) I can tell the whole idea is starting rather to appeal to her, actually, so I haven't bothered to disillusion her (much!). Now she's wandering around the house looking smug and virtually humming songs from *The King and I.* You see, you really have *no need* to worry about staying here when you come back. You don't need to 'keep a low profile' as you put it. You'll get a VIP reception!

Anyway, this gossip tells you there is as yet no news. Write and tell me what's happening to you soon; how your family reunion went, etc, etc. It's so hard not being able to imagine what it's like where you are. It feels as though you're in a void somewhere and will only really come back into existence at the end of September!

These air-letters are horrible, aren't they? Just as you get carried away, they run out. And I hate this blue. Next time, maybe I'll write on proper paper. Will it take ages longer to get there? I do hope this letter doesn't sound too complaining. I'm fine really. It's just because I LOVE YOU.

Sarah

PS. Make sure you keep this letter well away from your father's wandering gaze!

*

'I remember when I was compiling the pictures for the "Hunger" exhibition,' Mr Livingstone recalled. 'We were looking for some shots in a little place in Rajasthan. Its name escapes me. It's a lovely region actually, with those wonderful reddish hills, but this was a beastly little place – some dusty town in the back of beyond – and I can't think what we were doing there. And, to cap it all, it was one of the days when you weren't allowed to buy a drink. There we were, Johnny Callaghan and myself, stuck in that godforsaken hole waiting for our picture, so we decided to go for a spin out of town to see what we could see. We struck lucky almost at once when we came upon a child with a camel pulling a plough. You see them in that part of India. We stopped the car, got out, went through our little routine with the child and made ready to take the pictures. It was Johnny's picture, actually. Anyway, he went up to the camel, extended his lens, started focusing and said to the camel, "Stop looking so goddamn condescending. Look miserable, you beast." And he went just a little bit closer. Then he was quite ready for the picture and he said, "Come on camel, look wretched, can't you?" and the camel suddenly shot out a long stream of spit straight – wham! – into Johnny's lens. Bull's-eye! It was extraordinary, one of the damned funniest things I ever saw!'

*

21 July, London

Darling Ravi,

I am writing again, even though I haven't yet got your answer to my first letter, because a piece of news – however trivial – has broken the monotony of my days and since I think my last letter must have sounded very low, I thought I'd write again to improve the picture. Sunil Sircar came to visit me while he was in London, as you had suggested. He's been working in one of the libraries and staying with friends. We went for a meal in a Bangladeshi restaurant in the most sordid part of the East End – I didn't even know it existed – and heads swivelled when Mr Sircar and I walked in! We had a really good evening actually. He is very well and sends you his best wishes. He also sent you a message in Hindi, which I was supposed to write out phonetically, but I'm afraid I've forgotten it. It sounded rude.

Do write to me soon. I know the mail's awful and I can't expect a reply yet, but I've bet myself a double vodka and lime that I'll have one by the end of next week!

The weather here's dreadful; a real English summer with

torrential rain, washed-out garden parties – and colds! At least, no excuse not to embark on 'The Modern Novel'. I miss you, my Ravi.

Love, Sarah

*

1 August, Lucknow

My dear Sarah,

Thank you for your letter. For some crazy reason, it took nearly two weeks to reach me and then I carried it around in my pocket (my breast pocket!) until I could find a quiet moment to sit down and write back to you. That took until today!

I am leading a pretty hectic life after twelve months away, as I am sure you can imagine. I have to visit everyone and see everyone so as not to cause offence or tread on any toes. As well, people I can barely remember (and sometimes wished to forget!) keep turning up at my parents' house to have a good stare at me and see how I've changed while I've been abroad. Paler and thinner is the general verdict! I'm beginning to feel like a display model . . .

Next week I shall be at my uncle's house in Delhi, where it's probably best not to write to me. (I'll only be there for a week and it could cause problems.) But if you write to me here, I will get your letter when I come back.

I wish I had more time to work actually (and to write you a longer letter!) but my time here is hardly my own. My father has had one of his ridiculous ideas, which consists of my giving a talk at his social club on 'A Student's Life at Oxford University'. It sounds like a joke, but I shall actually have to look up some facts and figures, believe it or not, because some of those old fogies are bound to try and catch me out with their questions. I mustn't imagine that you are sitting in the front row or I shall burst out laughing.

I must stop now, as I have rashly promised to take Asha and Shakun to the cinema and I can hear them fussing around outside. I have some rubbishy film in store for me!

Still, it is good to be back here with them, I must say (if you'll forgive me for it!), even if I have to work hard for my keep. But, by September, I'm sure I shall have had more than enough of 'home sweet home'. The 'noises off' are rising to a crescendo now and it would never do to miss the commercials! I must go. Cheer up!

Love, Ravi

*

Darling Ravi,

I got your letter this morning and I've read it three times already! I'm glad everything's OK and you're having a good time. I love the thought of you giving a lecture on 'A Student's Life at Oxford University!' Will you tell them about the loose morals of the female students too? I must say, I was miffed at being told not to write to you at your uncle's house – surely everyone must know by now that the letters you're getting are from me? – but since you didn't give me the address in any case, I have no option. But, sulk over. You are forgiven really!

Here, things are pretty much the same. Preparations for the holiday are well under way. Emily rang me last night in a sudden flap about money; she didn't know if she could actually afford the holiday after all!! I nearly killed her. But the panic's over and we'll be leaving on August 15th and coming back at the end of the first week in September. I hope Emily turns out to be all right as a travelling companion. I can foresee friction if she gets one of her loony ideas into her head or takes a fancy to some dark-eyed Adonis. Still, it should be fun, hopefully. We're flying to Split and getting a ferry down through the Adriatic. I'll write to you from somewhere really gorgeous. (Desperate attempt to make you feel envious!)

Now I suppose I should make a last attempt at finishing my 'Modern Novel' reading. I haven't done nearly as much as I should, I fear. I ended up getting a waitressing job three nights a week in an American hamburger restaurant (just the kind of place you would *hate*). It works out quite lucrative with tips etc, but leaves me totally drained the next day. Still, sunny South, here I come!

Lots of love and I wish September 30th were sooner.

Love, Sarah

PS. What do you mean by 'problems' at your uncle's house? I'm most intrigued. Please explain. Love, S.

*

24 August, Mykonos

Oh, darling Ravi!

I'm lying on a rock about thirty feet above the most brilliant blue sea. The sun is beating down out of a matching sky and Emily and I are basting slowly like two fowl on a spit. (Please forgive odd spots of suntan oil!)

The holiday so far has been great – no problems of any kind. We had one close shave in Athens when Emily insisted on investigating the night life in a distinctly sleazy part of town. I won't go into sordid details but it ended up with us running – well, not exactly for our lives, but certainly for our virtue (!) – down a dark alley with two swarthy Athenians in hot pursuit. Honestly! Otherwise, things have been fine. These islands are so beautiful, it's incredible. (I have fantasies of coming here one day with you!) Just imagine – totally white villages piled up on the hillsides like sugar lumps, stray rickety windmills and all around the most dazzling sea. Every night, we go down to one of the little tavernas on the waterfront and listen to bouzouki music and drink ouzo or retsina – and I miss you so much!

We had quite a good time in Yugoslavia too, although it wasn't one hundred per cent hedonistic like here. It was pretty interesting but in places inland the country was a bit depressing, sort of poor and primitive, with little dark children running around. We were secretly glad to get back to the sea and holiday proper!

We have about a week here, then we move on to another island called Paros which apparently is even more beautiful and unspoilt. Now it's time to turn over onto my back again, I think, to roast my front. Mmm . . .

If I didn't have something to look forward to at the end of September, I think I could stay here for ever.

Lots of love,
Sarah

*

My dear Sarah,

Another letter – and another! What have I done to deserve this? My father remarked suspiciously this morning, 'Your friend S. Livingstone is a prolific correspondent.' I agreed! I would of course have answered much sooner, but I knew you would be away. Hopefully this letter will arrive in time for your return anyway. I'm sure your holiday was a great success and I very much look forward to hearing all about it (with tales of excitement and adventure, I bet!). I have had little of either here, but a great deal of toing and froing. I ended up staying in Delhi for nearly two weeks, instead of just one. My uncle and aunt were very welcoming, in fact nearly too much so. It was one round of dinners and parties and visits. He is a pretty big wheel in the Government now and has a lifestyle to match. I also visited some old college friends – members of the clandestine radio group, remember? It was good fun. Then back here for a few days before another trip to Kanpur to visit some old family friends. That went quite well too, but it was all pretty exhausting and now I need a few days to recover!

There is also talk of another visit to my uncle's house just before I leave for England. He is very keen, but I'm not so sure if I am. Still, we shall see.

You ask one or two searching questions, which I cannot evade entirely! In all honesty, no, I have not told the whole family precisely who my faithful correspondent is, only my brother Ramesh. For reasons which I am sure you understand, it would probably only cause more trouble than it's worth. (*My* mother would not go around the house humming Broadway musical songs!) As regards not writing to me care of my uncle, frankly I'm surprised you ask. I think you can probably see why; it would cause a million and one raised eyebrows when I come for such a short stay – as if the letter must be so urgent that it couldn't await my return! My uncle is also quite a big shot and, for all I know, his mail may be scrutinised. Your letter could give rise to all sorts of complications.

But these are trivia; why am I devoting so much precious air-letter space to them?

Look at the date, Sarah; only thirty days to go! Till then, I think of you.

All my love, Ravi

＊

9 September, London

Dearest Ravi,

I found your letter when I got back yesterday. It was lovely to find it, as everything else felt a bit flat. The holiday was marvellous, but you know how it is when you get back – all the normal everyday things seem doubly hard to put up with. I hope you got my letter from Mykonos and I also sent a postcard later from Paros, but it didn't say much. There weren't too many 'tales of excitement and adventure', as you put it, but Emily did have her beach-bag pinched on Paros. Luckily there wasn't anything of much value in it, but some swarthy Greek probably made his lady a generous gift of Emily's bikini!

It certainly sounds as though you've had your share of gallivanting around too. I looked up the places where you'd been (Kanpur etc) in the atlas. (On my father's it seems to be spelt Cawnpore?) I wanted to get some sort of idea of what it was actually like where you were, but needless to say failed miserably. Still, you'll be able to tell me all about it yourself soon enough – in twenty-one days precisely. Let me know your flight so that I can come out to the airport to meet you. Then let's go back to Oxford as soon as possible. I don't fancy sticking around here any longer than I have to. The next three weeks I shall have to work like mad catching up on everything I haven't done. So it's just going to be a question of putting my head down and sitting tight until you appear.

By the way, there was no need to get into such a state over what I said about not writing to me. All that I meant was that I hoped you weren't keeping me a shameful secret and I'm quite sure now that you're not. You know, misunderstandings occasionally creep in over four thousand miles.

I love you in any case.

Sarah

＊

102

Dear Sarah,

Just a quick note to say please don't be angry with me, but I will not be flying back until October 5th. There has been a last-minute change of plan and I will now be staying on in Delhi at my uncle's house for an extra few days before I leave. I didn't want to do this, but it seems there is no way out of it. It's a complicated story, but I'll explain everything when I get back. Less than a month to go now in any case! I can hardly wait . . .

All my love, Ravi

*

In the morning on the verandah, with the koels calling in the coral pink cool, Ravi drank his tea and thought about flying back to England with mixed feelings. Part of him couldn't wait to be gone, away from his family and the female relatives and the fuss. But part of him convulsed in a cowardly longing to cling on to this family cosiness, the way he had clung tightly to his mother as a child when he was frightened of falling into the murky depths of the latrine.

*

Sarah met him at the airport, at seven o'clock on a raw October morning. She had travelled out to Heathrow jubilant on the Underground. Ravi came out of the Arrivals door, smaller than she remembered him and cluttered by the crowd around him. After she had run to him and hugged him, there was first a problem to solve over a missing bag and then other luggage and transport to sort out. It was only when they were actually on the Underground again, going back to the house in the white crescent where Ravi had agreed to stay for two days, that they both realised that the bond between them had lasted and, disregarding the stiff passengers, clutched each other in exultant triumph.

Ravi had a funny little brown string tied around his wrist, which Sarah noticed as she held his hand.

'What's this?'

He tucked it under his cuff, dismissed it. 'Shakun put it on.'

103

'Your little sister Shakun? Why?'

'Oh, it's for a safe journey. It's nothing.'

'Well, you've arrived safely. You can take it off now.'

'No, no. It's a good luck thing; you keep it on until it wears through.'

They giggled and kissed.

Later in the day Sarah noticed the string again, when Ravi was asleep in her parents' guest room, exhausted by his journey. His arm was hanging down over the edge of the bed and the little brown string – firmly knotted, she now saw – sat smugly around his wrist. It looked to her like an ownership label and she had a jealous urge to snip it off.

The two days at her parents' house, much dreaded and debated, went easily. Ravi had never wanted to come there before, out of nervous embarrassment she thought. But the visit was quite a success. Her mother and father were elaborately polite to him, her younger brother simply ignored him and Ravi, well used to tuning his behaviour to please people like Sarah's parents, was almost effortlessly charming and appreciative. He looked at Mr Livingstone's photographs of India and shook his head in wonder, repeating, 'Oh my, oh my!' He ate amply of the studiously spicy dinners which Mrs Livingstone had prepared. He was deferential and attentive.

But at night, in the little guest room which Mrs Livingstone had given him, Ravi looked out at the street-lamp through the flowered curtains and felt odd and ill-at-ease – a little like a trespasser in the soft lumpy bed, as if he had been let into the house through mistaken identity and given a prodigal's welcome. He had never wanted to come before because it would have seemed to put a stamp of public acknowledgement on the seriousness of their bond. Now, he regretted that he had succumbed to Sarah's pressure. Until Mr and Mrs Livingstone had gone to bed and Sarah came creeping giggling across the landing to him, he seemed to have no business being there and when she tiptoed back in the morning, he felt doubly strange. He was glad when the agreed two days were over and left for Oxford at the first possible opportunity.

*

'God, I missed you so much in the summer, I thought I would *die!*'

'I missed you too.'

'Did you? Did you really?'

'Of course I did. I used to go out into the gardens at night and howl at the moon.'

'Oh Ravi, why aren't you ever serious? Honestly!'

'This is hardly a position for being serious, is it? Naked in your bedchamber at . . . two a.m.?'

'No, but I *want* to be serious. We've got so incredibly much to talk about.'

'I didn't come all the way over here tonight to be serious, Sarah; through all that wind and rain and kamikaze cyclists—'

'Sometime we have to be serious.'

'Sure, sure, but not tonight, OK?'

'Oh Ravi, that's just the easy way out.'

'Speak for yourself, Miss Livingstone! OK? Agreed? It's a deal?'

'It's a – a deal. Oh, Ravi!'

'Good, so not tonight.'

*

In the third year, they both had new rooms. Sarah chose a room in a turret because it had no neighbours; it looked in two directions from ill-fitting windows, over the red buildings of the college and out along the suburban street. A small architectural frivolity at the end of an institutional wing, Ravi called it her 'ivory tower'. It was a good choice because it was so isolated that no night porter ever came to check on her or discovered Ravi's almost constant presence in her room. But it was cold, so cold that Ravi began to catch his germs again. Almost as soon as they got back he fell ill, smitten by the contrast between Lucknow and an English October, and Sarah had to nurse him. She loved nursing him, a quite unexpected pleasure for she had always thought she was hopeless with invalids. But Ravi, weak and dependent on his back, was more within her grasp than ever before and, for the first time, she felt she possessed him entirely. His illness began as an ordinary cold but progressed alarmingly into a combination of bronchitis and 'flu. He lay in bed in his room, wheezing and sweating while Sarah fussed around him with hot lemon drinks and blankets. Ravi luxuriated in this nursing and Dev and Sunil, only recently returned from their protective families, looked on enviously at this female care.

Certain things had always seemed to Sarah to sum up the stigma of being English and one of them was having a cold. Ravi said, 'When I arrived here, I thought sniffing was the national language. I didn't know how much information could be conveyed by mucus.' And in a gorgeous, hideous imitation, he had snorted his way through a whole spectrum of English emotions: prudishness, arrogance, insularity, disdain. Sarah had giggled, but when she caught a cold herself she remembered the jibe and kept away from Ravi. The accompanying ugliness was bad enough and she did not want to be ridiculed for her classically English complaint.

But Ravi's cold was far more dramatic, life-threatening. The college nurse, called in when his temperature rose, was unsympathetic. 'Too many people in here, for a start,' she said, eying Sarah, Sunil and Dev grimly. 'The first thing you need is a good night's rest.' They did not call her in again. The starchy phrase 'a good night's rest' became a private catch-phrase, which one of them would sometimes murmur smugly after sex.

It was November. Sarah rode through the fog on her bicycle and one afternoon was hit by a delivery van which materialised out of the grey mist. Stricken, Ravi rushed to fetch her from the Casualty department of the hospital. They mourned over her five stitches and an enormous but amusingly located bruise. Ravi was secretly rather impressed that Sarah did not cry at all; she was even tougher than he had thought. She vaunted her injuries afterwards like battle scars and told the story of the accident all over again to an admiring audience. She also seemed to have no idea how horrid her wounds looked. Ravi watched her sleep that night and was touched with pity for her poor arms, stretched repugnantly black and battered on the much-laundered sheets.

On Guy Fawkes' night, there was a party given in Ravi's

106

college. At first, Sarah was secretly amused to see how excited Ravi and his friends were over fireworks. She thought it was endearingly uninhibited, their usual exuberant selves. But she found out that they were actually celebrating their own childhood memories, far removed from 'Penny for the Guy'. The bright flames in the dark reminded them of Diwali, the festival of lights, when in India the houses are decorated with tiny oil-lamps. Their exuberance had nothing to do with the boyish fun of bangers; they were miles away. Sarah suddenly felt left out of their evening, for she had no idea any more what the party was about. Ravi wrote her a message in the dark with a sparkler, but she couldn't follow it. 'I don't know what you're going on about,' she said snappily. Sunil filched some Roman candles from the communal store and took them away for a private display afterwards. He, Dev and Ravi stood and watched them burn in utter silence. That night, Simon Satchell was badly burnt while fooling around with a Catherine wheel.

Emily Williams gave another party to which she invited Sarah and Ravi, and Sunil and Dev as well. At the party, Sunil made a pass at Emily which Sarah and Ravi watched with incredulous amusement.

'We've started a trend,' Sarah said happily to Ravi, as they went to bed afterwards.

But Ravi did not reply; oddly, Sunil's behaviour repelled him, although he could not have said exactly why. He had found the sight of his friend fondling Emily Williams in the dark of the party peculiarly unpleasant. He felt somehow implicated in the murky scene and did not want to dwell on it, so he pretended to be exhausted and already half-asleep.

Perhaps there had been the occasional difficulty, dwarfed by memory: meeting David Whitehead at a small lunch party. But Ravi had coped well, had come out of it better, in fact, than David who had appeared gauche and churlish. Sarah had felt disconcerted afterwards, wondering how she could possibly have been fond of David. That seemed a different incarnation now: rugger shirts and crumpets, vicars and tarts parties, playing games with a blond schoolboy hero. Ravi had been most diplomatic afterwards, had made no comment until Sarah pressed him. Perhaps there had been the occasional argument too – not many, but the chance eruption of some unimportant grievance; the issue of the pillow-case, the unexplained air-letter, the beautiful sari lent by Nanda which Ravi had refused point-blank to let Sarah wear to a party. And there had been Christmas.

Everyone became slightly frenetic in the build-up to Christmas and Sarah, whether she wanted it or not, found herself caught up in the excitement too. Only Ravi it seemed to her, stayed aloof, wouldn't be inane and jolly, wouldn't join in. And funnily, it had never occurred to Sarah that she might have to give up Christmas. Before, she had condemned it unthinkingly, never imagining an English winter without it. Now she berated Ravi at first for being a killjoy and told him he was middle-aged before his time. It was only when he eventually got annoyed with her and snapped, 'Oh, for heaven's sake, run along and enjoy your Christmas,' that the truth hit her. Then she was devastated by her chauvinism. How could she have been so stupid? She dropped Christmas like a scalding dish, studiously avoiding all the parties and carols but underneath bearing Ravi a grudging resentment for depriving her of them. For his part, Ravi did not like to see Sarah going to such lengths to please him. It was almost as embarrassing as her sari-wearing or her eating with her fingers. He hated to be responsible for her happiness and persuaded her to go to some of the lesser Christmas festivities.

Together, they went to a vegetarian Christmas dinner given by a girl in Sarah's 'Modern Novel' class. The girl, Rowena Archer, had collected everyone she could think of to whom Christmas was alien and, declaring it an alternative festival, sat them down to an ersatz Christmas feast. There were four Jewish students who clearly found the whole thing obscurely insulting, two timid Malaysian Chinese girls who simply giggled helplessly at yet another instance of bizarre English behaviour, and Ravi and Sarah, taken aback by this heavy-handed philanthropy. Rowena's boy-friend, a well-meaning left-wing theology student, tried to engage each of them in turn about their own cultural background and repeatedly failed to see that he was being snubbed. It was an unhappy compromise. At the end of the meal, Rowena served a carrot-based Christmas pudding – 'Beef-suet-free', she beamed at Ravi – and in trying to flambé it, set her oven glove alight. Afterwards Sarah and Ravi made fun of the dinner, but that time their laughter rang a little hollow, for it had made them feel momentarily exiled to a no-man's land where no one was at home.

Both he and Sarah boycotted their colleges' Christmas dinners and went instead to the Shah Jehan. The waiters had put up holly around the flock wallpaper and a gaudy banner on the door wishing all their customers a 'Merry Xmas'. 'To deter them from smashing the windows,' Ravi said bitterly. By then, Sarah felt confident enough not to suffer a pang of national guilt and gloomily agree, but answered impatiently, 'God, you're cynical.'

*

Ravi spent the Christmas vacation in Sheffield again. There had been some brief discussion about his coming to stay at the Livingstones'. But both of them knew that would be impossible – Sarah because of the constraints and her parents and Ravi because it felt too much like a trap. In any case, the Christmas vacation only lasted six weeks and they shortened this by staying up in Oxford until the very day the colleges closed. Sarah saw Ravi go with a fair amount of resignation. It was a parting from which he was guaranteed to return.

*

They both came back to Oxford early, before term began, and continued where they had left off. It was so bitterly cold in Sarah's room that it became one of their jokes; neither of them could bear to get out of bed in the morning – they had to take it in turns to dart across the room to switch on the fire. The shadow of the final exams first fell across their horizon that term, a worrying grey blotch which obscured what might lie beyond it. Sarah's attitude was one of erratic panic, Ravi's a grimmer determination. In a way, perhaps they almost welcomed them, for they hid the less well-defined obstacles which would follow.

They liked to work at different times of day; Ravi slept

late and it was sometimes three or four o'clock in the afternoon before he got into his stride. After dinner, he would go back to work and then quite often sit up until two or three in the morning, reviving himself with a wet towel wrapped around his head. Sarah got up at about nine and hurried to the library, only to be lured out by some distraction a few hours later: coffee with a friend, an invitation to lunch. By dinner-time, she usually felt that her day's work was done. Sometimes they accused each other of being a distraction and once, when Ravi had done badly in a test paper, they had a real argument about it, their first since the pillow-case.

They always seemed to be short of pillow-cases; wherever they slept, they invariably ended up with just one. The spare pillow-case was a humorous bone of contention which travelled back and forth between their rooms. One day, Sarah discovered to her annoyance that Ravi had filled it with his dirty washing and left it by his door in a way which seemed to imply that the washing was her responsibility.

'What's this supposed to mean?'

'Oh, you said you were going to the launderette tonight, remember? I thought, as you were going anyway and you wanted the pillow-case, you wouldn't mind taking my stuff too. There's not much.'

'Oh, Ravi, honestly!'

'All right, all right, don't. I didn't think it was *such* a great favour to ask.'

'It's only the third time! I'm not your maidservant, you know.'

'Oh Sarah, don't exaggerate. I never thought you were.'

'Ah, but you'd never dream of doing mine for me, would you?'

'Bras and coloured panties would look a bit funny in our laundry room.'

'Funnier than underpants and men's shirts in ours?'

'I thought you said your laundry room was always overflowing with rugger shirts and size ten socks.'

'That's not the point! It's the principle – why should I go on doing your washing if you're not prepared to do mine?'

'OK, don't do it, don't do it! But you'll have to go without

110

the pillow-case then, because I certainly shan't have time to do any washing for a couple of days yet.'

'Oh, stuff the pillow-case!'

'Sarah, I wish you wouldn't keep saying things like that—'

'Why not? Is it because it makes me jar with your image of how a woman ought to be, all nice and quiet and subservient?'

'What on earth are you going on about now?'

'You don't like it when I'm crude and unladylike, do you? Deep down, I suppose you still believe in all that crap about women being meek and docile and knowing their place.'

'Sarah, what rubbish! I don't think women should be meek and docile.'

'Oh yes, you do.'

'No, I *don't*. Look, how many times have I told you that the very first reason I liked you was because you were independent, you were precisely the opposite of what I was used to?'

'Oh yes, that's fine. It's great to be independent, so long as I'm still prepared to do your washing and I don't contradict you in front of your friends.'

'What *are* you talking about?'

'You know perfectly well. Last night, when we were talking about racial prejudice among intellectuals with Sunil and Rajiv Mehrotra and you said you thought most dons were really racists underneath and I said you'd got a racists-under-the-bed complex, you looked daggers at me.'

'It was such a crude way of putting it.'

'What did I say? Underneath, you would really like me to be demure and know my place.'

'Sarah, this is totally ridiculous. I don't want you to touch my feet in respect – or to wait to eat until I've eaten for that matter, either.'

'No? Why not? Is it because you don't view me in the same way as Indian women? Is it because I'm not pure enough to be put on a par with them?'

'Sarah, what has got into you? What you're saying is preposterous. I'm not a barbarian, you know. My God! All I asked you to do was carry one extra bag to the laundry. Is that really so demeaning? Listen, I just want you to be you, all right?'

'And do your washing? And not use bad language?'

'Oh Sarah, stop it! Forget the wretched washing! Forget it! This is so silly. One bag of dirty laundry!'

'It's not just one bag of dirty laundry, it's a whole issue. You just won't admit that you would view me completely differently if I was Indian.'

'If you were Indian? Is that it? Sarah, don't you realise that if you were Indian, probably none of this could ever have happened? We would never have got into this situation in the first place.'

'Because you would have considered me too unattainable to lay a finger on me? Out of bounds? But English girls come into a separate category, don't they?'

'Shut up!'

'I will. I'm going – and I'm leaving you your bloody dirty washing because it's my pillow-case and I'm taking it anyway. There!'

'Well, you've certainly done your best to be "crude and unladylike", I'll give you that.'

'Bully for you.'

'Oh, you're so *silly*!'

'And you're such a cheat!'

*

They probably argued more often then because of the pressure of work. January and February were dreary months, unrelievedly drab and cold. The prospect of Finals swelled from a grey blotch to a sooty mushroom cloud beyond which the rest of the world was hidden. Ravi and Sarah shut themselves away in their small universe of timetables and revision. They blocked up Sarah's draughty windows with Ravi's socks stuffed with newspaper so as to make her turret room easier to work in. In a way, the exams actually helped them because they were a legitimate reason for shutting out the rest of the world. For a short while, they could barricade themselves inside their doomed fortress and let nobody in.

At Easter they went on a short holiday together – five days in Cornwall in a borrowed cottage. It had been Sarah's idea;

the cottage belonged to one of her parents' friends. But everyone agreed that a quick break from revision was quite essential. So Ravi left his desk too, where anxiety was gradually glueing him, and together they went down to a windy little bungalow above the sea where, for the first time ever, they really were quite alone.

The ocean tossed at the bottom of the cliff and sand found its way into the cottage, even with all the doors and windows shut. When it rained, the wind flung solid sheets of water at the windows and the whole ocean disappeared. They could have been anywhere in their draughty pastel-pink house and it was cold.

There were hardly any tourists as yet in the village to which they walked to buy eggs and milk and sliced white bread. They struck up quite a friendship with the cheery fat Cornishwoman whose shop sold little else. She took a fancy to them and asked Ravi where he came from and, on Easter Saturday, gave them each a free chocolate cream egg. They walked back to the cottage with their green nylon net clanking with tins and, in the evenings, Sarah cooked amusing combinations of tinned luncheon meat and tinned spaghetti and tinned rice pudding and tinned peaches. After supper, they sat in the borrowed living-room and read by the poor light of two pink-shaded standard lamps.

One evening, they were sitting there with the fake log gas fire on and sipping at surreptitious glasses of 'borrowed' brandy. A wet squall was making the ocean thud outside. They were both reading: Ravi a new interpretation of England's economic decline ('half work'), and Sarah a gorgeously lowbrow bestseller which she had found on the bookshelves. Suddenly, she looked up and said, 'What's going to happen to us?'

'We'll both get starred Firsts,' Ravi answered.

'No,' Sarah said. 'No. Afterwards. I mean, what's going to happen to us after Finals?'

Ravi looked up from his book. 'What's suddenly made you bring that up?'

'It's not sudden, I've thought about it a lot. But being here together, all normal and relaxed and knowing it can't last . . .'

113

'Let's enjoy now.'

'That's easy to say. I would enjoy it a lot more if I didn't know it was going to end so soon.'

'Well, we can't stay here forever, can we?'

'I don't mean *here*, Ravi. I don't mean this grotty little house and our pink double bed. I mean everything; don't you realise that in less than four months' time we'll have left university? What are we going to do *then*?'

'I've thought about that too,' Ravi said, 'and I don't know.'

'You'll go back to India, won't you?'

'Yes, of course.'

'Well, and what about me?'

Suddenly Ravi felt trapped in the little pink living-room, felt it had all been planned – that he had been lured down to Cornwall on purpose, shut up in this remote cottage where he had loved Sarah more than ever before, and now she was rounding on him and demanding payment. She had arranged it all.

Instead of the pity and guilt he had started to feel, he was suddenly unexpectedly angry; he had been tricked. He answered her more callously than he had intended to: 'You said you might try for a job in publishing.'

He saw her flinch and, quickly, he tried to moderate his harshness. 'I mean, until we work something out.'

'What?' Sarah said shrilly. 'What can we work out? If you're going back to India and I'm supposed to stay here, what exactly can we work out? Be pen-friends?'

'I shan't go immediately,' Ravi said. 'I won't hop on a plane the day Finals finish and vanish for ever, you know. I shall still be around for a while afterwards.'

'Oh, big deal!' Sarah said. 'I can look forward to two weeks helping you to pack.'

'Sarah,' Ravi said slowly, almost as if he were afraid to let the words out, 'what did you expect when all of this began?'

'I didn't expect anything,' Sarah said hotly. 'I didn't think my maharajah would sweep me off to his glamorous Eastern palace, if that's what you mean. But I suppose I didn't think I'd be dumped at the end like this, either.'

'Dumped?' Ravi said indignantly. 'Dumped? Who's

talking about dumping? I didn't pick you up, Sarah, and I'm not going to let you drop. I thought you were an independent adult human being. Stop talking as if you were a passive package. If you're in a situation that you don't like now, isn't it fifty per cent your own choice?'

For a moment Sarah, who was lying on the level of Ravi's feet, stared at them as though she hated them. Then she looked up into his face and answered, 'My own choice is to come to India too.'

Ravi was stunned by the threat. It had never once occurred to him that Sarah could produce it. He stared at her, astounded. A moment ago he had been justly accusing her of not being far-sighted enough. But in fact she had arrived by her own route at the hurdle which he had acknowledged all along as insurmountable, and here she was prepared to jump it. He gaped. 'What?'

'Why's that so shocking?' Sarah said. 'Wouldn't you like it if I came?'

'You can't come to India.'

'Why ever not? Other people have.'

'Sarah, you have no idea what you're talking about. You . . . you don't know what India's like. You couldn't behave or do anything there the way we do here.'

'Don't you want us to go on?'

'Of course I do. But—'

'Then let me come to India . . . Marry me.'

If she had hit him instead, attacked him with great violence, he would not have been as shocked. The thought which had lain behind everything – behind those summer letters, behind his uneasy insomnia in her parents' guest room, behind their argument about the pillow-case, the thought which had gone to and fro between them as they said different things, behind the sunny Indian dress and then the sari, the thought she had no right to fling into the open – now lay between them.

'Sarah!'

'All right, all right. I wish I hadn't said it—'

'Oh, Sarah, don't cry!' And then he did exactly what he had least imagined he would do. He got out of his chair and crouched down beside her, taking her carefully into his arms, prepared for her to hit out and repel him.

'Oh, Sarah . . .'

She said nothing, but she did not push him away.

'That was such a brave thing to say.'

'I take it back, I take it back!'

'No, Sarah, don't cry. What you said was tremendous. Sarah, I love you.'

Then she did repel him, pushed him with an almighty shove which knocked him to his seat.

'No, you don't. If you did really, we wouldn't be having this discussion.'

'Sarah, you don't understand. Everything's totally different in India—'

'You're always telling me that! You're always telling me I don't understand, I can't understand. India's *different*. Well, why have you got to keep your life in two separate compartments? Why can't you let me come and find out for myself?'

'Because it would probably be the end of you.'

'It will be the end of me if you just go off to India and I have to stay behind here with nothing. I won't be able to take it.'

'But, Sarah, this is your *home*, you belong here. You've got all your family and your friends, everything you know. One can't just drop all that one fine day for an adventure. And India – Sarah, *you* in India, you in India as my girl-friend, as my . . . my wife, is like imagining some outlandish flower trying to survive in the English winter. You'd droop, you'd grow sour and reproachful. It couldn't ever possibly work, Sarah, not in a million years.'

'I don't believe you.'

'You must, Sarah, you must. If you came to India, imagining we could set up house just like we have here, you'd have the most terrible shock.'

'I don't see why we can't *try*.'

'As a holiday, for a jaunt, that would be one thing, but to come out imagining you were going to make a go of it!'

'People do.'

'Not you, Sarah. Not me.'

'Why *not*?'

'Can't you see? Here we're left to our own devices. We can live in this little toy world we've made up for ourselves.

116

Everything's on our side. But there, everything would conspire against us; we'd have nothing.'

'We'd have us, we'd have us!'

'Sarah, my darling, that isn't going to be enough for ever. Look, stop crying, please. Come for a holiday, by all means, come sightseeing if you must, take a look, but don't kid yourself. Really, I know what I'm talking about.'

'Have you known that all along?'

'Known what?'

'That we hadn't got a future? That this was short-term only?'

'Sarah, I didn't look so far ahead. I wasn't thinking when we were walking round the playing fields that time, "Right, I'll fall in love with this girl for two years".'

He was pleased to see her giggle forlornly through her tears. He pressed his advantage. 'I thought the great thing about us was that we weren't part of the predictable order of things, we didn't fit into a conventional ready-made pattern. You liked that too, didn't you?'

'Yes, of course. But now—'

'Now?'

'Now, I want to go on to the next stage and you're not prepared to. You don't dare.'

'I don't *dare*? Sarah, you always talk as though this were some sort of game we were playing. It's not a question of "daring". I know what would happen if you came to India and I don't want that to happen to us. If we have to part, I would like us to part with pleasant memories of all the good times we've had here, not with acrimony and misery.'

'And I'll only ever have known half of you. I want to see what you're hiding.'

'What I'm hiding?'

'Yes, you've always kept your Indian life a secret from me.'

'I've got a harem of nautch girls—'

'Oh, shut up. Be serious. We've always been lopsided. You know where I come from and my past and my parents, but I haven't got a clue about you.'

'Well, come and see what there is then. Come out and

117

take a look, if you want to. Just don't imagine that you're coming for good, that's all.'

'All right, I will. I'll get a job after Finals and save the air fare and I'll come out in the autumn. For a visit.'

'I'll look forward to it. Is there any more of that brandy?'

*

After that exchange, how was it possible for them to go back to Oxford the way they did and carry on as before? How was it possible for Sarah still to fall asleep beside Ravi with one hand left across his stomach to make sure that in the morning he would still be there? And for Ravi to lie back after they had made love, still crowing triumphantly: 'One all!'?

The summer term was pretty wretched. Overshadowed utterly by Finals, the weeks went by in a numb routine. They worked all day, as often as possible together in one or the other's room, and only broke off to eat dully in the college dining hall. Once a week or so, they allowed themselves the treat of a visit to the Shah Jehan and at night, they made love enjoyably and often. Those were their only recreations. They had to spare a little time for Sunil, who had become alarmingly weird from overwork. He had pored over his philosophy for so long that he could no longer take any of it for granted but felt obliged to question everything. The fixed certainties of his universe were receding into a frightening void. He didn't sleep at night, but wandered through the city streets debating with an invisible opponent. He ate his dinner at four o'clock in the morning, or not at all, took a bath at six and was found asleep in the library in mid-afternoon. Emily Williams was not coping too well with the pressure either. She found she could only sleep after sex and, in order to overcome her insomnia, embarked on a series of desperate one-night stands which racked her days with panic and remorse. She had also virtually stopped eating and her hair began to fall out. Sarah and Ravi clung to each other and felt relatively safe. In the face of such an awesome trial, they thought of little else.

Two weeks before the exams, Sunil collapsed. He walked into Dev's room in the middle of the afternoon, announced,

118

'Either you get a First or you go mad,' and fell headlong to the floor. Horrified, Dev tried to revive him with a splashed tooth-mug of water and then ran for the college nurse. She was having tea when Dev rushed in and, he reported, when told what the trouble was she exclaimed, 'Why do you lot have to make such a song and dance about everything?' Sunil was taken to the college sick bay. When he came to, he was silent and inert, apparently resentful that he had been revived. Dev and Ravi, defying the nurse, came in to see him in the early evening and were shocked out of their selfishness to see how ill he looked. 'So you've decided to lie back and be waited on, then?' Ravi joked uneasily, but Sunil stared back at him quite blankly. ('Why not get a First *and* go mad?' Ravi said afterwards to Sarah.) The following day Emily Williams came to visit Sunil, unannounced, with her sparse hair hidden under a dramatic kerchief. From that visit a feverish affair developed, out of the unhealthy atmosphere of the sick bay, which lasted with neurotic intensity until the exams were over.

The last weekend before the exams, Ravi and Sarah took a break as recommended, but they were too keyed up to relax and enjoy it. They went to the Livingstones' holiday cottage in Wales; Sarah had long looked forward to taking Ravi there as the consummation of her triumph over her upbringing, but they were both restless and unable to appreciate their pretty surroundings.

'Gosh, England is so small,' Ravi said when they arrived at the spruce cottage. 'Everywhere is someone else's back garden.'

Sarah said, 'We're not in England.'

'We've come all this way,' Ravi went on, waving around at the narrow valley. 'Here we are in the middle of nowhere and yet it's all neatly parcelled up. It's all someone's nest. Look around at that landscape,' he said, 'it's all so *tidy*.'

Sarah shrugged. 'We could have gone to Brighton if you'd preferred.'

'And it's all parcelled up by people like your parents,' he continued, as they unpacked deep-frozen blackberries and Mrs Livingstone's quiche from the freezer. 'Have you noticed that, at their level, everyone in England is connected? They run the country like a jolly board game.'

'Look, I've got the message,' Sarah said, 'there's no need to keep going on about it. Just you wait – when I come out to India, I'm going to get my own back on you!'

For three days they bickered listlessly, and the ultimate triumph which Sarah had looked forward to – making love with Ravi in the Victorian brass double bed – did not take place because he was too tired and wanted to conserve his strength.

*

Ravi's exams lasted three days longer than Sarah's, so she had to wait to celebrate until he was through. During those three days she rested, worn out, and began to wonder what would come next. She lay on the college lawn, too tired and triumphant at having survived to summon up much feeling about anything else yet. The sky overhead was a distant blue and she would never have to sit another exam again in her life. The difficulties with Ravi would be resolved. For three days, she gazed up at the sky and waited for Ravi and was content. Counted on the fingers of one idle hand against the grass, the months between the beginning of August, when Ravi would go home, and October when she would fly out to join him, were a tiny span – pitiful, a mere three dots on the lawn. In those three months she would earn her air fare, she would start learning Hindi properly and get ready to turn her back on England. For three days she practised waiting for Ravi and it was so easy, such fun on an Oxford lawn.

Ravi finished his last paper at five o'clock on a sweltering afternoon. He wrote his last sentence almost without realising it, superstitiously perfected his punctuation and when the invigilator announced that the time was up, left the hall in an estranged daze. Across the hall Dev signalled to him jubilantly and, out in the corridor, they hugged each other and beamed. Feeling almost hollow from fatigue and exhilaration, Ravi walked outside. On the steps, his friends were waiting to meet him. Still oddly drained of emotion, Ravi walked over to them. Their babble of greetings and congratulations broke over him, but for a moment he just looked blank and almost puzzled. Of course one of them was Sarah, but in his peculiar numb state somehow he could not single her out and put his arm around her. Nanda had to push her forward bossily and say to Ravi, 'There's someone here who's got something to say to you.'

'Quite dazed, my poor Ravi,' Sarah said, taking him in her arms and he let himself be taken as if he were paralysed. All the others cheered and Sarah lifted the foaming mouth of a bottle of champagne to his lips and fed him with it like a doll.

Gradually, his trance cleared. The joy of achievement dawned on him and celebrations started to fill the void left by the exams.

Ravi's tutor, Professor Elstree, gave a party for his third-year students and halfheartedly Ravi went along. He had never had much time for the professor, whom he considered pompous and insincere. Although he had not told Sarah about it, Professor Elstree's reaction when he discovered that his Indian student had an English girl-friend had filled Ravi with an unforgettable rage. Sarah had been introduced to the professor at Christmas at a drinks 'do' he had held for his students. Ruddy and genial as always, he had shaken hands with her and later in the evening, when the mulled wine had dissolved his reserve, he had come across to Ravi – quite bluff and congratulatory – and, clapping him on the shoulder, had nodded at Sarah who was talking animatedly to his wife and declared jokily, 'You've done very well for yourself there, Ravi my boy!' The implication, as Ravi promptly saw it, that he should be grateful for having won Sarah, that she was somehow a trophy he should acknowledge with humble pride, had cut him to the quick. He had looked back at Professor Elstree with a frozen face and wished he could vomit the Christmas cake and the mulled wine, vomit the party from his consciousness. Since he told no one about this incident, it rankled with him for a long time and although Sarah never knew about it and certainly could not have been held responsible, it came between them insidiously.

The party for the third-years was held in the garden of Professor Elstree's sprawling, suburban house; there were jugs of fruit punch on a table covered by a floral cloth and, in the dining room, a buffet of cold meats and flans. 'Hey, a great spread,' Sarah murmured to him as they were shown through into the garden. When the time came, she heaped her plate with game pie and multi-coloured salads and Ravi, who helped himself rather frugally as a matter of pride, found the sight of her sitting on the verandah steps and tucking into Mrs Elstree's handiwork unreasonably annoying. He could hardly blame her, of course; he had not explained to her that she was feasting on an enemy's offerings. But quite unfairly, he was prepared to find her irritating.

Professor Elstree came up to them as they were eating and boomed, 'Well, what are you two going to do?'

'I'm going back to India,' Ravi said quickly.

And Sarah had to chip in, 'And I'm going out there in the autumn.'

'Are you?' said Professor Elstree. 'How fascinating!' He turned to Ravi and asked, 'What have you got in mind? The Civil Service?'

Although Ravi had of course considered taking the Civil Service exams, he found the assumption that he would be such a run-of-the-mill conformist rather galling. 'No,' he answered impetuously, 'I was thinking of giving journalism a go.'

He sensed Sarah looking round at him in surprise. 'It's one of several ideas I'm playing with at the moment,' he went on airily. 'It all depends which way the wind's blowing when I get back.' It pleased him to imply that there were things about India that Professor Elstree could not understand.

'Really?' Professor Elstree said. 'But it's definitely to be India, is it? No question of staying on, as it were?'

Ravi's toes curled with relish at the possibility of snubbing Professor Elstree. 'No,' he replied, 'I think three years here is quite long enough.'

If he was slighted, what with bonhomie and punch, Professor Elstree gave no sign of it but laughed heartily and soon moved away to another group.

'Honestly!' Sarah said to Ravi afterwards, 'did you have to say that to Professor Elstree? You might need him for a reference one day, you know.'

Although the thought did give Ravi a momentary qualm, he answered hotly, 'Professor Elstree's one of the main reasons why I shall be glad to shake the dust of this place from my feet.'

Their last afternoon in Oxford was spent, as Sarah had once sadly predicted, packing Ravi's stuff. Mrs Livingstone had driven up to collect Sarah's belongings the previous day and commented wistfully that it seemed only yesterday when she had brought her there for the first time. Querulously, she expressed concern that Sarah should be leaving the university with her future so undecided. Sarah was rude to her, annoyed that her mother should have identified her own worry so accurately. She helped Ravi sort his belongings into those worth packing and sending home and those to be left behind. He did not suggest that she took anything as a keepsake, but then that was not his way. And what would have been the point, anyway, when they were only parting until the autumn? Both of them hated sentimentality, above all. Sarah had to wait until Ravi was temporarily out of the room in order surreptitiously to retrieve a slightly torn silk kurta from the discarded pile and slip it into her handbag. Mended, she would wear it as a nightshirt until October.

In the evening, of course, they went to the Shah Jehan: Ravi, Sarah, Sunil, Dev, Dilip, Rajiv and Nanda. Sunil, wonderfully recovered, had been offered a grant to stay on and study for a doctorate. He viewed everyone else's emotion at leaving with patronising phlegm; he had evaded the future which terrified him. Dev was going to America. He would stay for a while with his married sister in Washington and then he planned to travel for a bit, to see something of the world. Dilip, Rajiv, Nanda and Ravi were going home. And although this struck Sarah as the most cowardly option, she noticed that they seemed to treat the others with a kind of contempt, as though they were the cowards dodging the issue, while the four of them had taken up an invigorating challenge. Nanda was going to be a teacher (the most unadventurous profession imaginable, Sarah thought) and yet she seemed the most stridently convinced of them all that her path was the most challenging, the most irreproachable. It was almost excessively tolerant, Sarah thought, the way no one disagreed with her. When they had had some wine and lager, because it was their very last evening, Nanda even became rather shrill, shrieking, 'Rats! Rats leaving the sinking ship!' and giggling hysterically.

Sunil said, 'Ah, you'll all end up wishing you were me, well out of the hurly-burly in my little academic niche.'

Dev clapped him on the shoulder. 'That's right, you'll be our shining star, Mr Sircar, a scholar of world renown. We shall look out for your name in the newspapers.'

'Rat!' giggled Nanda. 'Rodent!'

'You mustn't have any more wine,' Sarah said to her with mock solemnity. 'You're becoming an embarrassment.'

'Oh, leave her alone,' said Ravi. 'She's not doing anyone any harm.'

'He springs to my defence!' Nanda boasted. '*He's* not a rat.'

'No, he's a lizard,' Sarah said, 'wriggling quickly out of reach because he's frightened of being caught and losing his tail.'

Those who had heard burst out laughing and Ravi flushed with annoyance.

'Talk about the pot calling the kettle—' he said to Sarah. 'How much have *you* had to drink?'

'Only enough to dull my feelings,' Sarah said, 'only enough to drown my sorrows.'

Dev said he would come back to India around the world, via California and the Pacific.

Sunil looked pensive. 'Maybe when I've done my doctorate I'll get a fellowship in the States,' he said. 'Do you think Berkeley would be interesting? Or better, Harvard or Yale?'

For a moment Nanda, Dilip, Rajiv and Ravi looked at him enviously. But then Rajiv crowed, 'Sold your soul, old boy! Sold your soul.'

*

And then, the next day, Ravi and Sarah caught a train to London. They walked to the railway station holding hands and sat side by side for the short journey, not saying much. Still, they could not believe that this was the end. Still, it seemed, they would take up again in the autumn – not there

124

maybe, but only somewhere else. Later on they would not be able to remember that departure; sometimes it is not the real events which remain, but the accompanying irrelevances which linger unwanted for years. It was a hot day and the caked train window was jammed shut. Ravi kicked off his sandals and put his feet up on the empty seat opposite them. Half-way to London, a ticket collector pulled open the door of their compartment and looked down at Ravi with distaste. He was lolling back with one arm around Sarah and simply held out the other to offer the man their tickets. 'Feet off the seat, if you please,' the man snapped. 'We don't do that in this country.' The shock stopped either of them from expressing their rage and the ticket collector was gone with a vicious bang of the door before Sarah thought of exclaiming, 'Bloody racist!' and Ravi shrugged disdainfully, 'Ignorant peasant.'

They had a month. As a concession to Sarah, Ravi was staying on in England for four extra weeks. There were ways in which he could easily explain this to his parents: waiting to hear his exam results, clearing up business matters and belongings, saying goodbye to friends. At some expense, they rented a rather unpleasant little room in South London, for it would have been intolerable to spend those last weeks at Sarah's parents' house. Her parents accepted this, perhaps dimly hoping that the dilemma might be resolved in favour of their daughter. The one dinner at the house in the white crescent which Ravi came to during that time was still an awful experience; he sat under what he felt to be their silent reproach and could barely chew his chicken. Mr Livingstone made one or two bluff male attempts to pretend that this was not the case, that of course Ravi was under no pressure at all, but his ham-handed questions – 'Well, what will be your fondest memory of England, visually speaking?' – only left worse silences in their wake. Mrs Livingstone said goodbye to him with large and what he imagined to be imploring eyes; at the door, she actually darted forward and gave him a little kiss, saying, 'Now, you know you'll always be welcome here.' They were glad to go back to their gloomy room. 'I'm sorry they were like that,' Sarah said to him. 'Honestly, if I'd known, I would never have gone.'

125

In different circumstances, they could have enjoyed playing house in their poky room. But the communal kitchen was unappetising and, in any case, they did not feel like creating a cosy domestic illusion. They had very little money, so they could not eat out every night, which would at least have given them the impression of extravagance, going out on a high note. They ended up bringing back take-away meals – neon-pink Chinese food and suspect kebabs – and eating them on the bed because there was no room on the table. There was no proper way to do their washing either. Although Ravi had suggested it, pride stopped Sarah from taking their laundry home to put it in her mother's washing machine. Instead, they resorted to washing things in bits in the wash-basin and hanging them precariously around the room to dry. The bathroom at the end of the corridor was something of a joke; it was so nasty that they pretended to be frightened to use it. In fact they were frightened of being infected by the house's gloom.

They only had a month, so they tried to enjoy it. During the day, they went to one of the parks or to an exhibition. Sometimes they met up with Sunil, who was also staying in London until the results came out, and the three of them talked idly for hours. They went to pubs and cheap cafés. Sarah could not help feeling it was a bit of a shame to be in London in the summer. She would have preferred to be at the cottage in Wales. But Ravi needed to be there to arrange his departure. Every day there was something connected with it which had to be done: luggage to be registered, final gifts and unobtainable medicines to be bought. A spate of imperious letters arrived from Lucknow requesting essential items which Ravi was to bring. They were addressed to the family with whom Sunil was staying, where every few days Ravi and Sarah went to collect them. Usually Ravi read them aloud, chuckling and raging, 'Five badger shaving-brushes! *Badger?* What am I supposed to do? Organise a hunting safari?', but one day, he did not read the letter and flung it aside in a rage.

'What do they want now?' Sarah asked. She was beginning to resent these querulous, almost daily reminders that Ravi's duty lay elsewhere. 'What do they want now?'

Ravi dismissed the letter with a disgusted gesture. 'It's rubbish.'

'Who is it from? What do they say?'

'Oh, never mind.'

'No, go on, tell me. We've got so much to get anyway.'

'I said, never mind. It's not about shopping.'

'What is it about then? It's from your father, isn't it?'

'Look Sarah, forget it, it's of no interest.'

'It's of interest to *me*.'

'Well, you're mistaken. It's just a stupid crackpot idea he's come up with, which isn't worth explaining.'

'I think it's a bit much, when I've spent all this time traipsing around the shops with you getting things for them and then when I ask you one simple question, you won't answer it.'

Ravi considered her flushed face across the room. For less than a second, he wondered what her reaction would have been if he had picked up his father's letter from the floor and read out to her: 'Upon your return, I propose that we have a discussion on certain pressing matters, of which you are well aware. I am sure that you have not forgotten Major Mehrotra's charming and sweet-natured daughter . . .' But of course he just shrugged and sighed and for the rest of that day, Sarah noticed, he seemed sullen and depressed.

Perhaps Ravi slightly resented that extra month he had given Sarah – for that was how he saw it. It was not that he was raring to go home; the letter had reminded him that, God knows, there would be problems enough for him to face there too. But he found it infuriating that, having extracted this month from him, Sarah was now spoiling so much of it by bickering and grumbling.

Imminent separation exaggerated everything, of course; this was the last week, the last weekend, the last chicken curry, the last sex. Walking through the streets of London, Ravi saw them very clearly because he was about to leave them for good. He supposed the same must go for Sarah too. He certainly saw her very acutely during those last few weeks, though whether that was just because she was behaving more noticeably, he could not tell. Of course, he was going to miss her a lot. Her lovable qualities were highlighted, as well as her cantankerous shrillness. But since they had to part, he told himself there was no point in dwelling on those. Did he ever question that necessity, ever wonder privately if perhaps he was wrong to be so adamant? Maybe, who knew, perhaps their crazy experiment could work after all? Of course, awake in the middle of the night, eaten up with regret and guilt, he tried to imagine it. Sarah was sitting up beside him, painstakingly memorising his face in the dark, and this proof of the scale of her love devastated him. He wanted to open his arms and take her, saying, 'All right, come with me, let's give it a try.' But just as he began to open his eyelids, panic seized him and he thought, 'My God, I'm out of my mind. What am I doing?' and he forced his eyes to stay shut, pretended to be fast asleep, with a harsh expression on his face. Their parting was going to be hard enough, without his adding to the anguish.

*

She was looking forward to her trip already. Without the promise that in the autumn she would be going away – not just away to Ravi, but away from England as well – she would not have known how to face the future. What was there in England, for heaven's sake, as exciting as Ravi Kaul? What was there in the tiny world of English job options that her friends were now entering, which could compare with the prospect of travelling four thousand miles to a different life altogether? She relied on her dream and she clung to Ravi because at any moment he might disappear.

She knew by then – had long known – that Ravi Kaul could get on fine without her. Sometimes she imagined herself injured, drowning in front of him, so that he would be forced to act and to show that he cared about her. But it was ridiculous after all to expect him to want her as much as she wanted him. Things were different in India and it would have been presumptuous to expect Ravi, who had grown up with a different set of rules, to convert to hers just like that. So she explained to herself what sometimes looked like indifference. And even if really, deep down, he had wished himself rid of her, her dream actually no longer needed reciprocation. It could sustain her love by itself.

They decided to do something really lavish on their last evening. Otherwise, it had been an unremarkable day. They had packed, argued over the size and quantity of Ravi's suitcases and remembered, in a panic-stricken rush, to reconfirm his flight. In the early afternoon, Sunil had turned up and sat slightly irritatingly with them as they finished packing, a wistful expression disguised as wry irony on his face. 'Homeward bound,' he murmured, shaking his head at the expanse of hand luggage and wide-open suitcases. Sarah did her best to turn her back on him, not in the mood for a facetious exchange, but Ravi – unaccountably smug – looked up from where he was squatting, rolling a gift cassette recorder inside a pair of jeans, and joked back, 'You're green with envy!'

Sunil jeered, 'What rot!' but his expression betrayed him and he stayed sitting there in silence, following the presents and souvenirs going into the suitcases like a hungry child watching someone else eat dinner. Sarah began to resent his presence, for he distracted Ravi who kept swapping joky repartee with him and reminiscing about their treatment at the hands of Delhi customs men. The last straw, she felt, was when Sunil produced a shoddily wrapped parcel from his shoulder bag and asked Ravi to take it to his brother in Delhi.

'Honestly!' Sarah wanted to exclaim, 'hasn't he got enough?'

But Ravi took it without a word and tenderly found a place for it near the top of his larger suitcase, to Sarah's fury moving to a less favourable position four paperback books she had bought him as a leaving present. She did not even give Sunil a look. This afternoon of all times, she thought, surely she had a right to have Ravi to herself? But it seemed that Sunil might stay all evening. In the end, towards six o'clock, when already she saw their plan for a lavish evening shelved in favour of a threesome in an Indian restaurant, he tapped the spot where his watch would have been if he had been in the habit of wearing one, and announced with mock solemnity, 'The hour draws nigh.'

Ravi stopped tidying and straightened up. 'You've got to push off, then?' he said, to Sarah's indignation. Suddenly she sensed that both of them had wanted to put off this separation, for different reasons, and that silently Ravi had been willing Sunil to stay there. She sensed it like a betrayal as they stood for a moment facing each other, looking deep into each other's eyes. As if they were the parting lovers, she had to look away tactfully as they embraced and she cried breezily, 'See you around, Sunil,' when he turned to her and said, 'Goodbye, Sarah.'

'That's right,' Ravi added, as though the idea had only just occurred to him. 'You two must keep each other company.'

And although Sarah had felt nothing but dislike for Sunil a minute earlier, merely to take revenge on Ravi she agreed flirtatiously: 'Well now, Sunil, that's an idea, isn't it?'

They dressed up and went to a smart restaurant in the West End. Since they had no money to speak of, this felt more lavish than it was. Sarah wore her Indian dress and the little silver necklace which Ravi had brought back for her from India the summer before. Ravi combed his hair and put on a clean shirt. To begin with, they had to be artificially cheerful and pretend to have nothing but celebration on their minds. But quite soon they found they were genuinely cheerful because the evening was, whatever else, a welcome change. They came under the influence of their festive clothes and by the time they were sitting opposite each other in a little, dark red Italian restaurant, the scraping waiters and cockaded napkins were sufficient to make them quite jolly. And there was, of course, an additional reason to seem unconcerned, because it had always been part of their policy to scoff at solemnity.

They made a great business of choosing their dishes. 'Because,' Sarah said giggling, 'we'll remember what we had here for ages.' And Ravi imperiously ordered quite an expensive bottle of wine.

They had already drunk two glasses each by the time their starters arrived. Ravi poured their third glasses and joked, 'OK, come on, let's drown our sorrows.'

Across the table, they held hands and fed each other forkfuls of avocado and fish paté. By the middle of the main course, they could talk about the next day and still be cheerful.

'You know, you really transformed my whole time in England,' Ravi said grandly as he rolled up his pasta with a flourish.

Sarah giggled. 'Gee, thanks!'

Ravi smiled. 'I'm serious. Before I met you, I was actually quite wretched here. I felt totally alone and ostracised in a cold, hostile environment.'

'A "before and after" commercial,' Sarah joked. 'Depressed? Unloved? Miss Livingstone can change your life. Take her twice a day; once before breakfast and once last thing at night.'

'Wow, give me a break,' Ravi protested and together they laughed and laughed.

'In India,' Sarah said, 'will we have to be awfully prim? I mean, not smooch or hug each other in the street?'

'Oh, awfully,' Ravi said teasingly. He reached across the table and playfully laid his fingers on her lips. 'Never, never, *never* smooch in the street!'

'Oh God, how will I bear it?' Sarah pretended to groan and Ravi answered mischievously, 'Oh well, it won't be for long, will it?'

'Where will you be this time tomorrow?' Sarah asked him as they lingered over their dessert. It was not in fact the next day which began to depress them as the meal came to a close, but more immediately their return to the grubby house. In the plush foreign restaurant, they found they were once more serenely immune to England and regained a playful cosiness they had not managed for a month.

'Let's see,' Ravi said, 'what time is it? Half-past eleven. That will really be about four in the morning, won't it? I expect I shall be watching the dawn come up over the Himalayas.'

'Oh,' Sarah exclaimed, 'you lucky thing!' But she added quickly, 'Still, not long to wait!'

He had to admire her then, although he might have condemned her foolishness. 'Good old Sarah,' he declared. 'Where there's a will, there's a way!'

When they could prolong their meal no longer, they paid and went out into the night. Ravi put his arm around Sarah's shoulders and said, 'Let's finish up in style. Let's take a taxi.' But, infuriatingly, at first no taxi would take them; the address was too far and too disreputable. By the time a surly driver on his way home agreed to take them, their festive mood was spoilt and when they unlocked the door of their room, the suitcases confronted them brutally.

Naturally, they did not sleep. Their love-making was ruined by a sense of its gravity and they would not have a chance to remedy it. At some time after dawn, Ravi fell into a transparent doze and dreamt that he was being disturbed by Sarah crying beside him.

In the morning, tired out and numb, they did the things that they had to do one after another: shut the suitcases, telephoned for a taxi to take them and the heap of luggage to the airport terminal and caught the bus out to the airport. On the bus they hardly spoke, daunted by the lasting significance their words would have. Just once, Sarah tried to joke: 'Too bad I forgot my passport, I could have come too,' and as the airport buildings appeared, Ravi squeezed her hand and muttered, 'Promise me you'll be OK?' They coped with the airport as best they could; stood patiently in an excited, mostly Indian queue to check in Ravi's luggage, paid his excess and sat down bravely in an echoing hall to wait. They were so sure that they would be able to manage it without some sort of messy collapse because they were two such resolute, exceptional people that when finally Ravi's flight was called, Sarah was completely aghast that he should begin to cry too and vanish through the passport gate, waving back to her with tears running down his face.

*

Beneath his plane wings, Ravi saw England shrink to pitiable proportions. There were miniature houses with red toytown roofs, mini highways busy with toy buses and cars and midget-sized people scurrying about on their tiny errands. At the sight of England reduced to this silly scale, Ravi felt a surge of incredible relief. He sat back in his seat and flexed his leg muscles. He would order an American Martini as soon as the seat-belt signs went off; he deserved it. He would order it imperiously, with a curt command, because he was on his way back to what he had been before. He imagined

Sarah down there as one of the midget people, walking jerkily away from the airport, going home and turning in automatically at the gate of her parents' sugar-lump white house. Thinking of her like that, safely back where she belonged, what he had done did not seem nearly so bad.

*

Sarah earned her air fare by taking a job as a holiday relief assistant in a shoe shop. It was in Kensington, not far from her parents' house, and every morning she enjoyed the comic transition from her parents' leisurely breakfast table with its freshly ground coffee and high-class marmalade to the stuffy little shop and its sorry employees. There was one other assistant and a would-be dictatorial manager called Mr Patel. Sarah was supposed to be at the shop fifteen minutes before it opened at half-past nine, although after the first week she was often late and then, unless there were a lot of customers, she sat on the fitting stools all day, talking to the other assistant, Julie. After a few days, she would dearly have liked to read, but the book she produced clearly annoyed both Julie and Mr Patel. Reading was not actually forbidden, Mr Patel stated in answer to Sarah's half-joking query, but it was clearly offensive to her colleagues. So, for two months, she sat and listened to Julie telling her about her boy-friend Kevin and their wedding plans and, in exchange, she told Julie about Ravi. If very well disposed and able to take time off from his endless ledgers and stocktaking, Mr Patel would contribute some humorous anecdote or interrupt their chatter with a little pun. He was not very forthcoming about his own life; he kept it rather primly to himself, like the packed lunch he brought every day and shut away in his private cupboard. Only occasionally odd details emerged, like the distinctive smells which escaped when he ate his lunch in the back office. He and his family shared a house in Ealing with one of his four brother's families. All four of them worked in the clothing trade – one in hats, two in frocks and saris and Mr Patel himself in shoes. 'Between us,' he quipped in one of his happier moods, 'we make up body.' He was obsessed by order and even though the little shop could have been managed with far less effort, he worked at it constantly.

If there was really nothing else to do, he pored over a Hindi film cartoon magazine. Once, quite unexpectedly, he burst into a soulful high-pitched song which made Julie snort with giggles.

At home in the evenings, Sarah cooked herself experimental dishes from an Indian recipe book and drowsily tried to concentrate on her Hindi primer. The house was otherwise empty because her parents were at the cottage in Wales and her brother away on holiday. Over and over again, she played the records of Hindi songs which Ravi had left her and traipsed rather ridiculously around the house in her sari.

Through August and into September, she worked in the shoe shop, compensating for her boredom by an elaborate calculation in which each hour in the shop represented so many of the four thousand miles between London and Delhi.

In mid-September, when she was due to book her ticket, she got a letter from Ravi asking her to postpone her visit because his grandmother, who lived with them, was seriously ill. She tried to overcome her disappointment and wrote back to him the same day, saying how very sorry she was to hear it and please to give the grandmother her best wishes for a speedy recovery. But at the bottom of the letter she added in capitals, 'LET ME KNOW AS SOON AS POSSIBLE WHEN I CAN COME.' She took out her disappointment on her family when they returned and on the irritating employees at the shoe shop.

Ravi took three weeks to reply to her letter. By then she had actually started to worry, to wonder if maybe this excuse would be the first of many similar; if, after her illness, the grandmother would need to convalesce or if she died, heaven forbid, that a visit to the family would be tactless and therefore out of the question. She lay awake at night and thought she saw her imagined future shrivelling to an impossible illusion. She tormented herself and once, in the early hours of the morning, she even wondered if Ravi's story was true. But by then she had also decided that she was going anyway. Whatever Ravi might write to her, or not write, she was going anyway. One day, in her lunch hour, she went impulsively into a travel agent's office and made enquiries about booking her flight to Delhi. As she left, it struck her quite forcibly that she was flying off into a void. But she had to go. If only to keep up appearances now, to preserve her dignity in front of her family and friends, she had to go to India. So when at last Ravi did answer and wrote that it was all right, that she could come in a couple of months' time even though his grandmother had died, she greeted his letter with rapturous relief. The qualifications and caution which detracted from it – everyone in the family was very gloomy, she must not be prepared for an enthusiastic welcome – hardly bothered her at all.

She booked her ticket for the thirtieth of November, then rang all her friends and told them that she was practically on the point of departure. With renewed energy, she flung herself into a round of Indian pastimes. The attempts she had maintained to hang on to some vestiges of Ravi seemed like positive preparations once more.

Getting ready – organising lightweight clothes and travellers' cheques and vaccinations – prevented her from thinking much about her journey. There really was an awful lot to do; as well as getting all her own stuff prepared, she had to buy a number of items which Ravi had written and asked for as soon as he knew for sure that she was coming and which she was superstitiously conscientious about finding for him. In addition, she wanted to bring an appropriate gift for each member of his family, as he had described them: the serious brother Ramesh, the giggling little sisters Asha and Shakuntala. She had no idea what she ought to bring for his parents, since she could not clearly imagine them; but in the end she settled on cufflinks for his father, (he would surely consider whisky wicked and she had never asked Ravi if he smoked), and a nice Liberty silk headscarf for his mother. Friends of her parents, who had known India long before she was born, deluged her with advice but she rarely listened. Their travellers' tales of mosquito nets and lethal drinking water seemed comically irrelevant. In fact, she barely thought beyond the miraculous moment when she would walk out of the Arrivals door at Delhi Airport and see Ravi, open-armed and beaming, waiting there for her.

Two weeks before she left, she had a farewell lunch with Emily Williams. Emily was beside herself with envy at

Sarah's adventure; she had always imagined that she would be exhilarated by the world outside when she left university, but was finding it a disappointment. Because she had no clear idea of her own preferences, she could not decide what path she ought to take. They all seemed plodding and, in contrast, Sarah's plans appeared superb. They sat over salads and coffee in a wine bar and talked headily about her future. Gradually, it began to seem to Sarah too that her destiny was utterly enviable, that her future was bright and glamorous and assured. She allowed herself to confide her secret misgivings to Emily: Ravi's reservations, his worrying reluctance, his family. But Emily brushed them aside reassuringly and Sarah left the lunch feeling more confident and excited about her journey than she had at any time since Ravi went home.

His last letter, which she received only days before her departure, reinforced that confidence:

My dearest Sarah,

Only fourteen days to go now – I can hardly wait to hop on the train to Delhi and come to meet you! This place is really intolerably small and stuffy; it is suffocating me with its wretched, petty restraints! My parents' mentality is frankly even more blinkered than I remembered and their behaviour over your intended visit has been a source of great rage. Let us spend just as little time here as possible and travel together to other places. Just you and I on the move, what a relief that will be!

To confirm, I will meet you off the Air India flight from London arriving at Delhi at 7 am on December 1st. You will recognise me because I will be wearing a broad grin – outsize measurement.

Don't forget the cassettes and the throat lozenges if you can manage to bring them. Also, the books – please, the books! Come prepared for a magnificent holiday!

All my love, Ravi

*

When she woke up, it was already morning. They were flying through a salmon-pink dawn over a country which looked bleak and inhospitable. Down below were villages in a barren plain, huddled around muddy pools, a village to a puddle, and between them pink fields pathetically divided and subdivided for ever. Involuntarily, Sarah shuddered; life looked awfully precarious down there.

She had not slept well, aware of Ravi approaching through her sleep, but now she beamed at the air hostess who brought her a steaming scented face flannel to wipe her face. Between scraps of almost conscious dreams, she had imagined this morning. She was taut with expectation. The air hostess brought her a plastic tray of breakfast and she ate it with relish, thirty thousand feet above the pink plain. She was surprisingly ravenous with nervous excitement and also suddenly acutely aware that comforts such as butter curls and sterile sausages might be about to vanish.

The 'Fasten Seatbelts' sign came on when she had eaten and she had an involuntary shiver of anticipation. Outside, there was now reassuring grass and trees as the plane came down towards a sprawling garden city and then landed with a self-satisfied bounce at Delhi Airport. For a fraction of a second, as she came out on to the aeroplane steps, Sarah wondered if she would be able to stand the brilliant, white-hot sun.

Everyone was so kindly to her at the airport – the fat, moustachioed Sikh at the passport counter, the little affectionate bank clerk, the inquisitive Customs officer. But she barely paid any attention to them, hurrying, jostling, and she was one of the first off her flight to rush out towards the exit where an excited crowd was waiting.

*

Seeing Sarah appear through the International Arrivals gate was like seeing a piece of his past return. He was already nostalgic for that recent past, for he had been back in India just long enough to miss it. The sight of Sarah Livingstone, so unchanged and eager, trotting towards him despite her heavy bag – oh, just as rosy-cheeked and cheerful as he remembered her – caused him a great rush of fond remembrance. And having lain awake for much of the night, worrying how he would react to her and how he would handle the difficult first days of their reunion, he now had no difficulty in seizing her and giving her an enormous hug for all the lost freedoms that she represented.

*

Although she had not really thought about it that much, Sarah had naturally assumed that they would stay at the political big-shot uncle's house in Delhi. Ravi had never actually *said* that they would, but it did seem likely in view of the hospitality of the extended Indian family and all that. She hardly questioned him though on that dazzling, wonderful morning when he told her that they were going to an hotel. In fact, she squeezed his hand conspiratorially because it must mean that he wanted greater intimacy. They were sitting on the airport bus when he told her, driving into the city along a wide avenue which for the first few minutes looked quite deceptively ordinary. Only then she began to notice oddities like women in saris riding side-saddle on the back of motor scooters and more women at the roadside digging a drain and, further on, a very brown, ragged family apparently camping under a tree. The city proper seemed a spacious, comprehensible place and the central 'Circus' where the bus stopped almost an eroded version of England. Only bit by bit did she catch sight of things which startled her, but then for a lot of the bus ride, she had had her face turned to Ravi.

It was not a very nice hotel; in fact, it was rather disgusting. But of course that didn't strike her straight away. They had taken a funny scooter rickshaw from the bus terminus, with her suitcase wedged across their knees. On the way, they had shouted silly pieces of news at each other above the racket of the engine and held hands and kissed, while the driver – a big and ebullient Sikh – kept turning round to giggle at them over his shoulder.

At a distance, beyond Ravi, Sarah became aware of an extraordinary, implausible place. It was not a tremendously long ride to the hotel, but in the course of it the city changed completely. The broad, reasonable avenues gave way to narrow, jammed streets and a cacophony of the most motley traffic surged around them: bicycles, buses, more scooter rickshaws, flower-painted lorries and cars. It did not seem

controlled by any obvious means and every vehicle aggress-
ively pursued its own path. There were so many people
on the pavements suddenly, although the avenues had been
empty; so many jostling arms and legs and, at a traffic light,
an arm with no hand on the end of it thrust itself under the
hood of their scooter rickshaw and poked up sickeningly
into Sarah's face. But Ravi bellowed at it and it disappeared.

Almost all her attention had been for Ravi. The indescrib-
able joy of finding him, the reassurance that he existed, that
he was here and that he loved her removed everything else
to a distant plane. The city seemed in any case confused
and dream-like. A haze of pink dust and sunlight would
intermittently come between them and the glimpses of the
city which she caught that morning seemed afterwards inco-
herent and unlikely. Her exhaustion from the overnight flight
blurred everything. What with the sunlight, the unremitting
noise, the chaotic traffic and the eddies of dust, in the end
she was glad to get inside their hotel and shut out everything.

She did register the dingy hall and the dirty staircase. She
noticed the horrid red splashes on the skirting board as she
followed Ravi up the stairs. But once they were in their
room, there was only Ravi and everything else receded.

For a day or two, or perhaps it had even been three, they
had more or less stayed in the hotel room, although it was
small and smelly. They had lain on the hard bed without
even a sheet over them, talking and making love. But they
had not mentioned anything important during that time.
They had simply lain together and *been*. For a while, Sarah
had slept and when she woke, Ravi was beside her reading
one of the books which she had brought him. Stray indi-
cations of India reached her from outside; shrill shouting and
the tiring sound of someone hammering in the midday heat,
a crescendo of car horns and later on – perhaps it was already
evening – the smell of spiced food cooking under their
window. When they got thirsty and hungry, Ravi had gone
down and brought back fresh limes and bottles of soda water,
samosas wrapped in brown paper and strangely pale oranges.
Later, when it was already completely dark, they had gone
out to have dinner at a little restaurant almost directly
opposite the hotel. Sarah had been so happy just to sit and

eat with Ravi again, and so careful also to observe the new rules and not kiss or touch him in public, that she did not take in as much of their surroundings as she might have done. They were run-down and crowded, that much she saw. Coming back across the street to their hotel, she heard a scuttling on the pavement behind her and looked round. A moan drew her attention down to the shape of a creature pulling itself urgently across the ground towards her. In the dark, it looked for a moment grotesquely as though its legs were only two bent bones and it was heaving itself along on a pair of straining, over-developed arms. She stood transfixed, but Ravi hustled her into the hotel. Again they lay together and again they slept.

In the morning – or perhaps it was already the afternoon, for at the beginning her jet lag had confused things even further – Ravi had come back from a shopping trip with a present for her, a sweet little brass bangle. For a day or two – or perhaps it had even been three – she had been perfectly happy to lie there in that stuffy room and not go out to see India at all. She had not asked Ravi what they were going to do; she had not even really cared about it and it was only on the third or fourth day that he started to explain what would happen.

They were not going to stay at his uncle's at all, it turned out. As ill luck would have it, there was a big congress on in Delhi right now and his uncle's house was overflowing. In fact, his uncle did not even know yet that Ravi was in Delhi; he was really too busy to be bothered. Ravi had told his parents that he would stay with an old college friend when he came to collect Sarah, but really the friend's flat was so small that it would be impossible for them to stay there for more than a night or two. He had thought it best to begin in comfort, he explained. Sarah, looking around at the scaly walls and the grubby, wasted curtains, did have a brief moment of apprehension then as she wondered whatever the next place might be like. But the glamour of being connected, however negatively, with a political congress of national importance made up for the disappointment.

They would stay in Delhi for about a fortnight, Ravi thought. Sarah would get a chance to do some sightseeing, he had one or two business matters to attend to. Since he came back in July, he had been rather lazy about looking for a job. He had felt he deserved a break. But now he was getting fed up with sitting at home in Lucknow and he had decided it was time to act. There were a couple of people in Delhi who might be able to help him. Only a bit put out, Sarah had asked, 'But won't you show me around?' And Ravi had answered, 'Yes, of course I will. And, anyway, there are bus tours.'

Their first outing was to visit his old college friend, Birendra. Ravi felt ridiculously nervous at presenting Sarah for the first time here. It was not that he was embarrassed or worried about how she would behave, but it was the very first time that his two lives would meet and he found it difficult to imagine how they would mix. But Birendra was an easy beginning; he laughed uproariously when they arrived, because he was not expecting them and was at work in the middle of a monumental mess. His small room was crowded with newspapers and books, and the remains of several uncleared meals were distributed on top of them. Ravi noticed that, amid his laughter, he was examining Sarah keenly, but he must have liked what he saw because he gave Ravi a friendly punch in the belly and crowed, 'Yes, you've quite forgotten what slumming is like, haven't you, old chap?'

He quickly cleared room for Sarah and Ravi to sit down and put a kettle on to boil on a camping gas cooker in one corner. Then he perched on the edge of his table, hugging himself with pleasure as he looked at his visitors in grinning anticipation.

Birendra had been one of Ravi's closest friends at college. In the distant life before he had gone to England, Ravi remembered that Birendra had desperately wanted to go too. But he had failed to win a scholarship and naturally self-finance was out of the question. He had failed – as everyone had known at the time – not because he wasn't clever enough, but because he had spoilt his chances by writing deliberately controversial things in his General History paper. The estrangement which might have resulted between them because of Ravi's good fortune had never materialised. Every time Birendra might have felt envious or less worldly-wise, he only had to remind Ravi of the compromises he must have made in what he wrote in order to be admitted to Oxford, for Ravi to feel morally his inferior and a sneak. Their friendship had always thrived on joky rivalry and right now, with his challenging job on a left-wing newspaper while Ravi sat unemployed at home, Birendra was well ahead. Did Sarah improve Ravi's position?

She had been frankly somewhat shocked by Birendra's flat. They had taken a bus to get there, her first real Delhi bus. It had seemed an incredibly long way; they had actually left the city and driven out along a wide avenue to another quite separate one. When they got off the bus, she had followed Ravi through a maze of small, nightmarishly crowded streets. People had gaped at her in a way she was just beginning to find unnerving. Birendra's flat – one poky room and a sleeping alcove – was at the top of a huge, dilapidated house. In England she supposed it would have been called a tenement, but somehow you could not put the same labels onto things here.

Anyhow, she had liked Birendra. She had taken to him straight away because, quite unexpectedly in the middle of all that upheaval, he had seemed somehow familiar. Despite the heat and the din outside and the sweat from the bus ride, it was suddenly almost as if she were sitting back in Ravi's room in Oxford, listening to him as he fooled around with Sunil and Dev. So she was able to relax immediately, although she too had been worried and nervous, and to behave quite naturally without any inhibition.

'No sugar, thanks,' she said to Birendra as he poured their tea.

Ravi giggled nervously. 'Sarah's been having a terrible time with our tea. She can't get over it coming ready sweetened.'

'You don't take sugar?' Birendra asked incredulously, pretending to scrutinise her suspiciously. 'I would never have guessed it!' He slapped his thigh and laughed at his own joke. 'Well, I have three, I'm afraid, and in fact four as there are guests.'

He put as many spoonfuls into Ravi's cup too and passed

it to him. Ravi took it and straight away sipped it appreciatively.

'Gosh, you take far more sugar here than you did in England,' Sarah could not resist commenting.

Ravi answered quickly, 'When in Rome . . .'

But Birendra gave another great laugh and cried, 'He's a chameleon, that's why. His behaviour is coloured by his surroundings.'

'He seems exactly the same as he was in England, so far,' Sarah replied in the same facetious tone. But in fact, as she said it, she made one mental exception; Ravi did not look quite the same. In four months he had shrunk somehow, grown less clear-cut. Or was it just that here he did not stand out?

' "So far!" ' Birendra exclaimed. ' "So far!" But you've only been here for three days. How are you liking it?'

Sarah hesitated, 'Well . . .'

'She's hardly been out of the hotel yet,' Ravi said. 'Jet lag,' he explained.

'That's right,' Sarah said. 'It sounds awful, doesn't it? Three days in bed! But, really, I was shattered. Now I can't wait to get started, though.'

'Where are you going to take her first?' Birendra asked Ravi.

Ravi considered and shrugged. 'Jama Masjid? Red Fort?'

'Oh, that's so conventional. Why not begin at the beginning; Qutb Minar?'

'OK,' Ravi said, 'and then?'

'Don't tell me you've forgotten everything already,' Birendra teased him. 'You're not a foreigner here.'

'Oh, cut it out!' Ravi responded. 'And then? Tughlaqabad? Of course, there are those bus tours, aren't there?'

Birenda hooted. 'Sure, sure, if you want air-conditioning and an American tripper's version of history.'

'Oh, no,' Sarah interrupted, 'I'd far rather have the real thing. I'm really not keen on guided tours. You know Ravi, I don't mind if I don't see all the traditional tourist sights. I'd be far happier just wandering around and getting the feel of the place.'

'Well, that's easily done,' Ravi answered flippantly. 'We'll take a stroll afterwards around Birendra's local haunts.'

'That's right,' Birendra agreed eagerly. 'I'll show you – and Mister Kaul – some local colour.'

For a short time at the very beginning, Sarah did still think that India could be the country it had been in England. For a short time, in the company of Ravi's college friends, she conceived a small private version of India, from which all the misery outside could be excluded. She thought it would be quite possible for her to feel at home in that India.

When they got up to leave Birendra's, he asked, 'So when are you two going to exchange the hotel for the delights of my humble abode?'

Although the remark had naturally been addressed to Ravi, Ravi turned to Sarah as though the decision were hers and she giggled nervously. 'Well, I'm not sure . . .'

'Some time next week, maybe?' Ravi suggested.

'We're going to be awfully in your way though, aren't we?' Sarah said politely and then felt dreadful because Birendra bristled and replied, 'I've put up four or five people in here, you know.'

'Yes, Birendra's actually planning to open a hotel in here,' Ravi said quickly.

And Birendra laughed at himself louder than anyone. But there was nevertheless an unmistakable awkwardness as the three of them said goodbye.

Out on the pungent stairs, Sarah said to Ravi, 'Was I OK?' and when he squeezed her hand quickly and answered, 'You were tremendous,' she added, 'Look, you'd better just decide what to do about where we stay, Ravi, I really don't mind.'

They ended up staying in Delhi for three weeks. Ravi's job interviews could not be arranged immediately. Sarah was aghast that he could spend the whole day sitting waiting to see someone and then at the end of it be told to come back the next day. But Ravi seemed to take it in his stride, telling Sarah wryly that that was the way things worked in India.

She went off on her own sightseeing. It was not what she had imagined – traipsing around monuments by herself with a guide book. In fact, she had not even brought a guide book. But Ravi got hold of one for her and, once or twice between assignments for his newspaper, Birendra came with her instead. She did not enjoy sightseeing on her own because, although she had set out on the first morning full of enthusiasm and independence, the experiences she had within her first few days discouraged her considerably.

For a start, she had to get used to being stared at. It was a new and distressing experience for Sarah Livingstone – to stand out in a crowd simply because of the colour of her skin. She was also nastily aware of being female. After a week or so she became perpetually conscious of her legs emerging, white and indecent, from beneath her skirt when all the other women's legs were covered up. Yet it was too hot and sticky to wear jeans. At midday, the monuments danced in a shimmering haze and she retired under the trees with her guide book and a bottle of the horribly sweet fizz which Ravi had said was the only safe thing for her to drink. Enchanted, she watched the pretty gilharis playing; Birendra told her that they were not some kind of fantastic striped Indian squirrel, but chipmunks. She noticed that the sparrows were not sparrows, but long-legged, yellow-billed monsters.

One day in the Lodi Gardens, a man came up to her as she sat writing postcards and asked her if he might practise his English on her. He was a student of literature, he said. Although she might otherwise have been suspicious, Sarah was beginning to feel lonely. She was still well-disposed towards people like him, so she let him sit down next to her – reproaching herself that it would be a form of racism to move her handbag out of his reach too obviously – and they began a rather stilted conversation about various English authors. For a student of literature, he seemed pretty ill-read. After a while, he leaned over to Sarah and suggested coyly that they went for a cold drink. Her first inclination was naturally to refuse, but it occurred to her that at least if something happened to her, it might prompt Ravi to come sightseeing with her. So she followed the man in the direction where, he indicated with a vague wave, there was a drinks stall. But this led them into a desolate, rather empty stretch of the gardens way beyond the ruined tombs, and as they walked under a row of tall trees the man made a sudden lunge at her and grabbed her around the waist.

'Get off!' she shrieked indignantly, aware of her prim little voice echoing in the deserted gardens. Although she tensed for a struggle, at the sound of her voice rising shrilly in the stillness the man let go of her and ran off, but the experience made her even less adventurous.

She liked it much more when Birendra came with her. He was terribly courteous and polite and, even more important, she could talk to him about Ravi. To begin with, he had been rather shy and silent when she had tried to broach the subject, but gradually he thawed and told her all sorts of stories about their college days which were a revelation. Far from being the maverick he made himself out to be, in Birendra's stories Ravi was the less daring of the two and had to be goaded to take part in their escapades. She and Birendra got on together so well, in fact, that it nearly made up for Ravi's repeated absences.

Ravi's job interviews were not going too well. Whether he was being too intransigent in his demands or whether there were simply no suitable jobs to be had, Sarah could not tell. But she rather resented the fact that, because of the delays, he had to spend so much time away from her. Quite unfairly, she began to blame him for this.

They did go together to Agra, at Birendra's and Sarah's insistence. Whatever else, Sarah had to see the Taj. And although Ravi fidgeted quite a bit while they were there, worrying about the opportunities which he might be missing in Delhi, later those three days were among Sarah's happiest memories of her whole stay.

'Attention, please! Your attention is solicited. Here you see gateway to mausoleum of Emperor Akbar, built by Akbar's son Jahangir in 1613. Within, we shall see splendours of mausoleum itself. Sadly, some splendours have faded. Restoration work has begun, but does not proceed apace. Ah well, your fantasy must fill missing sections. Rome was not built in a day. What can't be cured must be endured!'

It was very hot in Agra, but they stayed in a nice old colonial hotel with rotating fans and went to see the Taj Mahal three times. It was every bit as beautiful as Sarah had hoped and she tried hard to memorise it against future ugliness. They also visited Agra Fort and the enchanted ghost city of Fatehpur Sikri. Ravi bought Sarah a garland of orange flowers to lay at a shrine. Holding his hand as they watched green parrots dive through the sunset over the old red turrets, Sarah thought that she had been exaggerating the problems of adjusting to India.

When they came back to Delhi, they moved to Birendra's flat. Sarah did not really want to go there, but even the grubby little hotel was working out expensive, especially after their trip to Agra which of course she had paid for. They had discussed the pros and cons, but actually they did not have much of a choice; Ravi still had no job and so no money to speak of and after a fortnight, Sarah told him that if she was to stay in India as long as she wanted to, she could not afford the hotel any more.

It was pretty dreadful at Birendra's. They had a simple bed roll on the floor which they had to put away every morning. The racket from the surrounding flats was unbelievable; the walls must have been made of cardboard. The din out in the street began at 5 or 6 am every day and, most offensive of all, Sarah found, the lavatory was out on the landing.

But she pretended not to care. Ravi and Birendra slept through the racket and she pretended that she thought roughing it was a laugh. She learnt to say good morning in Hindi to the astonished neighbours. She even went shopping for their evening meal down at the little street market. When she came back Birendra told her, chuckling, that she had paid exactly twice as much for their shopping as he would have done.

Ravi seemed elusive. During the day he was preoccupied with his interviews; at night, next to each other, they could only whisper because Birendra lay on the other side of a translucent curtain. He snubbed her once when she suggested that now the congress was over, perhaps his uncle might have a modest room for them somewhere after all. It seemed to Sarah that the real reason for her journey was being obscured by a hundred individually unimportant but collectively insurmountable obstacles. One night as they lay in the stuffy

147

room, the sound of two people making love next door became painfully audible through the thin partition wall. For a while they pretended not to hear it, but then at last Birendra behind his curtain gave a snort of laughter and Ravi and Sarah joined in. The three of them lay giggling in the dark and Sarah did not realise straight away why there were tears running down her face. In the end, even though she knew that Ravi was not looking forward to it, she was glad when the time came to leave for Lucknow.

Two days before they left, they went to a magnificent party at his uncle's house. Ravi had eventually let him know that he was in Delhi, had gone off alone to pay him a formal visit and come back with the invitation. It was for all three of them: Ravi, Sarah and Birendra too. There was quite a lot of friendly sparring between Ravi and Birendra over this, since it turned out that Ravi's uncle did not exactly approve of Birendra's politics so he was in two minds as to whether or not he should go. But Ravi insisted he wanted Birendra to come; all sorts of important people would be there, it was going to be a really big do and Birendra would be a fool to pass up an invitation like that for some sort of half-baked principles. In the end, Birendra agreed to come and Sarah, who had been meanly hoping that he would not, had to hide her pique.

They went most of the way on the bus, but changed over to a scooter rickshaw when they were near the uncle's house because, Ravi said jokingly, it would never do to turn up there on foot.

The house was wonderful, Sarah thought. They bowled in at a pair of lovely old yellow gates, where a man in uniform was standing stiffly at attention, and bounced up to a neo-classical porch. It was part of a colonnaded verandah which ran the whole way round the house and where there hung a string of little multi-coloured light bulbs, looped from one pillar to the next. The house was not enormous, she considered, but it presented a picture of wealthy serenity. It looked, in fact, like the entrance to the version of India which she had once imagined – a place of elegance and glamour and extravagance.

There were a few people behind the columns of the

verandah, but the bulk of the party was at the back of the house. They paid the scooter driver, who threatened to make a scene because he thought the money they had given him was too little, and then climbed the steps to the porch. For a moment they hesitated, uncertain which way to go, but then Ravi said, 'Come on, let's find Auntie,' and led them into the house.

Of course, they did not see much of it – they walked straight through the entrance hall into a living-room which opened on to the garden – but Sarah was still deeply impressed by what she saw. Those two rooms were decorated with hangings apparently as splendid as any she had seen in the National Museum and the few elaborate-looking pieces of furniture held ornate bronze sculptures and little bejewelled boxes. She just had time to take all that in and to appreciate the high, cool ceilings, before they reached the French windows and stepped out again on to the verandah.

Already, as they came into the living-room, a manservant had gone scurrying ahead to announce them and as they appeared at the windows, a voluminous woman in pink came forward to greet them.

Sarah was astounded by the speed with which Ravi changed – instantly, immediately. He had still been Ravi as they walked through the house, but before that outsize woman who was, for heaven's sake, only his aunt, he was cringing and scraping like a toadying schoolboy. Sarah watched him, aghast. And in that instant she saw at last what she was up against; not the misery in the streets, not the blinding sunlight and the smells, but the imperious demands which his home made on Ravi.

'Hello, Auntie,' he was saying. 'You do remember Birendra, don't you? And this is Sarah Livingstone, a friend from university.' And he and Birendra, who had both been perfectly derogatory about the foolish fat woman when on the bus, were now bobbing and fawning in front of her as though they were children over-acting servants in a school play.

The aunt gave Sarah the briefest of smiles and trilled flirtatiously at Birendra, 'So you have spirited our Ravi away to your Old Delhi hideout? You exert such a fascination on him, you know.'

Ravi and Birendra shifted uncomfortably and Sarah wondered indignantly how anyone who had refused to put them up could be so outrageously hypocritical. Ravi had said he had hinted during his visit that they would like to come and stay, but the hint, he said, had been ignored. But meanwhile, Birendra was answering, 'Oh, I assure you, it is nothing of the sort. I could not possibly dream of trying to compete with the attractions of your home.' And the aunt, already busily aware of other guests arriving behind them in the hall, was gesturing them to move on into the garden and saying, 'Make yourselves at home. Soon, we will eat.'

The crowd which filled the back verandah and spread out across the lawn was made up of kaleidoscopic groups of stately, well-dressed, confident-looking Indian men and women. Men outnumbered women quite noticeably, so that what women there were stood out in their strident silks. Sarah picked out two other white faces because they had both turned towards her as she came out. Everyone was chattering, laughing, sipping. Between the groups, lithe uniformed men were deftly making their way with trays of drinks. For a moment, it was quite intimidating.

They took drinks – there was a choice of everything – and stood together near the verandah steps while Ravi pointed out the important people to Birendra. There seemed to be quite a few of them. They stood there for a while, Sarah enjoying the change to an atmosphere in which she felt at home. A little bent old man in a dhoti came up to speak to Ravi and praised him and ingratiated himself in a way she found quite embarrassing. He asked inquisitively who Sarah was and twinkled at her salaciously when they were introduced. As soon as he had gone, Ravi dismissed him rather arrogantly as 'one of uncle's hangers-on'.

Soon they were summoned indoors to an immense buffet spread. A whole side room had been lined with huge tables of elaborate dishes. Ravi and Birendra helped themselves eagerly and Sarah, overcoming momentary misgivings at the sight of so many unfamiliar dishes, followed suit. Some lesser female relatives, Ravi explained, had been instructed to help the guests and to make sure that everyone had plenty to eat. With heaped plates, they went back out into the garden where they joined a largish group sitting on rugs on the lawn around one of the dignitaries. As she ate, Sarah did her best to follow the puzzling conversation.

In the middle of the meal, Ravi's uncle came up to their group. He was making the rounds of his guests spread over the lawn, stopping for a few minutes with each group.

He stood over them beaming and nodding, joined his hands in greeting to the dignitary and nodded benignly at everyone else. To each of them he spoke a few words, smiled, implied how pleased he was to welcome them in his home. Before he moved on, Sarah was introduced to him and he paused, his face expressing benevolence and concern for her welfare as he said, 'I hope our Ravi and Birendra are looking after you?' At the mention of Oxford, he asked her knowledgeably which School she had taken and when she said English, he nodded again wisely as if that was only to be expected. Delighted to find him so well-informed about her background, Sarah would have begun to talk enthusiastically about favourite authors and works, but his eyes were already moving beyond her and on to his next guest.

She was left with the impression of someone soft and infinitely accommodating but whom, perhaps because of his bulk, it would be impossible to move.

Later on, she slipped inside to go to the lavatory and as she sat there, enjoying the calm of the big vaulted cloakroom, she thought what a terrible pity it was that they were not staying there after all; everything would have been so much nicer, so much closer to the adventure she had imagined.

Before they left, the three of them went up to the uncle to say goodbye. He asked Ravi when he would be going home to his parents and when he heard it was so soon, exclaimed, 'Well listen, young man, next time you just must stay here with us, do you hear?' He turned to Sarah and asked her kindly what her plans were. She laughed and answered, 'Oh, I'm going to Lucknow too.'

The uncle paused and for a second seemed to look at her more attentively than he had all evening. 'Are you?' he said. Then he turned to Ravi and gave him a searching stare.

＊

Two days later, they caught a train to Lucknow. Sarah
thought she was quite an old hand by then. She knew what
to expect when they entered the railway station and steeled
herself. But even so, stations always shocked her; there were
whole families apparently camping on the platforms and
unclaimed children working their way through the crowds.
It seemed incredible that out of such a commotion she and
Ravi should eventually find themselves in the right carriage
of the right train, even if there were so many other people
jostling and shrieking and squabbling in there too that she
really did wonder how they could all reach their destination
without a riot breaking out. It was dreadfully hot to begin
with and until the train got going, creating a feeble breeze
which brought in the ubiquitous dust, Sarah worried about
how she would cope with the ten hours ahead.

Ravi began the journey in a filthy mood. He was going
home without a firm offer of a job, only a hazy promise –
of which he did not hold high hopes – of a position in a new
social survey outfit, which would not be decided on for a
couple of months yet. That he was going home was bad
enough, but with no prospect of getting away for good and
with the humiliating admission that he had so far failed to
find a post, it was unbearable. Sarah was really the last straw.
Since she had blurted out to his uncle that she was coming
to Lucknow with him, Ravi had found himself becoming
increasingly irritated by her. Time and again, she proved that
she simply had no grasp of the realities of Indian life. Despite
all the overwhelming daily evidence to the contrary, she
persisted in hanging on to her stubborn little idea that
somehow or other she could fit in here. Whereas in truth she
stuck out like a sore thumb. In the long run, it exasperated
him. Now she was sitting beside him, suffering nobly in the
heat and the cramped space – as though millions of people
did not put up with that as normality every day of their lives
– and cultivating an expression of glazed affection for the
people around her. That, Ravi thought, annoyed him most
of all: the sentimental fondness she tried to show for Indian
types for whom he had no time. It was insulting; it was as

though she imagined that they must somehow be dear to him, whereas in fact they left him cold. He wondered how she would have reacted to a parallel, in which he romanticised the sturdy shopkeepers and doughy college servants of Oxford. How was it that she could not see the unbridgeable boundaries which separated them? He had thought that a week in India would open her eyes. Up to the last minute, he had hoped that she would see sense beforehand and not come with him to Lucknow. But his family would open her eyes for her, soon enough. And at the thought of his family and the scenes ahead, his bowels constricted.

*

They sat side by side on the wooden seat and although they did not talk to each other much, they were united by the stares surrounding them. Sarah was the only foreigner in the carriage and fair game to while away the tedium of travelling. An hour or so into the journey, an old man opposite them, a self-elected spokesman for the passengers nearby, started to question Ravi about Sarah. After a while, Ravi said rather rudely, 'Ask her yourself!' So the old man cleared his throat and in quaintly archaic English, put the same questions to Sarah all over again. Although this annoyed Ravi, at least it saved him the effort of answering and he sat back rather sullenly and stared out of the window, lulled by the mechanical banality of the old man's questions and Sarah's well-meaning answers.

When Sarah could stand it no more, she turned to him and whispered, 'Help me out, you lazy so-and-so.'

'Get out your book,' Ravi answered.

'Oh, but Ravi, that's such a put-down. Why are you in such a bad mood?'

'I'm not. Look Sarah, you create your own problems, then you protest and make an outcry. It's like the Lodi Gardens all over again. You encouraged him.'

'I did *not*! I was just polite, that's all. What am I supposed to do? Confront them all with a stony stare?'

'We might get a bit of peace and quiet if you did.'

'Oh Ravi, you're being a pig.'

During this exchange, the old man had been painstakingly

translating his conversation with Sarah for the benefit of the passengers who did not speak English. Now he had finished and leaned forward again, waiting with new questions from the others. Continuing their argument became a way of shutting out the rest of the carriage.

'I don't mean to be. I'm just getting fed up with you landing in sticky situations all of your own making and then turning to me, wide-eyed, for help. You're not as naïve as you pretend to be.'

'Yes, I am!'

'Well then, you won't have an easy time in India.'

'I'm not *having* an easy time in India! I'm having a bloody difficult time in India and you don't lift a finger to help me. Or is *that* a sticky situation all of my own making too?'

'Hah!'

'Oh God, you're the *end*!'

'Sarah, we're not going to have a row in a railway carriage.'

'Why not? We've had one just about everywhere else.'

'Gosh, you can be so childish.'

'And you're such a despicable conformist!'

'Attention please,' the old man interrupted. 'Ahem! Your attention, please. This old lady on my left wishes to ask you one very foolish question. Is your mother white-haired?'

'Just a minute,' Sarah said. 'Just a minute.'

'A conformist?' Ravi repeated in genuine surprise. 'That's a new one.'

'Yes,' Sarah repeated bitterly, 'a bloody weak-willed conformist. You care so much about what people think, don't you? You just don't dare defy them. All the things you blamed on India aren't India at all; they're you!'

'I see,' Ravi said coldly. 'You mean it's my fault that this is such an impossible country and that you're not having a nice time here? Is that it? Well, if you remember, I did warn you.'

'Yes, you warned me,' Sarah burst out, 'but you didn't tell me that that was how you *wanted* it, that you didn't actually *want* to fight against it, that you were quite happy to be part of this . . . this travesty.'

'Let's go and stand in the corridor,' Ravi said. 'I don't want to make a spectacle of myself, even if you do.'

154

They squeezed outside. The pink plain slid past them in the late afternoon sun, pockmarked by the occasional village, a pustule of huts. They stood at the open window and observed a moment of truce. Sarah looked so miserable, staring out at the foreign landscape, that Ravi briefly put his hand on her shoulder. She did not shake him off.

'Why didn't you tell your aunt and uncle who I was?' she asked after a while. 'Would they really have been that upset?'

Ravi withdrew his hand. He looked out too onto the late afternoon landscape, bathed in the peaceful coral light of exhaustion, and his expression was remarkably similar to Sarah's. 'In a word, yes.'

'But *why*?' Sarah asked. 'Why? I mean surely they're perfectly on the ball and they realise that things like this go on? And anyway, would it really matter? I mean, basically – so what if they get upset?'

Ravi went on staring out of the window. So many things were going wrong; it was hard to separate Sarah from the general mass of difficulties. He resented that she had come now, bringing her extra intractable problem, when it was more than he could do to stay afloat here on his own.

'Sarah,' he said, and he sounded very tired, 'you knew when you came here that it couldn't be a long-term thing, didn't you? We'd had it all out. You knew we wouldn't be able to carry on here like we did in England, so it's totally ridiculous of you to keep on insisting.'

Sarah rounded on him. 'I knew it wouldn't be easy,' she retorted. 'I knew I would have to fight, but I didn't know you wouldn't make any effort at all. I didn't know you were such a stick-in-the-mud!'

The word aroused him; it was so quaintly incongruous in that dusty train, spat against the tired orange landscape. He knew then that Sarah would never free herself from the legacy of the playing fields, that she would judge every country she encountered by the rules of her own checker-board country. And he laughed. He did not mean to be callous – he laughed in recognition of his helplessness, as much as anything. It was as if Sarah had flourished a hockey stick at him and that was the girl he had first loved: Sarah Livingstone at her best. He would have liked to hug her, to show her what he felt, but his laugh had hurt her too much. She laid her forehead on the window ledge and quietly began to cry.

Later, they did talk more affectionately. In the evening they unwrapped their picnic supper and made fun of Birendra's mammoth scale of provisions. They were unusually polite to each other, offered each other the chapatis and the pickles; the confrontation in the corridor had shaken them profoundly. Afterwards they sat in silence, while opposite them the old man read aloud from his newspaper to a group of attentive passengers. They watched him and smiled. Everyone in their carriage was relaxed and cheery and eventually someone started to sing.

Sarah sat looking out of the window at the huge, unbroken night. The dark was soft and total. She breathed in the sugary smell of bidis and shut her eyes. For a while she imagined that she was by herself on the train, travelling alone through a quite different adventure, and she admired herself for her courage. The country around her was weird and wonderful and with her eyes closed, she began to enjoy it independently of Ravi for the first time. She fell asleep in a benign trance, but woke soon afterwards when the train stopped at a small station. She woke several times during the night, once to see a long naked foot dangling down in front of her face from the bunk above. It was unexpectedly cold in the carriage and the last time she woke up, she was glad to see that the sky was paler because the wretched night was nearly over.

*

Maybe if she had not come down with a tummy bug the very day she arrived at Ravi's home, everything might have worked out. Maybe if she had been more on the ball at the beginning, more receptive, she could have sensed what was going wrong and retrieved the failing situation. But as it was, Sarah's introduction to the family was a write-off.

She had begun to feel queasy on the train, but had put it down at first to the bad night and the motion. They arrived at Lucknow early in the morning. She told Ravi that she felt sick as they got their luggage together, but not surprisingly he must have thought she meant with nerves, because he answered her brusquely, 'Don't worry! I doubt if there'll be anyone there to meet us.'

Since he had not let his family know when they were coming, it seemed unreasonable to suppose that anyone could be there. But all the same he seemed to look around expectantly – or was it apprehensively? – as they got off the train and, in fact, between the train and the exit from the station they did run into two people whom he knew. Considering the size of Lucknow, that seemed extraordinary to Sarah, but Ravi and his two acquaintances appeared to take it for granted, exchanging enthusiastic but not astonished greetings and clapping one another on the back. The second one turned out to be a friend of the family, who had arrived by first class off the same train and was being met by a car. He offered to drive them home. Not terribly enthusiastically, Sarah thought, Ravi accepted, the man's persuasion being hearty and forceful. He and Sarah sat together in the back of the car while the man himself climbed in beside the driver and turned round over the front seat so as to carry on talking to them on the way. He and Ravi had an animated conversation, mixing Hindi and English, but Sarah, sitting in the corner and fighting her rising nausea, did not take in a lot of what was said.

It was a nice house, not a patch on his uncle's but pretty all the same. That was her first impression. It stood in its own small garden in a street of similar cubic white bungalows. Judging by its style, it must have been quite modern, but already its white walls were splodgy and ageing.

As the friend's car stopped and hooted at the gate, a scruffy little girl ran out to open it and Sarah, fuzzily thinking that must be Asha or Shakuntala, gave her a groggy wave. Of course it was the servants' child and anyone who had noticed her wave must have thought how very uncouth she was.

Two older, smarter girls rushed out onto the verandah and clapped their hands. Behind them a shadowy figure, not emerging fully from inside the house, must have been Ravi's mother.

They got out of the car and the friend went forward first to say hello. Asha and Shakuntala, for that time it was them, came skipping down off the verandah to throw themselves on to their brother, but at the sight of Sarah checked themselves and greeted them both with restraint.

'Hello,' said Sarah, 'I'm Sarah. How fantastic to meet you at last.'

'How do you do?' the two girls replied solemnly. They looked at Sarah with huge eyes.

'Sarah's quite worn out from the journey,' Ravi said bossily. 'Let's come inside.'

His mother welcomed them quietly. She took Ravi into her arms, nodded and smiled at Sarah and she was asking them softly what refreshments they would like after their journey, when there was a bellow from further inside the house and, at the end of the passage, Ravi's father appeared. Mrs Kaul seemed to shrink even further, Sarah noticed, and her question trailed away into the general hubbub. She turned to go to the kitchen, but before she went, Sarah whispered to her urgently, 'Please, I would really like to go to the bathroom.'

She caught Mrs Kaul's look of surprise and dismay just as Ravi's father descended on them. He was not tall, but he was a heavy man. He came billowing down the passage, dressed in a loose white shirt worn outside his trousers, waving his arms about as he called to them. He had a fleshy face, whose handsome features had succumbed to fat. Had he been thirty years younger and maybe as many pounds lighter, he could have been the spitting image of his son Ravi.

He greeted them both formally. He questioned them about the journey, about Delhi and asked after his brother and his brother's wife. He wanted to know if their train had been late, how late. Then he told them to come into the living-room and sit down, and he despatched his wife bossily to the kitchen to organise some tea and snacks.

Sarah could barely concentrate; her bowels seemed about to burst and she felt cold sweat break out over her as Mr Kaul beckoned her into the living-room and then, as she hesitated, cried, 'Come on in, come on in!' She managed a ghastly smile, 'I'd like to go to the bathroom first, please.' And she saw a look of shock and offence on his face too, before Ravi's mother helped her – now grey-faced, all pretence gone – into the bathroom. Perhaps it was then,

158

sitting on the Kauls' lavatory with her bowels gripped by that excruciating pain, that Sarah finally admitted the likelihood of defeat.

His family had been expecting her, that much was clear. A room had been prepared for her and she was happy to collapse into it. But as the worst of her distress lifted, she realised that of pleasure or intimacy or even inordinate interest, there was no sign at all.

Her first three days were terrible. Ravi blamed it on the restaurant lunch they had eaten before catching the train, Sarah (privately) on Birendra's picnic. But whatever the cause of her upset, it ruined her arrival. She only saw Ravi's family on her painful way to or from the lavatory and, if one or other of them came in to see her, she was usually too wretchedly embarrassed to talk to them. Worst of all, on the second day his mother prepared her a special delicate dish of curds and having eaten it with difficulty, out of politeness, she was immediately violently sick.

By the time she was better, she felt the chance to make a good impression was long lost. The family saw her as what she was – a bothersome guest, who was too faint-hearted or finicky to fit in with their life – and they turned their backs on her. Afterwards, when she dared to look back on that awful period, Sarah wondered if her illness had not been the beginning of the dislike which the family showed her so sharply at the end.

But, once she was better, her first fortnight was fine. Apart from expressing surprise that Sarah should choose to spend so long in a city which had comparatively few tourist attractions, Ravi's parents were perfectly amicable to her. Most mornings, Mr Kaul would organise a little sightseeing excursion for her, although actually she would have been quite content just to sit around and get to know them. But Ravi's father organised the whole household and everyone's activities came under his scrutiny. At breakfast, which seemed to last in stages from about half-past six until nine o'clock, he would cross-question each member of the family as they came to table on how they intended to spend their day and then offer criticisms or amendments. Sarah was amazed that none of them objected.

159

At Mr Kaul's instigation, she trundled around Lucknow in a tricycle rickshaw, accompanied by a bad-tempered Ravi and either Asha or Shakuntala. She found the way the two girls doted on their elder brother frankly irritating. It was not as if his shortcomings were not patently obvious. But they plainly worshipped him and competed to accompany him on these outings. And it made him doubly difficult to challenge, being back in surroundings where his every judgement was greeted with admiration and respect. The girls were invariably polite and prim to her. Of course, she would far rather have gone out alone with Ravi, but everyone seemed to take it for granted that one or other of the girls must come with them and she did not want to cause further offence to the family. So they would set out, a sulky little party, and 'do' the Great Imambara or the Hussainnabad or the Residency. It annoyed Sarah especially that Ravi did not dream of trying to get round this imposition – bribing his little sister to hop off in town. He never suggested staying out for lunch in a restaurant or simply going off somewhere on their own. He yielded blandly to what Sarah saw as unspeakable tyranny.

The family was like an irredeemable tangle of string from which it was impossible to extricate the strand which was Ravi. All day, from one room to the next, their activities coiled on, apparently involving everybody, and no one could have turned their back on them and shut the door. Nor, Sarah marvelled, did they seem to want to.

In the evenings, Mr Kaul came back from his office and everyone took part in his homecoming. Dinner and the frequent after-dinner visitors required everyone's presence and when Sarah, exasperated by this constant communal activity, wanted privacy, the only place to retreat to was the garden.

She had thought there would be more room in the house. Although Ravi had said it was small, she had never imagined that she would actually be sleeping in Asha's and Shakuntala's bedroom. It made her feel doubly awkward and embarrassed in front of them. Not only did they obviously suspect her of designs on their precious big brother, but she had turned them out of their bedroom as well. For her convenience,

160

they were sleeping on makeshift beds in a tiny laundry room. She tried hard to ingratiate herself with them by talking about English fashions and pop music, but without ever saying anything ungracious, they politely repelled her advances. Although they were only sixteen and fourteen, they made her feel clumsy and indelicate. Physically too, she began to feel that she *was* clumsy and indelicate: she was in the way, she was a nuisance, she was too gauche for their small house. One day, eagerly trying to help clear the table, she broke a beautiful painted bowl.

'Oh my God, I'm so sorry, Mrs Kaul!'

'Ai-yai-yai,' pronounced Mr Kaul. 'Smashed to smithereens!'

'Oh, I'm terribly sorry. Listen, can I . . . may I get you another one? It was so pretty.'

And Mr Kaul replied with a loud, mocking guffaw, 'Indeed it was, Sarah. Indeed it was. But I'm afraid you cannot replace it, even if we were to let you. It was an antique object.'

'Oh no, was it awfully valuable? Oh, God—'

'No, of course it wasn't, Sarah,' Ravi broke in. 'It was a present from someone who died.'

'It was of sentimental value, Sarah. Do you understand that? It was of great sentimental value.'

For the first fortnight, she told herself that the trouble was only a matter of novelty. On Asha's and Shakuntala's part, it was shyness and on his mother's, it must be reserve. Mrs Kaul did not talk to Sarah very much, but then she did not say a great deal to anyone. She was clearly an important power in the household, but much less vocal than her husband. She asserted her will by means of pungent day-long silences and lingering sorrowful looks. If Sarah had drawn up a table of which members of the family represented the greatest threat to her ambitions, then little self-effacing Mrs Kaul would have come out way ahead of her big, blundering husband.

Despite all that, there were definitely things which Sarah enjoyed at the beginning. Her days were not all awkwardness and unhappiness. The gilharis which frisked outside her bedroom window in the mornings made up for a lot. The lizard scampering on her bedroom ceiling kept her company. And once, she slipped out of the house by herself for an adventure. Asha and Shakun had taken her a few days previously to a wonderful bazaar, for she had expressed enthusiasm for the pretty local embroidered muslin and, hearing her, Mr Kaul had promptly decided she must be taken out to buy some. The shop which Asha and Shakun had taken her to was comparatively big and grand and its display of embroidered muslins was magnificent. But on the way there, they had ridden down a street of smaller, more picturesque-looking shops and Sarah would have preferred to go into one of those. When she suggested this, however, Asha and Shakun tittered and when she persisted, they had dutifully insisted on taking her to the shop their father had named. 'These shops,' they assured her, 'are *cheap*.' So one afternoon when everyone was resting Sarah had sneaked out of the house, relishing her mischief, and gone off to the bazaar on her own.

It was easy getting there: stopping a rickshaw and repeating the name of the bazaar twice, carefully, to the driver. Only he had whirled her off eagerly to quite the wrong bazaar and when she had tried to redirect him, repeating the right name angrily, he had just cycled faster and answered, 'Yes Madam, yes, Madam.'

So she had tried to go shopping there instead. There were little shops, with bales of cotton and muslin. But a crowd of children followed her into the first shop she entered and stood in the doorway watching her and chirruping. When she left the first shop in embarrassment they followed her into the next shop too and then into the one after that, growing in noise and numbers. They set upon her out in the street, when she decided the whole thing was getting just too unbearable, and screeched for money and beat at her with their hard little hands. In the end she had to break free and make a dash for the nearest rickshaw, although the children still came after her and one of them threw something.

When she got back, luckily no one had noticed her absence; they were all still resting. But Ravi was aghast when she confided in him where she had been and made her promise never to do something like that again. Sarah was fed up and she sulked.

The atmosphere in the house was often fraught with tension, but that did not seem to be just because of her. Nor did it seem in any apparent way to be due to their grandmother's death. She was referred to once or twice, wistfully, but her departure did not seem to have left the cloud of mourning over the household which Ravi had depicted. It was more, Sarah thought – especially as time went on – due to the intolerable constraints which the family put on one another; expecting each member to be first and foremost a compliant part of the whole rather than an independent individual. Every time selfish interests clashed with the interest of the community, the community, like a bully, won. Sarah watched this for a fortnight. She thought it was dreadful.

Ravi's brother Ramesh, whom Sarah knew he would have relied upon for understanding and support, was away in Bombay. The rest of the family closed about Ravi like a fortress. It was impossible to get through to him. But what Sarah had not been prepared for was that as soon as he crossed the threshold, Ravi would become part of the fortress too.

Sometimes she told herself that she was being unfair. She had known all along that his family would be the biggest obstacle. She tried to go along with their idiosyncrasies and their restrictions. She kept up the pretence that she and Ravi were strangers to each other's bodies. But she could not keep it up indefinitely. She had not come to India to look at mosques, to sit genteelly on the verandah after dinner and discuss parliamentary democracy with Ravi's father. She signalled to Ravi increasingly desperately that they had to break out of this frightful predicament. She said to him, in the garden, that she was going crazy. When would they go off somewhere together, like he had suggested to her in his last letter? But he had no money. He had to stay at home in case he heard from the social survey outfit in Delhi. Even though they were within sight of the house, Sarah wildly caught hold of his arm. She could not bear it, did he understand? She just could not bear it any more.

163

It was to avoid scenes like that that Ravi agreed that they should at least go out for evening strolls together and these strolls were such a welcome release, walking alone in the cool of the evening beside the river, that for a while they relieved the worst of the tension.

It was only in her third week that the trouble started. Apparently Ravi's mother had complained to him that the neighbours were gossiping about Sarah's prolonged presence in their house. ('What do they think I am?' she shouted at Ravi. 'A leper?') They were dropping round for tea and looking her up and down. And Ravi – pathetically susceptible to pressure, Sarah raged – admitted that his mother had a case.

'It's not that I care a hoot what the neighbours think,' he told her. 'You know I couldn't give a damn. But one has to think of their point of view, of Daddy's position.'

'But why – what's wrong with me?' Sarah raged. 'Am I a social embarrassment?'

Ravi twiddled the leaves he had pulled from a scented bush. He shrugged: 'In a way, you are.'

Sarah turned to him, genuinely intrigued. 'What do you mean?'

He puffed, as though the effort of explanation were too much for him. 'People will say all kinds of peculiar things about my parents if they imagine that their eldest son has serious intentions about an English girl.' He gestured at the quiet side-street where they were walking. 'It isn't jet-setting Delhi here, you know.'

Sarah looked at him nastily. 'I don't see why that should bother you,' she retorted bitterly, 'since you haven't.'

They were walking close to the river, past the grounds of a big boys' school. On a patch of bare ground, a group of young boys was kicking a ball around. Their thin bare legs flickered up and down their makeshift playing field and in order to interrupt their argument, Ravi and Sarah stopped to watch them. Playing for their audience, the boys' movements grew wilder and fiercer. They hurled themselves frenziedly up and down. Sarah and Ravi exchanged looks of amusement and, walking on, continued their argument less acrimoniously.

His mother's complaint was not the only problem. And while Sarah was naturally hurt by it, she could of course see that she was inconveniencing them. The growing knowledge that she could not stay there oppressed her, but something else had happened which was equally ominous.

Two days before, sitting out on the verandah as usual after dinner, they had received a visit from one of Mr Kaul's office cronies. As soon as he arrived, Mrs Kaul and the girls had as usual retreated into the house but Sarah had been kept outside – as a diversion, as a curiosity, she said to Ravi bitterly: 'That's how they treat me; as an amusing curiosity. It's fine just so long as I remain an entertaining conversation-piece, someone who will perform their party tricks and drink whisky, but as soon as I want to discard that role and actually take part, then it's curtains, isn't it?'

The visitor had questioned Sarah about her impressions of India. He was a ponderous, solemn man, in many ways rather similar to Ravi's father. He had taken all her answers very seriously, analysed and assessed them. At one point, he asked her if she had been disappointed by India or if it had lived up to her expectations? Sarah, by that time quite irritated at the interrogation, felt a foolish urge to shock the two old men with a forthright answer. 'Oh, I knew what was in store for me,' she answered, pretending to roll her eyes. 'Ravi had prepared me. I mean – he and I have known each other so well for such a long time!'

Ravi laughed nervously. The visitor leaned forward. He patted his fat moustache. 'Ah, you two have known each other well for a long time?'

'Of course,' Ravi answered briskly, 'Sarah and I were at Oxford together.'

Their visitor sat back with his arms folded and looked quizzically across at Ravi's father. He raised his eyebrows, which were plump and trim like his moustache, and he smirked. There was an embarrassed silence before Ravi went on, 'I mean Sarah and I are old buddies. She knew quite a few other chaps from this neck of the woods as well.'

Still the visitor said nothing. He shifted his ponderously ironic gaze from Mr Kaul to Ravi. Then he simply said, 'Is that so?'

But Mr Kaul had started perceptibly at his friend's look. He turned to Ravi and Sarah with an expression of bewildered, disgusted alarm.

When the visitor had left, uttering genial platitudes into the night, Mr Kaul stiffly excused himself to Sarah and asked Ravi to come out into the garden with him. For ten minutes the two of them walked up and down the short lawn, arguing in an undertone. Ravi said that his father had been adamant; this whole business had gone on for long enough. His friend's insinuation had cut him to the quick. It was all very well for Ravi to carry on as he liked away at the university and to give whatever unfortunate misleading impression he chose, but if he and Sarah were going to flaunt their easy-going ways here and bring public embarrassment on himself and Ravi's mother, then he would have to put an end to it.

'But, for heaven's sake,' Sarah objected, 'surely they must *know*? I mean, surely you told them once that I wasn't just a college friend? Didn't you?'

'Of course I implied you were,' Ravi answered, 'but you've seen for yourself what they're like. I could hardly spell things out, could I?'

'But you told them who I am? I mean, they do at least know I'm your girl-friend, don't they?'

Ravi looked at her teasingly. 'I told them what was necessary,' he said, 'not specifics.'

They were still sitting in the garden talking about it, so late that everyone else must have gone to bed. And, in the dark, Ravi reached out his hand and flicked her nearer nipple playfully. 'Not specifics.'

Sarah pushed him away. 'Oh, you're just horrible,' she shrilled, 'and anyway, why shouldn't I tell people that we're not just college friends? It's the truth.'

And then, to top it all, there had been that unfortunate incident with Asha. Sarah had not thought much of it at the time and hadn't even mentioned it to Ravi, hoping that Asha – only a very naïve sixteen-year-old – would not know what to make of it and would dismiss it. But later she was sure that Asha had understood perfectly well what she had seen and had reported it to her mother. It must have been that which in the end precipitated the crisis.

What had happened was this: Sarah had been sitting on her bed that morning, taking her contraceptive pill from its cellophane card and thinking ruefully how unnecessary it was, since it was already nearly a month since she and Ravi had managed to have such privacy, when she realised that Asha was standing in the open doorway watching her. Instinctively, she pushed the card under the sheets and gave Asha a guilty smile. 'Stomach pills,' she said brightly, tapping her stomach as though Asha were slow on the uptake.

'Oh dear,' said Asha. 'Are you feeling bad again? Should I tell Mummy?'

'No, no,' Sarah said. 'No, I shall be fine. These are quite good pills actually.' She laughed awkwardly. 'Really, Asha, it's nothing.'

Asha shook her head. 'Are you sure? You mustn't fall ill again.'

'I won't,' Sarah assured her. 'This time I've nipped it in the bud.' And even as she said that, she had been cockily pleased with her little joke.

For a moment Asha stayed in the doorway, silently accusing, then she came in to collect the sandals she had come for. As she turned to go, Sarah called, 'Promise me you won't tell anyone, Asha. I don't want them to worry.'

All in all, by the time the storm broke it had been brewing for several days.

It was quite late and already completely dark when Ravi and Sarah set off to their favourite destination. They liked to walk to the grounds of a nineteenth-century mausoleum near the river called Shah Najaf. It was an ornate, fancy building, but in the dark it became something more ancient, simpler. The first time they went there together in the evening, the caretaker had switched on the lights inside to show them a collection of murky memorabilia. He had given them an eager explanation of his showpieces in Hindi ('He's talking utter rubbish,' Ravi whispered), but Sarah had found the shadowy rooms under the collection of multi-coloured chandeliers and lamps wonderfully atmospheric. From then on, they just walked in the garden and usually sat down in a secluded corner to talk and make amends. It was not a popular courting place, Ravi knew, and there was no reason why anyone should have come snooping after them.

They sprawled in their corner and discussed their predicament. It had reached a stage where they were temporarily reunited by the imminence of defeat. The weeks of bickering and frustration had worn them out. Suddenly it seemed they had no more hostility, only bitterness and the admission of failure.

After a while they grew calmer and, talking over what remained to them, they grew more affectionate towards each other.

Because he felt sorry for her and, in his heart, perhaps also a little guilty, Ravi stroked Sarah's hair. She had brought so many extra problems down on him. They were not major problems, certainly, but in his low state of irritable depression they had exasperated him. Rickshaw drivers charged him a higher fare at the sight of Sarah; he couldn't be a local. People stared in shops and restaurants and made quite audible speculative remarks about the two of them, as though somehow like Sarah he couldn't understand. When she had put her arms around his neck one previous evening in these gardens, he had seen her as a stone – a living stone, slung round his neck and dragging him down into a muddy pond of entanglements and compromises in which he would inevitably drown. Perhaps that was the reason why in the end, he had simply stopped sticking up for Sarah when his family criticised her and why, when his mother had asked him when he thought Sarah might leave, he had answered resolutely, 'Soon.'

It was not his fault, of course, that Sarah had insisted on bringing this trouble on herself, but now that she had done so the least he could do was to get her out of it. He looked at her, wretchedly playing with a strand of her yellow hair and repeating, 'It just seems so pathetic to leave now when I've hardly seen anything of India.' Even though there were tears trickling down her face, it was still nice to be lying there beside her on the grass with the background of night birds and crickets. He tried to comfort her, 'No crickets in the college gardens, eh?' he joked.

And Sarah sniffed. 'No, I don't know how I shall put up with England now. What will I do?'

Ravi tried to hide his relief, but his heart soared; openly, Sarah was at last admitting that this thing was over.

He took her fretful hand away from her hair. 'You'll go back home,' he said gently, 'and you'll live happily ever after.'

Sarah rolled onto her back and spoke sourly to the sky. 'I haven't got much option, have I?'

They were very close to each other. They had nothing else to take comfort in. And once Ravi had begun to fondle Sarah, a perverse desire to shock and commit public sacrilege made him go further, to get his own back on the place which had made him carry out this betrayal.

It was delicious lying together in their corner, hidden by the dark shapes of the bushes. The night was protectively full of other squeaks and rustles and they were sure that no one could possibly have seen them, for around them the gardens were impenetrably black.

Things were still all right that night, because it was very late by the time they got back to the house and everyone was in bed. On the way, Ravi worried that his parents would have noticed their long absence and suspect what they had been up to. 'You're like a well-brought-up young lady who's been led astray,' Sarah teased him. 'I'm the man in all this!' And to show how little she cared, she kissed him extravagantly on the front porch. They went silently to bed in their separate bedrooms. Before she got into bed, Sarah looked up a reproduction which she remembered in a glossy art book she had bought in Delhi; it was one of a series of miniatures, depicting Krishna making love to a milkmaid. They were lying horizontally, apparently floating, under a tree in a nocturnal garden. Krishna's skin was deep blue and the girl's an uncanny ivory white. She studied it for a little while, grinning, and then dog-eared a corner of the page as a memento.

When she woke in the morning, Sarah became aware of a noise which she thought at first was a new bird calling in the garden. It was piping and shrill and repetitive and it was only as she woke completely that she realised it was Ravi's mother crying. She stayed in her room, petrified, convinced that if there was trouble in that house today, then somehow it must be connected with her. She heard Mr Kaul's booming tones interrupt the crying and she listened for Ravi's. When they came, they were barely recognisable: shrill and anguished. The shouting rose and Sarah waited for someone to fetch her. She waited for an hour. When at last silence fell, Ravi came to her room. His face was tear-stained and contorted.

'Ravi! Whatever's the matter?'

'God bloody damn it!'

'What's happened, Ravi?'

'Can't you guess? Oh, damn, damn, damn, damn, *damn*!' He fell onto her bed and furiously pounded the pillow.

'Ravi, for heaven's sake, tell me! What's going on? I heard your mother—'

Ravi lifted his swollen face from the bedclothes. 'Isn't it obvious? We were followed last night. Someone saw us at Shah Najaf.'

For a moment Sarah was so aghast that she could not respond. Then the dreadful, obvious explanation occurred to her and, even though she already knew what his answer would be, she asked, 'Who?'

Ravi groaned. 'Asha.'

She deserved everything – that was her second thought. Whatever catastrophe, whatever nightmare now descended on her, she had asked for it. She had not understood anything; she had viewed Ravi's family as a comic cameo and Asha as a sweet little stereotype who would never alarmingly come to life. She had not credited her with normal perceptions, normal reactions, because after all this wasn't England. Whatever retribution the days ahead had in store for her, she deserved it all.

When she did not respond, Ravi went on, 'I just can't understand it. For the life of me, I can't see what could have made her *do* such a disgusting thing. There's no sense in it; it's just not *like* her.' He thrust his fists into the bedclothes, but drew them out as if he did not know who he wanted to hit. 'She must have suspected something,' he said, 'but it's so coldly calculating. What can have made her *want* to do it?'

Sarah couldn't tell him, of course. How could she admit – after everything else that she had done wrong there, all the mistakes she had made – that she had done that too? So she just stood, stricken in the middle of the room and, after a minute or two, asked, 'What's going to happen?'

'You'll have to leave,' Ravi said without moving.

Of course, she knew that. She could not sleep another night in that house, which she had turned upside down. She could not go on sitting with the family at table in the ghastly silence, which now filled the house. But where could she go?

She looked down at Ravi, defeated on the bed. He offered no solution, no comfort. He was sprawled across it, over-whelmed by his own misfortune. But then, she did not feel that sorry for him either.

'Where to?' she asked.

Ravi made an impatient little movement as though that, for heaven's sake, were the least of his worries. 'I'll get you a train ticket.'

'I'm not going back to Delhi.'

Her decision surprised her. 'I'm not just going to be packed off home like a naughty school girl. I've hardly seen anything yet.'

'Haven't you seen enough?' Ravi asked and Sarah was suddenly enraged that at that frightful moment, he could be so sarcastic.

'No, I'll go to Benares.' (Their train from Delhi had been eventually bound for Benares. Reading its destination on the station board, she had imagined going there with Ravi.)

'Varanasi?' Ravi said.

'Yes,' said Sarah, 'I'll go to Varanasi. Why should I miss that too?'

Ravi shook his head. 'Are you sure? On your own? You could go back and stay with Birendra for a bit.'

That decided her. 'No, I don't want to stay with Birendra. I want to go to Varanasi. I can cope. I shall go and spend a few days in Varanasi and then . . . then maybe I'll go to Khajuraho and have a look at those temples.'

Ravi looked amazed. For a moment, he seemed about to argue with her, to try and persuade her for her own good not to go. Then he shrugged. 'It's your decision.'

And losing any remnant of control she had kept, Sarah shrieked, 'Yes, it is!'

Wildly she tugged her suitcase out from under the bed, roughly pushed aside Ravi's dangling ankle and started to fling her belongings into it, with tears running down her face.

*

Of course, afterwards she still had to face his parents. She couldn't get a train ticket just like that, she couldn't evaporate. They were both grimly correct to her, as though it cost them dear even to look at her. When she finally dared emerge from her bedroom, ('Look, I don't care,' she had said to Ravi, 'I've just got to get some tea,') the house had at first seemed deserted. Waiting for a howl of fury, she had made her way as far as the kitchen corridor and gingerly coughed. One of the servants, Ila, shot out of the kitchen and gestured wildly at her not to come in. Sarah thought sadly, 'She thinks I'll pollute it.' She said, 'Chai,' tea, one of the first Hindi words she had ever learnt, and turned back to her room. As she turned, she caught sight of Shakuntala gaping at her from the other end of the kitchen corridor, but Shakun at once scurried away.

Ila brought them both tea, her face bunched and sorrowful. Sarah remembered long ago Ravi telling her that Ila had wept when he went away to England. She wondered what thoughts were running through Ila's mind now as she contemplated the end result of that foolish journey. Ravi got up off the bed and washed his face. They drank their tea and discussed what they should do next; Sarah's hysterically half-packed suitcase lay unavoidably at their feet.

They went to the railway station to fix up her ticket and on the way, Ravi said again, 'You know, you don't have to go haring off into the blue. You're quite sure you don't want to go back to Delhi? You could always stay at the YWCA.'

But Sarah answered, 'Sure. Why should I miss Varanasi on top of everything else?'

Ravi looked doubtful. 'It's a tricky old city.'

Sarah shrugged. 'It's hardly been a bed of roses here.' Because she had been thinking, in the meantime, that this was her last chance. If she turned her back on India now and fled home to safety, then she would never really have come face to face with her adventure. Naturally she was scared stiff, but that fear in its way was exciting. While at first she had been reluctant to turn to mosques and temples for lack of Ravi, her surrogate interest had turned to a real one. She found that immersing herself in that brilliance gave her an almost comparable thrill. And anyway, if anything went wrong, then her fate would be a punishment for Ravi.

Ravi said, 'I wish I could come with you.'

Sarah answered, 'No you don't, Ravi. It's too late to pretend now.'

When they came back to the house, it was already lunch-time. Mrs Kaul was setting dishes on the table. At first she pretended not to notice them come in.

'Sarah's going to Varanasi tomorrow afternoon,' Ravi announced unnecessarily loudly. 'She wants to see the big sights before she leaves India.'

His mother nodded primly, merely acknowledging that she had taken in this piece of information, but still she did not look up at them.

They ate the meal in near silence. Neither Mr Kaul nor Asha was there and naturally Sarah did not dare to ask where they were. She hardly ate anything and, for once, Mrs Kaul did not try to push more food on her. She sighed gustily at intervals through the meal and once or twice pressed her fingers to her suffering temples.

In the afternoon, Ravi and Sarah went out for a walk, walking well apart and not holding hands. They went automatically in the opposite direction from the night before, to the ruined Residency in its neo-classical park. There they sat under a tree and, in the end, were surprised by how little they had to say to each other.

'God, I'll be glad to get out of this place,' Ravi said.

His family had never felt at home in Lucknow and, in bad times, they always remembered it. They had come there unwillingly, uprooted by the imperious demands of Mr Kaul's Government job. They had come determined to resent the stuffy provincial city, a far cry from Delhi where they had been so at home. And they doggedly resented it, even

173

as children, outnumbered at school by cocky indigenous classmates. Only, in time, involuntary associations had grown up and all of them found themselves occasionally, despite themselves, feeling affectionate towards Lucknow. Eventually they even settled there and knew that when Mr Kaul retired, they would not have the motivation or the energy anymore to return to Delhi. But when things went wrong for them, they still remembered that they had never wanted to come there and they blamed Lucknow for their misfortunes.

Around them a few families strolled through the Residency compound, surveying the smashed arches and columns with a contrived, educational interest.

'When do you think you'll be able to get away?' Sarah asked conversationally.

Ravi shrugged hopelessly. 'God knows. I suppose I might hear soon if I've got that job in Delhi. If not, I shall have to go back and start looking again.' He hesitated. 'Let me know when you intend to get back there, won't you? I'll try to come up then so that I can see you off.'

Sarah didn't answer.

'You're really going to go trekking off on your own?' Ravi asked her. 'Promise me you'll take care.'

Sarah rounded on him. 'I don't know why you're keeping up this pretence!' she exclaimed. 'What's the point?'

They sat a little longer without speaking. Then, finding the silence between them harder to bear sitting still, they got up and started to walk back to the house. Ravi made one or two further attempts to talk on the way, but nothing came of them and by the time they got back to the house, they were both on the verge of tears.

That night Sarah wanted to miss the family dinner. But she realised that staying in her room would only make things worse, if that were possible. She walked into a hostile silence in the dining room and her 'Hello' sounded fragile and tinny. Only Mr Kaul replied severely, 'Good evening, Sarah,' and Ravi said in an artificially cheery voice, 'Have you finished packing yet?'

She sat down in her usual place on Mr Kaul's right, opposite Ravi, and looked down at her plate. Still none of them said anything and a ripple ran around the table – of revulsion, Sarah thought. She wanted to run away at once, to escape from that solidly united censure. Asha passed her the potato curry and she insultingly took a ridiculously tiny helping of it so that they should all see what she thought of them. After all, what, for God's sake, had she done wrong? She did the same with everything else which Asha silently passed her, until Mr Kaul announced stiffly, 'You'll need more than that for your journey, Sarah.'

'I'm not hungry,' she said sullenly.

'I think none of us are,' Mr Kaul replied reprovingly, 'but we are still managing to eat.'

Sarah looked around at the family and the family looked back at her. It was not really true that they were managing to eat: Mrs Kaul certainly hadn't taken a mouthful and only Ravi was miserably putting food into his mouth for lack of anything better to do. Asha sat huddled and silent; she had a fiercely stony expression as she stared down at her place, but whether she was triumphant or appalled at the disaster she had brought about, Sarah could not tell.

Throughout the meal, very little was said. The atmosphere was painful and everyone got up and scattered as soon as possible when it was over.

Ravi and Sarah went out into the garden. Ravi said to her, 'That was "The Last Supper",' and Sarah giggled sadly. It was their last joke.

*

Of course it was awful that, in the end, Sarah had to leave so suddenly, so sordidly. There was something horrid, Ravi thought, about the way his parents wanted her packed out of the house straight away, as if she carried some shameful germ. They had been beside themselves at the revelation – quite naïvely, he considered, for surely they must have had some inkling of his relations with Sarah? But he knew it was not the revelation in itself which upset them, so much as its implications: if a child like Asha had found them out, then who else might not have done? Ravi knew that, in his father's mind, a circle of his office colleagues stood around them at Shah Najaf, looking on in outrage and scandal as his son disgraced himself. There was A. B. Habibulla, their pompous visitor of the other night, puffing and pontificating; there was 'Nonesuch' Nair and there was Major Mehrotra, the father of the charming and sweet-natured girl whom Mr Kaul had still hoped that Ravi would one day marry.

Now that the truth was out, even if so far it had been kept a family secret, what was there to stop other people finding out in any case? The family might keep its mouth shut and expel Sarah like a serpent from its bosom, but once such a superlative piece of scandal became public it would be impossible to suppress it. In a gossipy provincial place like Lucknow, even the ceiling lizards told tales.

In the end, he was genuinely upset to see Sarah go. With her departure the last link with his university days was being severed and he knew that for years to come he would still sometimes miss her. He was sorry that she had decided to go off, so innocent and ill-equipped on her touring. But his life would be, oh so much easier when she had gone.

Even as he watched her pack, even as he took her to the railway station, he could not ignore the treacherous little voice which whispered under his sorrow, telling him that although today might be terrible, ahead of him at last his destiny was clear.

*

In the morning, after a virtually sleepless night, Sarah put the last few things into her suitcase. The art book with the dog-eared page she pushed down to the bottom, because she was afraid that later on the sight of it might make her cry. She forced down some breakfast and managed to reply quite calmly when Mr Kaul said goodbye to her before leaving for his office. Asha and Shakun had avoided her, skittering off to school as soon as she was up. Mrs Kaul had one of the servants prepare her a picnic for the journey and Ila brought it to her wordlessly as she closed her suitcase. Sarah felt as though her very presence were unhealthy.

Her train left at two o'clock, so she and Ravi set off to the station soon after one. Asha and Shakun were out and only Mrs Kaul stood stiffly on the verandah and watched them go, her face a composition of distrust as if she suspected that Sarah might still spirit Ravi away and he would never come back.

They did not say very much, even on the way to the station. What was there to say in the face of such an irredeemable mess?

Ravi said, 'Make sure you put your handbag under your head if you go to sleep on the train.' And, 'Don't miss going to Sarnath from Varanasi, will you? It's supposed to be really interesting.'

Sarah said, 'I get down at the Cantonment Station, don't I?'

'Look, you're sure the rickshaw men in Varanasi will know where this hotel of yours is?'

They went in silence past the school where they had watched the boys playing football. Nearer the station, they just talked about platforms and tickets. Everything was very rushed once they got there and, in the end, they did not even say goodbye to each other properly because that very morning a letter had arrived to say that Ravi had got the job in the social survey outfit in Delhi after all. So they just agreed that when Sarah's adventure was over, she would get in touch with him there.

*

Varanasi Station was no worse than any other station she had been to and the hotel, which Ravi had given her the name of, was no worse than any other hotel. There were plenty of foreign tourists there, which reassured her until she remembered that really she ought to be disappointed.

She went down to the Ganges to watch the sun rise on her first morning and saw a sight which made her forget for a good two hours that she no longer had a reason to be there.

The pink disc of the sun moved up over the wide silver river and all along the steps which lined the river bank, people were plunging. They bathed, absorbed in their ritual, and paid no attention to the foreign tourists standing watching them. They held up brass cups of water to the rising sun. As it grew brighter, individual ceremonies emerged from the general washing: a shrunken old woman in widow's white squatting in the mud, a contorted, emaciated yogi doing

177

exercises on a stone slab, a powerful matron in an infinite sari wading into the water. They were at one with the spreading morning and as the colours entered the crowded ghats and temples, the bathers too grew livelier and more jubilant.

That afternoon Sarah wandered through the chaotically narrow streets of the old city. They were alive with such feverish excitement that it seemed impossible that it could be an ordinary day. Every inch of space was given over to encouraging the excitement – shrines, stalls, garlands, incense. Now and then she would cross a wave of jostling, shrill pilgrims, who plunged past her as though she was invisible. Only their occasional kohl-eyed babies, their great eyes magically increased in size, would stare at her over the hurrying shoulders. In one small alleyway she came face to face with a cow, which butted its way absently past her as though she had no business being there at all. She spent the day in a state of happy shock, marvelling at the weirdness of it all, the adventure she had found for herself. She got lost, had no idea where she was, no idea what was going on. In a moment of whimsical abandon, she even bought herself some incense and a garland. In a busy temple, she met some French tourists from her hotel and, in the evening, she went out to eat with them in a restaurant full of the sweet fumes of dope.

On her second day, she went to the Durga Monkey Temple and the Shiva Temple. Little bells rang around her, informing the gods of the visitors' presence. She was briefly shocked from her happy trance when a monkey snapped at her ankle. She went back to the old city again as well. She had no idea how long it would last, but, for the moment, she was having a lovely time. In the evening, she went with the French tourists to listen to some devotional music. One of them, a Christ-like blond hippy called Jean-Marc, put his arm around her as the sitar pulsed and tenderly caressed her breasts through her thin muslin kurta. For two or three days, everything worked out fine.

But on the morning of the fourth day, she woke in her stuffy hotel room and realised that she felt dreadfully ill. Below her window, someone was cooking on charcoal and it took her a moment to separate her sickness from the smell.

She was suffocating. But when she threw off her sheet and sat up to go and switch the ceiling fan onto a faster setting, the sudden movement made her head spin. She lay back and assessed her condition as the fan croaked round infuriatingly overhead. She must have a fever; obscene little trickles of sweat were rolling down between her legs and her hair, spiky with damp, all seemed to be lying in the wrong direction so that her scalp hurt. Her mouth, foul with the taste of the previous evening's smoking, was dry and stuck together. She must have caught something. As she lay there, wondering how ill she really was, panic came over her in a cold sweat; she was going to be taken ill here, she was going to be overwhelmed by India. And she whimpered with self-pity; the prospect was just too terrifying for words.

She had to get up. Several times during the next couple of hours she told herself that and found the certainty comforting. At last her thirst forced her out of bed and, shuddering, she washed and dressed and went outside.

She went to Ahmed's Kola Korner, a small dingy restaurant frequented by foreign tourists where she had taken to having her breakfast. It was already nearly eleven o'clock and most of the customers she knew by sight had gone. The restaurant, which was really just a small hole in the wall of a larger Import–Export company, was empty and quiet. Sarah sat down thankfully. It was dazzlingly bright outside and as she walked down the street, the lurid colours of the little shop-fronts had seemed to hammer at her eyes. She was relieved to reach the dark cavern of Ahmed's, prop her head on her hands and shut her eyes.

She ordered tea and toast. Ahmed did a lively trade in mock European cooking. The toast came soft and utterly pliable and Sarah sat in front of it for a while, playing with it and feeling sick. Ahmed – at least she imagined he was Ahmed – watched her from his corner. His blank gaze annoyed her. But the tea helped a bit and after two or three cups, she began to think that she might be better. Ahmed came over to offer her some more tea, and they had a stilted little conversation about her health. It did her good to reduce her illness to simple terms: heat, fever, stomach, fatigue. By the end of their conversation she felt quite reassured, convinced that as Ahmed said, it was only an upset. She sat on in the restaurant for a while, idly watching the morning.

Walking back to the hotel, she was suddenly sick in the gutter. Her main concern was that Ahmed should not see her and be offended. But it was hard to vomit inconspicuously because a circle of street children immediately gathered around her, and pointed and commented.

She lay down in her hotel room, telling herself that it had been Ahmed's unspeakable toast, and dozed for most of the afternoon. But the fear of admitting that she really might be ill forced her to get up and go out again later on. She took a tricycle rickshaw down to the ghats and sat by the river in the pink peace of the dusk, watching the quieter evening people come and go. A little way away from her squatted a young American, his face glazed, his muscular legs contorted in an imitation of an Indian crouch. That time she felt no elation, only a sense of her own redundancy and defeat.

The next morning, she felt worse. She had sweated a lot in the night and her sheets were damp and chilly. Her head was swimming. At first, she even wondered if she had the strength to get up. But staying in bed would have been an unbearable admission of illness. She forced herself to get up and was promptly sick again, except that not having eaten anything much the day before, all that she could do was retch hopelessly over the washbasin, thin viscous liquid. After that, she thought she felt better and dragged herself into her dirty clothes. As soon as she put them on, she began to feel intolerably itchy. She gathered her things to go out with painful care, hoping that the concentration would pull her together – bag, sunglasses, purse, key. She walked out past the staring receptionist with an expression of frozen dignity on her face. She knew she must look a fright.

She walked slowly down to Ahmed's, fighting against rising waves of nausea. Whereas the day before the gaudy little shop-fronts had seemed blindingly brilliant, today they had receded to an uncertain frieze. The street danced at a great distance from her, on the far side of a shimmering layer of exhaustion peopled by jerkily gesticulating pin-men and women. It surprised her that the children in the bazaar still noticed her and called.

It took her eyes a minute or two to become accustomed to the total blackness inside the restaurant, and she groped her way to the same table as the day before. Ahmed was not in his corner and she sat down glumly to wait for him; he seemed to take ages coming. It was chilly and damp in there, she was the only customer and it seemed mournful and eerie. She fidgeted unhappily. Where the hell was Ahmed? This was really a nasty, sinister little hole. Whyever had she come here? As she tried to peer into the back of the restaurant to make out some sign of life, it suddenly struck her that the room was actually getting darker. She blinked and shook her head, her mouth filled with cold saliva and a wave of panic swept over her. She realised that she was about to faint and tried to get up and make for the bright open doorway, but it was too late.

The waiter and his brother retrieved the unconscious English girl from the floor where she had fallen. Acutely embarrassed, they made one or two discreet attempts to revive her with patting and prods and then called the brother's wife. But when none of their measures had any effect and the wife noticed how hot the girl's head was, they became frightened and the waiter shouted for a tricycle rickshaw and they took her like a parcel to the hospital.

*

'Is there any history?' Two doctors stood out in the corridor of the dilapidated hospital and an immense Indian sun spilt through the windows onto their white coats. From her bed in the large, silent ward, Sarah half heard them discussing her, a trifle dismissively. She was not presenting any of the usual hippy traveller's symptoms, they said; she had not got hepatitis or dysentery or malaria. Yet she was clearly ill. She lay repugnantly white and bony on the much-laundered sheets and tried to roll her eyeballs inwards away from their probing examination. Her illness dispensed her from her well-brought-up inhibitions and before their hands, she gave way to hysteria and recoil. Their brown and smiling faces bobbed above her and as they examined her, they seemed to make fun of her predicament. She wanted to explain to them that it was not what it seemed; she was not just another piece

181

of European flotsam and jetsam cast up in Benares at the end of a farcical quest for the wisdom of the East. She was there for another, quite admirable reason. But they had waggled their heads in amusement at her protests and gone on examining her. At that point, she gave up and let them see that she was simply utterly sick of India and, not surprisingly, that insulted them.

*

Afterwards it seemed so pathetic to think that she had been in and out of the hospital in only five days, when at the time her illness had held all the endless terror of a nightmare.

During the worst of it she could only cry and what were tears and what was sweat she could not really tell. She lay in the sad-smelling ward and dimly hoped that she would die, as a punishment for Ravi. Of course the worst of it could only have lasted a day or two, but she was not aware of that at the time. She thought she really might die under that scaly ceiling and, all in all, she found the thought quite attractive.

It came to her that she must have known all along that it would end like this. She must have known all along that her plan was impossible. Had she ever really seriously envisaged marrying Ravi Kaul and settling down in India? Or had she only embarked on this adventure because underneath she had known all along that it would lead her safely back to home?

She let herself float off into a feverish dream, because there was no hospital and no India there. There were no questions and no reproaches. There was only Ravi Kaul as she had imagined him long ago in a wintry city, the Ravi with whom she had walked on the playing fields, hand in hand with the promise of an adventure.

But sometimes she floated into an echoing white space where sing-song voices jabbered at her continuously, preventing her from completely drifting away.

'You're not as naïve as you pretend to be.'
'If you remember, I did warn you.'
'Spitting in Holy Tank is Quite a Bad Habit.'
'I could hardly spell things out, could I?'
'I told them what was necessary. Not specifics.'

'Attention, please! Your attention is solicited.'

'You're really going to go trekking off on your own? Promise me you'll take care?'

'You are wanting tea cosy?'

'Promise me you'll take care?'

And although she knew that the voices were inside her head, so she must be making them herself, still she could not silence them and eventually they made her cry too. She wanted to retreat inside her illness, where India was only an idea. It was almost with disappointment that she realised she was getting better.

When the worst of it was over, she lay in the silent ward and wondered what on earth to do next. The fever had been her last adventure and now there she was – washed up, alone, ridiculous, in the middle of a pink landscape which had nothing to do with her any more. She regretted bitterly that in a moment of weakness at the beginning, she had tried to ask the doctors who were examining her to fetch Ravi. Luckily, they had just laughed at her. Because now she was determined to get herself out of the nightmare on her own. She recalled Ravi's mocking voice on the train to Lucknow: 'I'm just getting fed up with you landing in sticky situations all of your own making and then turning to me, wide-eyed, for help.' So she visualised herself leaving the hospital and going grimly back to Delhi. She visualised herself booking a seat on an aeroplane and going quietly home again to England. For when the worst of it was over, she found there was nothing left.

One of the kindlier doctors said to her, 'This malady is, should I say, principally the effect of our climate. You know, here we have different constitutions, different ways. Your system, your metabolism is, should I say, acclimatised to London, to your English frost and cold. You are not made for our heat and brightness.' He looked down at Sarah pityingly and added, 'In your country, maybe *I* should fall ill!' And he gave a jolly laugh, as if to show how very unlikely he thought that was.

Sarah discharged herself from the hospital. She saw a weary, overworked administrator, who clearly found her a light relief from his usual duties. When she had filled in his forms, giving the hotel as her place of abode in India, he leaned across his desk and advised her to go home to England. And perhaps to demonstrate his command of English idiom, he winked at her and added, 'Go home. Home is where the heart is!'

She went back to the hotel to collect her belongings and found that a lot of them were missing. When she tried to reclaim them from the receptionist, he denied all knowledge of them. He implied with a condescending smirk that Sarah had invented them. Tears of helpless rage began to prick her eyes. She was not up to arguing with his smooth denials and she turned away, taking her pilfered case and walked unsteadily out of the hotel.

It took her a day or two to fix up a seat on a train to Delhi and she moved into a cheaper, nastier little hostel right opposite the railway station. Her room smelt dreadfully of drains.

She thought of letting Ravi know that she was coming back, but the queues in the Post Office looked interminable and she couldn't really be bothered to wait. She thought of taking a bus trip to Sarnath, the cradle of the Buddhist faith, but that didn't seem worth the effort either.

On a warm apricot-golden evening, which smelt locally of cumin and car exhaust, she crossed the road to the railway station and pushed her way in through the crowds of rickshaw drivers and beggars. She found the night train to Delhi and climbed aboard. By ruthless pushing, she got a place at the window and defended it with a nasty glare. Then she sat back on the wooden seat and shut her eyes.

*

On the train that took him to Delhi, Ravi thought about his future. What a change, what a marvellous transformation since the last time he had made this journey in the opposite direction. Then everything had been so hopeless, a dead end; he had been bogged down in the most gruesome mess. Sarah had been beside him, wide-eyed and enthusiastic but complicating everything tenfold by her presence. He felt a little pang of nostalgia as he thought of her and he wondered where she was by now. He was sure she was having a tremen-

dous time wherever she was and he could not help grinning
as he recalled how she had gone trekking off on her own
after that rumpus, undeterred by India, her usual headstrong
self. He thought ahead to his own destination: Delhi and the
glossy premises of the social survey outfit, new acquaintances
and new adventures, the first springboard of his career. Until
he found somewhere of his own, he had been invited to stay
at his uncle's house. Involuntarily he stretched in pleasurable
anticipation of all the parties and dinners ahead. He was on
his way to the utterly superior life for which he had always
hoped, to the prospect of prosperity, to success. Excitement
gave him an appetite and he unwrapped the substantial meal
which his mother had prepared for him. A last tremor of
misgiving vanished as he bit into the savoury pakoris; Sarah
would still reappear once more in Delhi. But he scooped
decisively into his dish of vegetables with a rolled-up piece
of roti. He would put her up in some little hotel near his
office. Everything would be quite different now that he had
embarked on a proper fulfilling life of his own. Sarah would
see there was no place for her in his future. He hoped she
would not be too troublesome and spoil the memories of
their good times, which he would cherish forever. No, she
would not do that; she had too much sense. Ravi squared
his shoulders. No, Sarah would not be a problem any more.

*

Sarah arrived back in Delhi on a dazzling morning. She did
not go to Birendra's but took a scooter rickshaw from the
railway station to the YWCA. After a shower and a rest, she
changed into her least soiled clothes and set out in the early
afternoon to Birendra's. She knew that Ravi would be out at
work, but she assumed that he must be staying there. She
thought she would drink tea and chat with Birendra until
Ravi came back from work and then give him the surprise
of his life as he opened the door. It had crossed her mind on
the train not even to say goodbye to Ravi, to leave the
country without getting in touch and let him come to the
crushing realisation after a few months that she was gone. But
that vindictive fantasy only served to console her. Despite

everything that had happened, her need to see Ravi one last time was stronger.

The house where Birendra lived was just as filthy and run-down as Sarah remembered it. She climbed the nasty stairs to his flat and for a guilty moment felt thankful that she would be leaving those stairs behind as well. In the minute before Birendra answered her knock, she thought she might keel over with excited, doom-filled apprehension.

Birendra seemed astonished to see her. He was hard at work on one of his shock-horror exposés and there was no sign that Ravi was camping in his room. He made her welcome though and, after a minute, commented with concern on how tired she looked.

'I've been ill,' she announced proudly. 'I was in hospital!'

Birendra looked horrified. 'What was wrong? I never knew . . .'

'Oh, you couldn't have,' Sarah answered airily. 'Ravi doesn't know yet either.'

Birendra blushed deeply. 'Look, you'd better bring me up to date.'

'The pig!' Sarah exclaimed. 'Hasn't he told you anything about what happened?'

Birendra shuffled. 'Sarah, I haven't seen him.'

That startled her. 'But you know about his job?' she asked falteringly. 'You know he got the job in that social survey place?'

Birendra nodded. 'I know that. I received a note about a fortnight ago from Mister Kaul, saying he was on his way. But he must have been rushed off his feet in the social whirl since he arrived in Delhi; I haven't seen him since.'

Sarah stared at him, then she blurted out, 'But where's he staying?'

Birendra looked at her gently, as though he thought that anyone that naïve ought to be protected, before replying, 'At his uncle's.'

Of course, she could hardly go and see him there. Not after what had happened in Lucknow and not after her hospital resolution. But Birendra said that he would get in touch with Ravi at once and later, as Sarah was leaving, he added rather abruptly that he would send him round to her hotel that evening.

She went off and booked her seat on the plane. For just a minute she was tempted to delay doing so until she had seen Ravi, but the thought of being able to tell him bluntly that she was leaving outweighed the imaginary possibility of his protesting that she should stay longer. So she made her reservation at the airline office and then went back to the YWCA and sat in her room and waited for Ravi.

So many things could go wrong in India that it was not necessarily through callousness that he failed to come. But when at ten o'clock there was still no sign of Ravi, she gave up hope and went to bed. Outside her window, a radio was playing an interminable succession of jangling, twanging songs. Maybe Birendra had not really meant what he had said. Maybe Ravi had not got his message. But she was so exhausted that she soon slept in any case and, in the morning, there was a note for her at the reception desk:

Sarah!!!

Welcome back! I hear from Birendra that you're back in town after quite some adventures. I do hope you're all right and I'm looking forward to hearing all about your travels.

I'm afraid tonight's impossible because my boss has fixed up dinner with some essential people whom I have to meet. But if it's OK by you, I'll definitely call round tomorrow evening. I'm sending you this note via Birendra since I can't get over myself.

See you tomorrow, Ravi

For a second Sarah thought of going out for the evening, or even changing hotels. Anything, to leave something to her imagination. She spent most of that day in the Lodi Gardens, imagining resounding endings. In the shadier recesses of the gardens, pairs of young Indian lovers acted out their passion in a prim, stylised mime. But by six o'clock, she was back in her room at the YWCA waiting for Ravi.

He arrived at the hostel at half-past nine. The foyer made him chuckle; with its stern English decor and institutional cooking smells, it was just the sort of place which Sarah would have chosen. He was buoyant with the party he had come from and slightly self-consciously aware of the spices and brandy on his breath. He was wearing a rather natty new suit and a bright tie. When he came into her room, he was suddenly sharply aware of the gulf between him and the bedraggled figure sitting on the bed who looked up at him with large, reproachful eyes. She did look awful and it was partly in an attempt to jolly her up that he began the conversation by exclaiming, 'Well, what's all this then? I wasn't expecting to see you back so soon.'

'I've been ill,' Sarah answered resentfully. 'I thought Birendra told you.'

'He did, he did,' Ravi said quickly. 'I was very worried.' Since she did not respond, he continued. 'What was the matter?'

'Oh, I passed out in a restaurant in Varanasi and someone took me to hospital. I had a temperature of a hundred and four.'

'Gosh!'

'Oh, it wasn't that desperate, really. I'll survive.'

'I think you still look a bit groggy though. You should rest.'

'I haven't got much else to do, have I?'

There was an unpleasant pause. Ravi felt Sarah slowly destroying all his jollity from the party and resented it.

'How long are you intending to stay in Delhi?'

'Don't worry. Not for long.'

'Oh Sarah, let's not get into a fight straight away.'

'No, that would take too much effort, wouldn't it?'

'Are you planning to do some more sightseeing?'

'No, I'm flying home.'

'Already?'

'Yes, already. There really doesn't seem much point in hanging around here, does there?'

'When are you leaving?'

'In three days' time.'

'In three days' time?'

'Yes.'

'Have you got it fixed?'

'Yes.'

'I'm sorry, Sarah.'

'Why sorry? You've managed to pull yourself clear of the wreckage quite nicely, haven't you? You're all right.'

That angered him. 'So will you be.'

She gave him a sour look. 'That's what you'd like to think, of course.'

'Oh come now, stop being so dramatic. Of course you'll be all right.'

She went on looking at him in that funny, hard way and didn't say anything, so he sat down in the regulation armchair and after a moment, said, 'Well, tell me what you saw in Varanasi, at least.'

She gave a sarcastic laugh. 'I saw the sights. I saw a lot of dope and I saw the inside of an Indian hospital.'

'Did you see the sun rise over the Ganges?'

'Yes.'

'It's superb, isn't it?'

'Yes.'

'Look, are you too tired? Would you rather I went away?'

She didn't answer him. She looked as if she might be about to cry. In a hasty attempt to stop her, Ravi said, 'Well, you saw Varanasi, at least.'

And then, to his annoyance, she giggled.

He asked her, 'What d'you think you'll do when you get back to England?'

The same hard expression returned to her face and she shrugged. 'I suppose I shall find something.'

He cast around in his mind for a cheery suggestion, but for some ridiculous reason all that he could think of was an Indian Art course. After a moment, he said, 'You thought about publishing, didn't you?'

She sighed. It was impossible, trying to have a conversation with this stubborn misery. Eventually Ravi lost patience and said to her rather coldly, 'Maybe I ought to let you get some sleep.' She made no attempt to stop him, so he stood up. He said, 'Goodbye, Sarah' as kindly as he could and walked to the door. He was disappointed that she did not reply. Before he opened the door, he turned round and looked at her; he thought he had never seen anyone look so totally wretched. He felt dreadful as he shut the door. It was as though he were stealing away from the scene of a crime. But on his way out past the snooty Anglo-Indian receptionist, he recovered a little of his self-esteem. He thought sadly how selfish it was of Sarah not to have asked him anything about his new job or his new life.

※

She did see him once again, on her last night, in a smart restaurant in the centre of Delhi. He had had his first salary cheque and he was treating her. He made her promise that they would still write to each other from time to time. But her flight left at ten o'clock the next morning. Of course, Ravi could not possibly take time off during the day so soon after starting his new job so, in the end, it was Birendra who came with her out to the airport and Birendra who saw her off.

※

England was wrapped in an all-enveloping cloud. It muffled the noises at the airport and the speeding traffic on the motorway into London. It shrouded everyone in a cocoon of selfish privacy and muted their words and movements, as if they might suddenly shockingly be found to be dead.

For a long time Sarah Livingstone stayed at home with her parents and did absolutely nothing at all. For a long time she could not even make herself get up in the mornings.

'But what did you expect?' said Sarah's mother's eyes over the breakfast table.

'That's that,' said her father's knife, smiting his breakfast egg.

She hung her room with the pictures and the silks which she had salvaged from her adventure. She went on wearing her Indian clothes and her sandals. In the autumn, she enrolled on a History of Art course, not out of any real interest but because it seemed something appropriate to do. Gradually, she met up again with all the friends she had known at university. For a while, she did enjoy the distinction of her tragedy. At a drinks party, she met a man who said to her, 'Hey, haven't I seen you somewhere before?' She moved out of the house in the white crescent and into a

190

shared flat. When she had completed her course, she got a job of sorts in a museum.

A year went by, another, bland years. It would be wrong to pretend that Sarah's whole life was ruined by her adventure; that she sat frigidly in the Indian Art department of the museum, cherishing the secret explanation for her expert knowledge of Mithuna erotic sculptures. Or that the taste she had had of brown skin stopped her from ever enjoying pink. Within five years Sarah Livingstone was married. But not one of her children's names would begin with R. In fact, it was Ravi who called his first daughter Sarla and rejoiced that her skin was so fair.

All Futura Books are available at your bookshop or
newsagent, or can be ordered from the following address:
Futura Books, Cash Sales Department,
P.O. Box 11, Falmouth, Cornwall, TR10 9EN.

Please send cheque or postal order (no currency), and
allow 60p for postage and packing for the first book plus
25p for the second book and 15p for each additional book
ordered up to a maximum charge of £1.90 in U.K.

B.F.P.O. customers please allow 60p for the first book,
25p for the second book plus 15p per copy for the next
7 books, thereafter 9p per book.

Overseas customers, including Eire, please allow £1.25
for postage and packing for the first book, 75p for the second
book and 28p for each subsequent title ordered.